# Bound By Iron & Blood

## The Metalist's Journey
~Book 0/4.5~
KD Lumsden

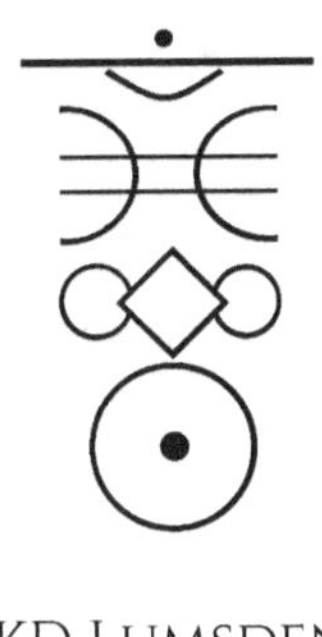

KD Lumsden

<u>**A KD Lumsden Production**</u>



ISBNs

EPUB: 978-1-959679-10-3

Paperback: 978-1-959679-11-0

www.KDLumsden.com

This book was made possible by my child asking me the best questions, forcing me to really understand Irwin's origin story.

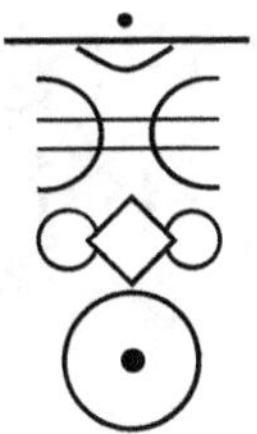

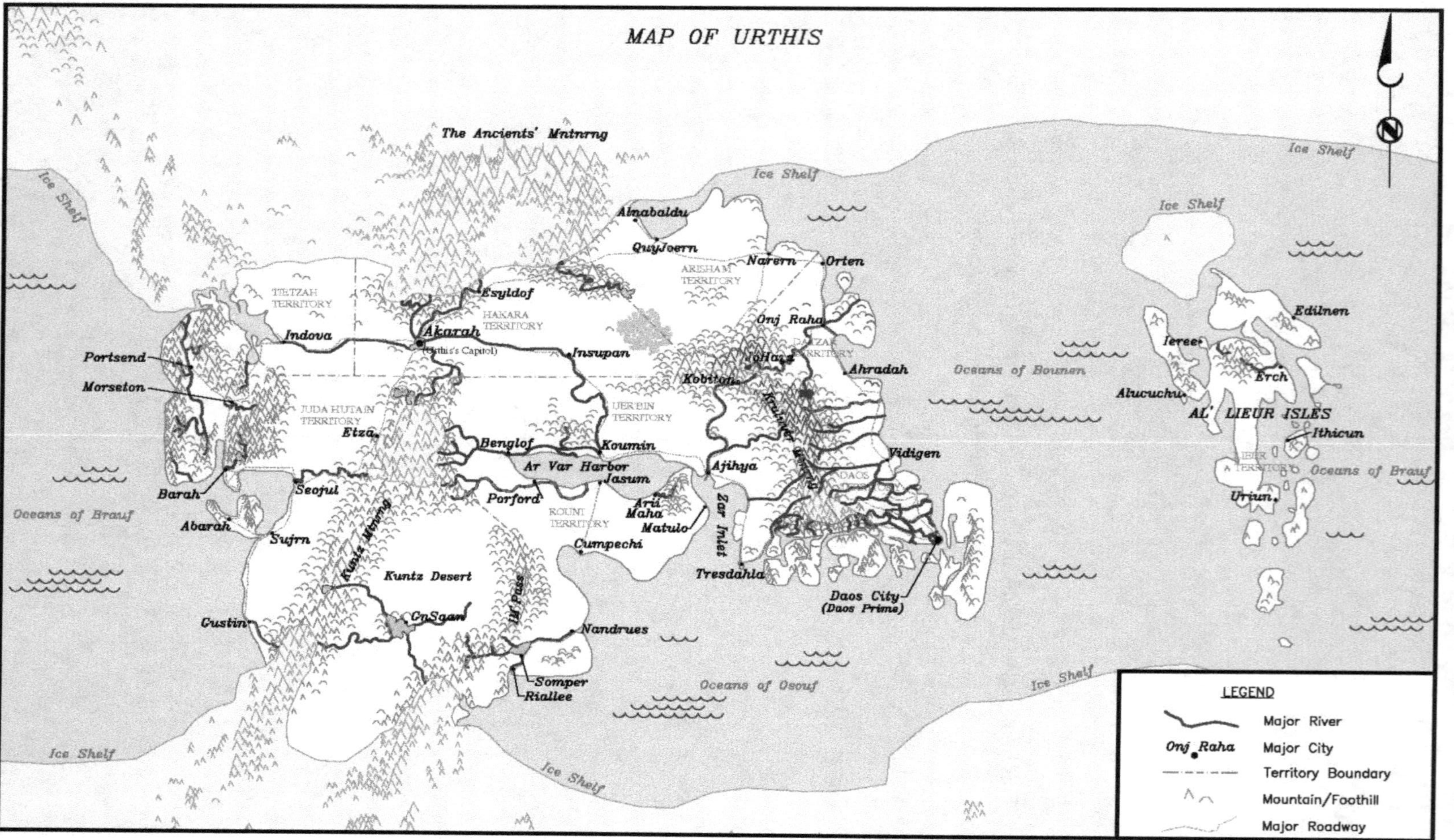

MAP OF URTHIS
N
The Ancients' Mntnrng
Ice Shelf
Ice Shelf
Ice Shelf
Alnabaldu
QujJoern
Narern
Orten
ARISHAM TERRITORY
Onj Raha
DAIZAE TERRITORY
JoHara
Ahradah
Oceans of Bounen
TIETZAH TERRITORY
Esyldof
HAKARA TERRITORY
Indova
Akarah
(Urthis's Capitol)
Insupan
Kobiton
Krulainet Umrmg
Edilnen
Iereee
Erch
Alucuchu
AL' LIEUR ISLES
Portsend
Morseton
JUDA HUTAIN TERRITORY
UERBIN TERRITORY
Vidigen
IBER TERRITORY
Ithicun
Oceans of Brauf
Etza
Benglof
Koumin
Ajihya
DAOS
Uriun
Barah
Ar Var Harbor
Jasum
Arú Maha
Matulo
Zar Inlet
Oceans of Brauf
Seojul
Porford
ROUNT TERRITORY
Abarah
Kuniz Mtnrng
Cumpechi
Tresdahla
Sujrn
Kuntz Desert
In Pass
Gustin
CnSgam
Nandrues
Daos City
(Daos Prime)
Oceans of Osouf
Ice Shelf
Somper
Riallee
Ice Shelf
LEGEND
Major River
Onj Raha    Major City
Territory Boundary
Mountain/Foothill
Major Roadway

# Contents

# PROLOGUE

The Warden stood at the edge of the northern road, hazel eyes fixed on Kobiton rising on the hillside ahead. The city's stone walls and tiered structures climbed the slope, crowned by the abbey and seminary at the summit. Early morning mist clung to the towers like spectral fingers, unable to hide what the Warden sought.

"We have found another two," the Warden whispered, though no one stood nearby to hear.

Born a man, the Warden no longer spoke as one. Decades of consuming souls had transformed him into something collective—a vessel filled with the voices of those he had absorbed through Hakra's malicious gifts. These dozens of consumed spirits watched the world through his eyes and sometimes spoke through his mouth—demanding acknowledgment. Thus, 'I' had become 'We'—a being of multitudes bound within a single form. Their master in the Ishik Empire could hear them all, every tormented voice that dwelled beneath the Warden's skin, a constant chorus of the damned that would remain until Death came for the body that housed them.

The voice that answered came from within, resonating through blood and bone. *How many heads have you so far?*

"Thirteen."

*Thirteen! Impressive. You've earned more than a dozen bags of gold! Very impressive. After this you can retire, live your life unbeholden to any master.*

The wind picked up and a cloud shifted the warm moment cold. But that was what they preferred. Change. The idea of retiring never entered their mind. This was the life they wanted to live—a life with purpose.

*Once you're done in Kobiton, you'll continue into Datzar Territory and return home.*

"As you command." The Warden's lips barely moved, features momentarily shifting like a magical cloud, obscuring what lay beneath. The voice was not meant for Mortal ears.

Their features shifted like a magical cloud, obscuring what lay beneath before settling back into human form. With a casual gesture, the Warden summoned their Erthin Powers and made a small flame dance above their palm, then extinguished it with a breath that frosted the morning air. Fire and air responded to their will as easily as earth had yielded a path through the mountain slopes days earlier, and as readily as water had parted before their horse at the river crossing. The fifth element—spirit—hummed constantly in their blood, connecting them to their distant master.

Their gloved hand patted the saddlebag where a heavy sack was secured. Thirteen heads so far, each bearing the same distinctive features—the prominent forehead, the arched brows, the peculiar set of the jaw, all blonde haired. All the adults and children were of the same bloodline. All threats to be eliminated.

The Warden's fingers traced the insignia sewn into their coat—not the mark of Hakra that the people of Kobiton would recognize, but another symbol entirely. The ecclesiastics and Head Mistress would not question a Warden's authority; none ever did. Blind faith made the task simple, and all of these executions performed by the individual incarnation—representing the whole of Hakra's authority—simple.

Their mount shifted restlessly, sensing the hunt to come. The Warden placed a hand on its neck, feeling the creature's pulse quicken beneath their touch.

"Patience," they murmured. "We shall have what we seek."

The Warden's mind reached ahead, sifting through the thoughts of those in the city above, searching for the distinctive mental patterns that would identify their quarry. Their telepathic probe slipped past the Telepaths within the PCP ranks with practiced ease, cloaked in the authority that came with their position. And then they found them. Two minds sharing the same curious resonance. The male was at the PCP Hall, training under a senior Telepath. The female was in the abbey's kitchen, her thoughts fluttering between herb mixtures and bread temperatures.

Something about those cooking thoughts tugged at the Warden's consciousness. How long had it been since they'd eaten a meal not hastily prepared over a campfire? The bland rations they had subsisted on for months now had become tiresome. Their stomach growled at the thought of properly seasoned food.

*Perhaps the female will be useful for more than one purpose. For a time, at least.*

The Warden's hazel eyes shifted, briefly reflecting an unnatural blue light before returning to normal. Their face rippled again, features becoming momentarily unrecognizable—a swirling vortex of mist and shadow. For an instant, they had seen through another's eyes—those of their master far away in the Ishik Empire. The connection faded, leaving behind the familiar hollow ache in their chest.

"We understand," the Warden said to the emptiness. "We shall not fail."

Their mount began its ascent toward Kobiton, toward the unsuspecting PCP Hall and Abbey just beyond. It would be a simple matter to plant the suggestion in both targets: *Hakra has requested your presence. A great honor awaits.*

No one would question. No one would resist.

By nightfall, they would be riding away from Kobiton, the male's head in their sack, the female under their control. The Warden's hand slid to the blade at their side, feeling its familiar weight. Their mission was nearly complete.

*Nearly* complete.

Far beneath the loyal servant's exterior beat a heart with its own ambitions. The Warden had smelled the female's cooking even from this distance, had felt the curious power emanating from her—a gift that might sustain long after this hunt was done. And when that usefulness came to an end ... well, there would always be room for one more head in the sack.

The true purpose of this hunt was known only to the Warden himself, hidden even from the chorus of souls he carried—not even their distant Master understood the full scope of their intentions.

"Soon," the Warden promised the blade, the road, and whatever forces might be listening. "We shall have what we truly seek."

The horse continued upward, carrying its rider toward destiny.

# 1

## <u>AWAKENING</u>

It was the sound of babbling water in a nearby brook that first caught Charlotte's attention. What was that sound right next to her head? Sounded like water percolating in a kettle getting ready to scream. Her stomach grumbled, and her eyes fluttered open. This was a new campsite. She knew that much.

How long had she been under the Warden's spell?

The Erthin-made campfire barely radiated any heat. Her breath's vapor floated up and dissipated into the chilly morning air.

Her memory was empty. But she knew she had to break free from this malicious creature holding her captive.

"Make us food!" The Warden stood over her, their hazel eyes demanding. They had exceptional powers—this one, a large person, could shape shift, yield the five elements, and mentally manipulate anyone they pleased.

Charlotte shook under their angry gaze. Somehow, she mustered the ferocity to say, "No."

"We could make you go another three days without food."

"Kill me already!" She continued to lie on the ground. Hungry. Weak. Charlotte wanted to make breakfast. Porridge—a tasteless meal—would be divine under these circumstances. But her will to be stubborn shone through the rest of these pressing discomforts. "Why don't you behead me like you did H'Eirwyn? We all know I don't deserve to live. You said it yourself. Just get it over with. Kill me now!"

She waited for the slice of the knife to carve her head off as this ugly creature had done with her friend. But that would not happen. The Warden's stomach growled even louder than hers.

"Make us food now!"

"I refuse." Once again, her stomach rumbled, and she flinched.

A wicked smile spread the Warden's thin lips. "We will let you eat, too. If you make us food."

She wasn't convinced. Nevertheless, Charlotte mustered enough strength to get up off the cold ground and calm the kettle and make porridge. Taking some herbs from a small pouch, Charlotte sprinkled some flavor into the mix of hot, lumpy oats. Flavor made from a Coterie spell of hers. She served the porridge into the wooden bowl provided.

She sensed the Warden wasn't sure what she put into the meal. The Warden watched her the whole time. Even as a child, Charlotte had known her connection to food went beyond cooking. Seeds sprouted at her touch; spoiled food became fresh again. The Abbey kitchen staff called it Hakra's blessing. Only she knew how deep the power really went. It was this power she used now, carefully measuring her herbs, knowing she could do far more than just add flavor.

"You eat first." They waited and watched as she took the first bite. Charlotte was ready to shovel more porridge into her mouth, but the Warden grabbed the bowl from her hands. They then scarfed every morsel of sweet tasting porridge, loudly scraping the bowl clean. Afterwards, they gobbled the contents of the pot.

She tried not to be disappointed, but her grimace was deep. Her stomach was angry and empty and now she had been denied a meal. And it let the world know—her intestines tightened, jabbing throughout.

"We leave now." The Warden tossed the bowl at her, probably hoping she would pick it up and put it in the packs to be washed later.

"I need to eat!" Charlotte pleaded.

The Warden was angered by her outburst. They slapped her. "Pick up those things, package them up. Get going!" As usual, the Warden would not wait for Charlotte. They had a mission. She was now the Warden's personal servant, not what Charlotte wanted.

Hands on her hips, she snarled, "I refuse!"

"Do you wish to be mindless for the rest of your life?"

"You seem to want me to be mindless!"

The Warden held their hand up in the air, readying to hit her once more, but Charlotte remained defiant. "Just take my head off already and go! I don't wanna live if this is how I'm going to be treated for the rest of my life!"

The Warden's lips twisted. "You cook better when you're aware of what you're doing. You do many things better when you're aware. Pack up. Now!"

She started the busy work but kept an eye on the Warden, a nameless creature who appeared to want more than Charlotte was willing to give. She dawdled on purpose; she was waiting for something to happen. Again, she was slapped and the Warden's harsh tongue prodded her to go faster, but she resisted.

"Please let me eat something! Anything!"

"You can have some of tonight's meal if you're good." The Warden's lips twisted with amusement, and they checked their horse's cinch.

It would soon be time to act. Charlotte knew not to think about what would happen next. If she did, the Warden would know too. She too was strong with powers, but nothing comparable to what the Warden could yield. Still, Charlotte kept a secret. Her powers made her aware of the food she touched. With a sprinkling of herbs, she could make any meal taste amazing or incredibly bland. Or turn it into poison. She also knew how deep into someone's digestive tract the foods she had touched had traveled—this was with everybody she fed but only at the time of the meal. Anyone who ate her food, she could feel them digesting it. Usually, Charlotte ignored that input from her magical powers. But today she would use that knowledge. She would use her secret power; she would attempt to kill the Warden.

She closed her eyes, reaching for the well of mystical Coterie Power within her. It surged up, warm and familiar, tingling through her fingertips. The air around her hands shimmered, tiny motes of light dancing in response to her will. She shaped the energy carefully, marveling as always at how something so intangible could have such profound effects on the physical world.

With a slight movement of her fingers, she inflicted a terrible pain that shot through the Warden—taking them to their knees. The large-bodied soldier cried out in agony, their blue eyes wild with anger, but Charlotte did not let up with her powerful magic. Soon they fell face down into the hardened soil from the pain. She used the porridge in the Warden's stomach and turned it poisonous. She knew Wardens were trained for this type of event, so she reached for their blade and went for their neck.

Even though the Warden was gravely hurt, doubled over in pain, they could still defend and deflect. They attempted to change her mind. The mental battle was excruciating. The Warden's defenses were like iron walls, unyielding and cold. Charlotte pushed harder, sweat beading on her brow. For a moment, she felt her control slipping, the Warden's mind pushing back with terrifying force.

But then she thought of H'Eirwyn, of all the others who had fallen victim to this monster. With a final desperate surge, the Warden grabbed the knife, turned it upon her, and pierced through Charlotte's thick wool dress drawing blood. She growled, pushed through it. This momentary infliction would not affect her too much. Her regenerative powers always healed her quickly.

She smirked and continued to weave her poisonous spell, twisting the food around in the Warden's belly, twisting the bottom of the esophagus, all the Warden's stomach cavity and upper digestive tract. She saw the glimmer of light in their dark, beady eyes falter. The smooth and sharp blade fell from their hand. Charlotte stumbled back, exhausted but triumphant. She knew this victory was temporary—she needed to act fast before the spell wore off.

She kicked the knife away as the Warden cried again before succumbing to the agony of it all. She then turned on her Succubus power. This soul-hungry power scared her, but the thought of dying at the hands of some rogue Warden filled her with the energy to follow through with this despicable task. Yet her dislike of this power sat heavy like a wet blanket. It was what kept her from following through with murder. She didn't want to live with someone's tormented soul tethered to her for the rest of her life (or so the teachers had warned). With this in mind, Charlotte proceeded to suckle the Warden's life energy, bringing them as close to death as she could. She had never taken a life, never thought of murdering anyone. And though she had been taught how to use this cursed power at school, she had always been afraid of it. As a youngster, she had been thrown into solitary because of it; yet it was that same fear which helped her steal the Warden's essence now. Though she wasn't sure she could extinguish the Warden's life this way, hopefully it would cripple them for many hours—long enough for her to escape far away.

She kicked the Warden's head. Every time her boot hit, she felt more victorious. She looked for breath and saw gobs of blood on their face.

"Good riddance." Her voice shook when she called out to no one in particular, and then she realized her whole body was shaking too. This had been too much for her, all of it. Being taken from the only home she had ever known. Leaving a lifestyle that she had worked so hard for. And her friend, someone she had known since a young age, had been destroyed right before her eyes. The Warden's motivations were unexplainable, inexcusable. She was still grieving for H'Eirwyn.

She lunged for the knife, picked it up and held it tight. Charlotte's heart pounded against her chest, in her ears. She surveyed the camp.

Should she take the horse?

Charlotte wasn't a sure rider. Yet she didn't want the Warden, if they resurrected from their infliction, to have the ability to hunt her down from horseback. Besides, the animal looked agitated from what she had just done to its master. It might throw her. Without another thought about it, Charlotte sliced the horse's throat. A quick death.

The young woman grabbed her meager shoulder bag and raced away from the crime scene.

Her heart thumped against her ribs. Her head ached. What had she just done? Charlotte hadn't known before now she had that in her, the ability to kill a person. She had killed many chickens and goats, and now a horse. She had only ever thought about murdering menacing individuals, but had never acted on it. She was thrilled and scared and wanted to return home at once.

The sun was out now, and bird chirps echoed throughout the wilderness. Charlotte was not a runner, but fear and adrenaline pushed her ahead. She hoped she was racing the right way home. None of this scenery looked familiar. She couldn't tell which way they had come or which way they were going. And the shadows that surrounded her gave no hints to her location in the Kruluver Mountains. She missed Kobiton. She missed her daily routines and seeing her friends.

Tears blurred her vision. The trees closed in, and the sky grew dark. Angry bird calls echoed from all around. Spooked, she didn't stay on the road for long, finding a well-used animal trail instead. Charlotte believed that if she hid in the forest, the Warden might not find her if they had survived the death knell she had dealt.

But Wardens were strong. They were trained assassins—trained for all types of defiance and violence, trained to sense people's actions before they act. Charlotte was not trained for anything other than cooking. There was no way her Powers could compete against the Warden's awesome Talents, even if she could turn food to poison and Succubus them to Death's doorstep.

She began to second guess her actions. They too had amazing Powers of instant regeneration of wounds. Did she really kill them, or was she now their prey?

As Charlotte stumbled through the forest, her mind raced. Freedom tasted sweet, but fear clung to her like a second skin. What if the Warden had in fact survived? What if they found her and killed her? Or worse, what if they died, and she would lose herself in this forest forever? She was lost. Which way was home?

But beyond all of that, a deeper fear gnawed at her: who was she now that she was away from everything she had ever known?

*I can't go back, but I don't know if I can go forward either.*

She continued to climb a steep slope. Her legs burned and ached; her breath heaved. She was sweating under her wool dress. Her shoulder bag was pulling on her and kept getting caught on underbrush and branches. She had found a prickly bush with her face, and it scraped her hands until she bled. Charlotte was frantic, fearful, and wondered if the Warden would pounce. She tried to put her thoughts to bed, knowing that they might pick up on them.

The trail intercepted another trail, and she took it. It wound around the hillside. From between the leaves laden with moisture in the thickening forest, she saw into the next valley. There was a river at the bottom of a rocky gorge, and Charlotte felt her thirst grow. She left the animal trail, turning her feet straight down the slope, and continuing to put space between her and the Warden. By now, all her senses were keen. She kept looking around, as if feeling the Warden closing in. Her cloth bag snagged itself on a branch, and she had a momentary argument with it before it released its grasp. Without warning, she began tumbling backwards down the hillside, gulping mouthfuls of dirt and moss along the way.

She landed at the bottom of the long slope, bruised and scraped. Branches and stickers poked and prodded her body. Possessions had fallen out of her baggage along the way—items she believed were now lost forever. She found her feet and dusted off her dress, pulling most of the larger sticks and moss from her hair, swiping at pools of blood on her arms and legs and neck. She was spooked and yearned to be anywhere but here.

Charlotte stood out in the open, shuddering at the sight of a dark shadow that passed overhead. She barely had time to look up and see the eagle tumbling from the blue sky toward her, mutating as it fell and shapeshifting into a vicious wild cat. Its loud yowl matched her blood-curdling scream as it tackled her. She was flung hard against a stoney surface near the edge of the churning river. Her head banged twice against the rocks, knocking her unconscious.

# 2

# <u>First Contact</u>

The metallic taste of blood filled Charlotte's mouth as she clawed her way back to consciousness. Her own Elementalist Abilities were strengthening, healing her at once. She became aware of the mountain's icy stones pressed against her cheek. Somewhere above, a falcon's cry pierced the silence. She wasn't dead—the Warden hadn't finished their work yet.

Above her loomed a furry-faced old man with silvery eyes that swirled like molten metal. Though his pale features suggested Mortal lineage, she sensed he was something else entirely—definitely not the Warden who had brought her to this place—attacked her—but perhaps something more dangerous.

"Oh. Sorry. I did not mean to startle you, Sweet Miss." The old man moved back, stood tall, and offered her a hand. "I did not believe you were alive, but now you are. Anything hurt?"

She didn't grab his hand and rose slowly on her own, taking in everything. A bloody trail was all that was left—that she saw at first—of the Warden who could have, should have, killed her. Charlotte studied the unassuming elderly man.

"How'd you kill it?" She asked.

"Took their head clean off, as one should when battling one of those bruits. They can live through most anything, except for that one."

She looked for the giant blade that would still be wet with the Warden's blood. There was none. This old man had no leather sheath affixed to his belt, and there was no axe handle protruding from the packs on his donkeys. She contemplated him, wondering how he knew of Wardens. He was old, probably had seen some things. But how would he know how to kill a Warden? They are creatures who did the bidding of Hakra—god himself—and were bred to encompass all the Powers; Clan-Duin shapeshifting abilities, wielding all five Elementalist traits (fire, air, water, earth, and spirit), and Telepathy.

The moss that covered much of the stony ground had been scraped off in spots. Just beyond, she saw a leafy, yet prickly, bush. A gloved hand protruded. Charlotte recognized that glove. She could barely make out the Warden's body, but knew it was stashed in the brush.

Bird calls echoed back and forth across this long narrow ravine. She heard the river rage behind her; tree branches swayed, making a soft ruffling sound. She could have silenced it to intimidate but knew not to show off what all she could do, her amazing Coterie Powers.

With a nod, she said, "Thank you, Sir, for killing it."

"Why did it attack you?"

Her toes tapped in her boots. She was afraid to tell the truth. Face now rouge, Charlotte was leery of his gaze. "I am the daughter of some noble. A nobleman's daughter, I mean. The Warden had been sent to retrieve me."

"A daughter to a nobleman? Huh."

She watched him, waiting, listening for any thought, but all she heard was the roaring water slapping against the gorge's walls.

He studied her, possibly contemplating her plain muddy clothes. "To what house?"

"I don't know."

"What do you mean, you do not know? How could you not know about your family?"

Her ears burned as hot as her face. "Um, well. I just found out. You see, I was a cook, I am a cook for …" She dropped her voice. "… Kobiton's Abbey and Seminary School." Her voice had returned. "The Warden came for me. Took me and my friend. Said we were requested by Hakra. But then later they said we were requested by my father. I'm sure it's all a lie. I think they captured us all for another reason. A sinister reason. I'm glad you saved me."

They stared at each other for a long time before he asked, "So, you are an orphan?"

"Yes, Sir."

"No Sirs with me. I am no Sir."

She bit her lip in the same spot as always. The mark of shame continued to grow. "I'm sorry for lying. You're just … I just can't believe you killed a Warden. That's just amazing! I mean, you look old, but you're obviously not feeble."

"What did they want with you?" His silvery eyes never left hers. "Wardens only chase the worst of the worst. So, I will ask again, why were they hunting you?"

It became hard for Charlotte to swallow. "Because I tried to kill them but failed. I wanted to avenge my friend's brutal death. They killed him. Killed H'Eirwyn."

A tear dripped, then a few more. She didn't want to keep crying for H'Eirwyn, but his death had been brutal, and she could not stop seeing it. For better or worse, she had thought of H'Eirwyn as family. Though they had different mothers, they were blood bound by their father, and that single link was precious to her. She was devastated that H'Eirwyn, the only family she knew, had been prematurely taken from her. In that moment, she wished she had known him better.

· · · ● · ● · ● ● · ·

H'Eirwyn and Charlotte looked much alike, meaning they had their father's features. She had been abandoned as an infant. He came to the orphanage at the age of seven following his mother's death. She would never forget the other children making fun of them, calling them 'by-blow babies.' But then again, most of the children in Kobiton's Abbey were either illegitimate or true orphans.

When the Warden came for her, her long-time friend, family, walked alongside the giant guardian who had come for them. Back then, H'Eirwyn had believed he was going off for the greater good. They were told the same story: that they had been asked by Hakra—almighty god himself—to follow the Warden back to Akarah. No hesitation. No questions. And they would be greatly rewarded for their efforts.

That time was marked by shared feelings of excitement and trepidation. As young teenagers, they embarked on a pilgrimage to Akarah, a journey everyone makes at least once in their life. Escorted by ecclesiastics and soldiers, the journey from Kobiton to Akarah took over a year to complete. But they had seen Hakra, gazed upon his black-skinned glory, stood fearfully under his azure-eyed stare, and had willingly pledged eternal servitude to him for this life and the next. Each of them questioned themselves and each other about whether their feelings for their savior would remain unchanged upon another encounter.

Two days into their journey, past the trash hole township known as Goshee, the Warden took H'Eirwyn's head off. One strike. He then placed his head into a bag filled with other heads, all with similar features to her own.

"If you don't follow my rules, you'll be next," The Warden's gloved finger pointed at her.

• • • • • ● • ● • • • ·

The old man asked, "There was someone else with you?"

She jolted out of her reverie and wiped away a drip of snot from her nose. "Yes. My friend. We were often teased for being what they called 'by-blow' cousins. Come to find out, we were more like half-siblings."

A falcon's call from above startled them, and once more their eyes were on everything but each other.

"The Warden killed H'Eirwyn, but not me. I don't know why I was kept alive. At first, I thought it was simply chance, but now ... now I'm not so sure. The way the Warden had watched me when I cooked, the strange insignia on their coat, did not add up. I knew there was something more going on, something I needed to figure out if I wanted to survive. That's when I realized he wasn't working for my estranged father. Or Hakra. He was working for something or someone else."

The old man was dismissive. "Wardens only keep people alive if warranted. They are well-trained bounty hunters. Always in it for the reward. Only called upon as a last resort. So, I will ask one last time—"

"I've told you the truth, Sir. I swear by Hakra's breath, I'm not lying to you. The Warden came to Kobiton, took me and H'Eirwyn. Told our superiors that we were requested by Hakra. But when he killed H'Eirwyn he told me that, both of us, H'Eirwyn and I, we were some nobleman's by-blow children. He was taking me to meet my estranged father." She saw a flick of emotion on the old man's face. "All I know is that he's some stupid yet powerful man who went around proliferating the landscape impregnating any sweet looking piece of honey he found along the trail. The Warden said he had requested his children to come home. But then we argued and ...." He had stolen her memories. "I now understand why I was abandoned and never adopted. No one wants an unidentifiably Talented child like me. Yeah, sure, I look like an Erthin, but I'm just as deadly as that Warden. I mean, you know, with some training, I could've been a match. Had Hakra any sight about women's strength, we could be Wardens too, you know. I mean, I could've killed them if I were better trained with my powers."

The beard made it hard to tell if he was smirking. "Are you saying you have comparable Powers to a Warden?"

"No. Oh, no. I mean, I'm not Clan-Duin, so no. I can't just change my appearance any ol' day. It's just creepy how they did it. I'm so glad it's gone. Thank you again."

"Are you telepathic?"

She didn't look like a Telepath with their bright blue eyes, pale hair and skin tone. Nor did she act like one. "Oh, no. No. I'm an Elementalist, actually," Charlotte replied. "Fire came first, when I was just a child. Then water and wind followed—gifts that made me valuable in the kitchen. I can create pockets of air to bake bread without an oven, summon water for washing without a well." She paused, her fingers tracing patterns in the air. "Earth came last, though it's less useful in cooking. And healing ..." Her voice dropped. "That's always been with me, though sometimes I wonder if it's more a curse than a blessing." She shrugged and looked at the stone slab below her thick leather boots. A long slug was crawling away from the running water and towards her.

"None of that makes you comparable in power to a Warden, if indeed you are being truthful about your Powers and your story. I am sure they would have sliced your head off without you knowing ... had there been no need for you, but you were obviously more valuable alive than dead. Until now, that is." His silvery eyes were full of skepticism. "So, what is your value? What kept you alive?"

The Warden had confessed much to her during the few times she was cognizant. Charlotte was never sure if the Warden had an ulterior motive with their conversations, or if they just wanted companionship. But there were moments, fleeting glimpses of something more.

Once, she caught the Warden studying a map marked with strange symbols, muttering about 'Ishik' and 'new orders.' Another time, she overheard a heated telepathic conversation with an unseen party, the Warden insisting they were 'still loyal' despite 'necessary deviations.' Each of these moments was a piece of a puzzle Charlotte couldn't quite solve. But now she wondered if her survival depended on putting it together, especially now that the Warden was dead.

"I'm a skilled cook." She tossed up her hands and smiled. "It's what I do. I love it. And you?" She sank back on her heels, her attention on him. But his eyes were now on the racing clouds. The blue sky and sunshine were gone, and it grew cold. Wind rattled dead leaves; a few fell with the grace of a swan.

He rubbed his hands together and jumped into action. "It is time for me to go." He sprinted away from her and began to arrange the tack on his lead donkey—the other ten donkeys were just attentive to the old man as their leader.

"Where are you going?"

"Chinochi."

"Chinochi? How far away is Chinochi from here?"

"You do not know?"

"All I know is the Warden stole my mind. After that .... I could see things, but I wasn't allowed to think. I don't know how long I was like that. And the few times I was allowed to have my mind was when I made food. But even then ...." She exhaled.

"Chinochi is about half a day from here," said the man who had introduced himself as Edwin. "But I need to hurry if I want to arrive before nightfall."

Her stomach dropped. "We're that close? The Warden stole my mind for many days then. Kobiton's at least half a moon's cycle away. And it's already late autumn. Winter will be here soon. I'll never make it home!"

"Indeed. And with no horse or provisions, it will take you longer. I know the snowline is at the pass, but give it a few days and it will be below that mark. Always happens this time of the year."

Charlotte fell to her knees and screamed. "Fuk!"

He gasped. "Dear Sweet Miss, who would have ever thought words like that would part your lips?"

She cried. "They should've just taken my head."

"Why? Why do you say that?"

"That's where all the heads went—into the bag on their horse. Over a dozen of us, all with the same features. Even a baby, no more than two!"

The old man took a deep breath and took up the lead lines tethered to the donkey train.

"I didn't ask for this, any of it. I don't want to be here. I never wanted .... I just ... I just want to go home." She sobbed.

"I understand, Sweet Miss. I do not desire to exist in this moment either, but here we are. Knowing that there was one Warden gives me much concern that there will be PCP on the prowl. They are bound, all of them. Every damn Telepath is tethered in one way or another."

Charlotte wiped her nose and brushed her tears away, fighting against the ceaseless stream. She couldn't look at him, yet asked, "Can I follow you?"

Contemplation pushed his salt-and-pepper colored eyebrows down, and soon he shrugged and harrumphed.

"Thank you, kind sir. Thank you so very much!" She practically fell over her words and feet, feeling more than sorry for herself.

The timeworn old man escorted her away from the bottom of the narrow but long valley. His lips were set firm, as was his pace as they made their way, zigzagging up the steep slope. Fir trees crowded the muddied trail, but her footprints were not on it.

In her mad dash to get away from the Warden, Charlotte had sidestepped what she believed was an animal trail and dove straight down the ravine. She had cut through the switchback path, and about midway, her bag had caught on a branch and tore. All the contents—beloved items—had been strewn along the steep slope.

As they hiked, Charlotte picked up all her belongings: her only other change of clothing, a favorite summer skirt, a scarf knit by her best friend Lori, a large pouch filled with many smaller pouches of herbs and spices, a small box with a carving of a great stag that held three pieces of jewelry, her favorite carving blade, and a leather-bound book, *Tomes for Children*. These few precious things brought her joy—beyond the friends left behind in Kobiton.

"Oh, I'm sorry. I never introduced myself. I'm Charlotte. And you are?"

"Edwin."

She waited for him to give her a last name, as most people did upon introduction, except for orphans. None was given. "How far away from here do you live?"

He pointed back the way they had come, but didn't reveal more.

"Have you always lived here?"

They hiked a long way before he replied, "No. But this is, by far, my favorite place to live."

Their boots were caked with mud by the time they reached the top of the hillside. Edwin pulled out a sharp hoof pick and scraped the mud off his boots. He had handed her a flask. She drank while he cleaned, and then they exchanged pick and water.

"How often do you visit Chinochi?"

"Once a moon."

"What's in the packs?"

"Coal. About two tons of it. Chinochi always has a demand for it. Easiest way to make silvers, I believe."

"Are you foolin' me?! Its soot clogs chimneys, smoke from it hurts lungs, and the occupation of it is more deadly than being a PCP soldier. And worse, I had a friend die from a cave-in a couple of moons ago. And they'd only been mining a few moons. It was the worst! Wasn't even twenty years old."

"Not everyone is meant to work in the underbelly of Urthis."

She nodded, passed back the hoof pick. He offered her one more drink, but she declined. Edwin pushed the flask back into a pack on the lead donkey and the two continued their grueling pace.

Before long, everything looked slightly familiar to her. The trail they followed, Edwin told her, was the one he frequented. Soon they found the road, packed firm with gravel—there would always be muddy parts, potholes, and puddles, but the structure had been maintained for a millennium. A soft mist began to fall. They stopped at the trailhead in the middle of the roadway for another water break.

"Well, Sweet Miss, here is the road. That way leads to Kobiton." She could only see a few hundred feet up the roadway where the gray cloud of rain swallowed up the green and brown forest. The view downslope was occluded too. The donkeys appeared ready for more walking, impatiently stomping.

Edwin passed her his flask. "Take this."

"You're leaving me?"

"You can follow me further, if you wish. Chinochi is still a good long walk from here. Most likely, it will be dark when we arrive."

With a nod, she gave him back the flask and onward they went.

Edwin led them down the narrow roadway that wound through the forest. They hadn't walked more than a kilometer before they found the Warden's campsite. The horse lay dead, its jugular sliced, blood soaked into the rocky soil. The sight sent a chill down Charlotte's spine—a reminder that in this world of power and secrets, nothing was ever simple.

The few possessions the Warden had owned were strewn about. It looked as if an animal had come through the camp, the contents of bags and foods were tossed and overturned. Everything was muddy. Only one sack remained untouched.

Charlotte stopped first. Edwin stepped alongside her to witness the atrocity. The day's rain only caused blood to flood the whole area—save the firepit, now an island.

She pointed at the untouched sack hanging in the air on an ethereal, magical tether. "That's the bag. It's got at least a dozen heads."

"I wonder how much they are worth?"

She peered at him. "You're not gonna kill me, are you?"

He was apathetic to her, or at least that's how he appeared through all that unkempt facial hair. "Anything here of any worth to you?"

She saw her cloak, soaked by mud and abandoned for freedom to run. Coming back for the worn piece of clothing, the offering of comfort it had brought her during torrential times, brought back a familiar melancholy. It made a sucking sound when she peeled it off the soaked ground. It was heavy and as weighted as she felt in that moment.

Edwin muttered, "You can leave it. When we get to Chinochi's mercantile, I will purchase you a new one."

Rain dripped down her face, forever etching this moment of time in her mind. Nothing would ever be the same. She wanted to cry. A deep and rare kind of sadness enveloped her and soaked her like the sopping old cloak she clung to.

**3**

## <u>CHINOCHI</u>

Edwin gave Charlotte some cleanish clothes and an oiled canvas. She changed out of her dirty and bloody wool dress and huddled underneath the canvas to stay warm and dry. Secretly, Charlotte created a pocket of Erthin heat that lasted until they reached the outskirts of Chinochi. She knew that if there were any Erthins in Chinochi, they would feel her coming if she maintained her spell. She had no desire to draw unnecessary attention. Not here. Not now.

The smell of Chinochi—fires, food, life—warmed Charlotte's soul. Edwin led her confidently to the mercantile, greeting the owner like an old friend. But the jovial old man shifted when the owner noticed Charlotte quietly standing with the donkeys.

Charlotte heard the merchant think; *I recognize that face!* "Who is this lovely lady?"

Edwin stammered, "Ah, yes, this … this is Charlotte. My daughter. Granddaughter, I mean. She wanted to see Chinochi."

"Well, good day to you, Miss Charlotte Miner. Edwin's never told me about you. She must be an older sister to Albert. Where have you been keeping her? Blocked up in that sooty ol' cave of yours? I'm surprised you haven't come down the mountain before now. Chinochi is a wonderful place to visit, don't you think Edwin?" The merchant's eyes were like the pools where Charlotte and her friends would swim on warm summer days. *That's the woman. We were warned about her. She must've killed the Warden, and now she's got Edwin under her control. Sly vixen. I must save him from her. Posthaste.* The man behind the counter came forward and reached for her hand, but she recoiled and hid behind Edwin.

Edwin's wrinkly hand grasped hers tight. It was then that she heard his thoughts. *… and the innkeeper is telepathic too. I forgot how many there are in this town. Where can we go so that she will be safe?* "Like I was saying, Gavin," Edwin pulled her along with him. "I brought over two tons this time. I was hoping to get the usual items. Pack up the line, get to the stables, and so on. It was quite a hard hike on Charlotte." He looked at her. "She said she has worked up quite an appetite."

"Yeah, I'm starving!" She dropped their contact and put her hands behind her back.

"As usual, Edwin, I can only give you store credit this time. You know me, I've never got enough silver for your coal," replied the merchant. "But, as usual, you can take anything you want. All my shelves are stocked for a cold winter." He continued to eye Charlotte like she was prey. "I even have warm winter cloaks lined with deer fur. Maybe your granddaughter would want to come and try them on. Come on dear, let me show you what I've got upstairs."

Edwin's hand brushed her arm, and their eyes caught one another's. He glanced back at the merchant, then back to her. Although he wasn't thinking anything, she understood what he was insinuating—he didn't want her to be alone with the merchant. She shook her head, hoping to agree with his hints, not wanting to go with this known Telepath who appeared to be considering her way too much.

Without a beat, Charlotte replied. "I'm here to help my papa." A smile drew up her cold cheeks.

The merchant, Gavin, unfastened the door to his storage room; soon they were bustling back and forth with heavy packs. Both Charlotte and Edwin were dripping sweat by the time they were finished.

"That went much quicker than it usually does. Thank you." Edwin patted her shoulder, pushing her along and out of the cold storage room. The donkeys—secured to a hitching post—stood patiently by the watering trough. He insisted they bring several empty packs inside the mercantile. Together, they walked up and down the aisles gathering provisions.

Edwin's grip on Charlotte's arm tightened as they wove through Chinochi's only mercantile. "Watch yourself," he muttered, eyes darting here and there. "This place is crawling with Telepaths these days."

Charlotte raised an eyebrow. "Really?"

"And they are about as friendly as a snake before it bites." Edwin grunted and sighed. "Ah, they are not all bad. Just ... keep your guard up, especially around Gavin."

As if summoned, the shopkeeper appeared, all smiles and hearty greetings. Edwin forced a grin. "Aye, Gavin. Why is it you never have any silver for me?"

Gavin's laugh boomed throughout the shop. "You know how it is, my friend. Times are tight. But I've got plenty of credit for you! Like I said, my store is stocked for the winter. Take what you need. Until then, I'll get the receipt started."

Gavin took off to fetch his ledger.

Edwin leaned close to Charlotte. "See those trinkets?" he whispered, nodding towards the glittering display above the door. "That man has more silver than the mountain itself. Just likes to keep us indebted."

Charlotte nodded, her understanding dawning. In Chinochi, it seemed, every smile hid sharp teeth, and every kindness came with strings attached.

Above the front counter there were silver and gold platters, both embellished and plain; fancy lanterns hung from small and stout and elaborately shaped hooks and chains; interesting knives and swords cris-crossed each other and gleamed; gilded pictures of many sizes were framed with nothing but the wood wall behind. There were countless fancy ornaments and different sized bells made from bronze, silver, and gold. The entire front wall glistened.

Charlotte saw several aluminum cookie cutters hung up like trophies, and she snickered remembering her favorite—very worn down—cookie cutters at the Abbey's kitchens. They too were hung up, but not for decoration, they had served a purpose; to bring a little bite of sweetness into an otherwise bitter life. Those trophy cookie cutters looked like they had never felt honey sweet dough rising against their tempered sides.

They filled all the bags. Almost finished, Edwin asked Charlotte to retrieve a few more cloth sacks from the donkey's packs. Upon her return, Edwin was at the counter talking to Gavin about the weather and other unimportant ramblings. He stopped mid conversation to address her, "Go find yourself those clothing items you needed. They are up in the loft." He used his nose to point out the direction for her. She darted away and up to the second floor that overlooked the long store's many aisles. There were piles of clothes, mostly new, some worn. And all along the far wall there hung wool dresses, skirts, heavy coats, and long cloaks.

She recalled his words about filling the bags with whatever, so she did!

Thick stockings, tall boots, a wool lined jacket and matching pants, two thick sweaters, and an undershirt to keep the wool from itching her too much. She also found mittens and matching caps, swatches of material, yarn, leather straps for fixing her bag, a wool lined canvas cloak, and anything else she wanted. Never had Charlotte delighted in such frivolousness, yet she reveled in it. Once done, she met Edwin at the counter. While she shopped, he had packed all the bags full of provisions onto his team of donkeys. The loyal animals, heads lowered, had waited patiently outside. The beasts were napping, and Edwin looked tired too.

"You hungry?" he asked as they left the building, hauling and breathing heavily with her bundled purchases.

"Yes, Sir!" Her stomach grumbled.

Once her belongings were secured, Edwin led his long line of donkeys to the local stable yard, Charlotte behind and wide-eyed despite her own exhaustion. They situated the dozen donkeys up for the night and hung the panniers and all their heavy purchases along the stall fronts. The barn quieted after all Edwin's animals were fed and prepared for nightfall.

Charlotte took a moment to change into some of her new warm clothing and returned Edwin's worn pants and oversized shirt he had shared with her. All done, they trudged out into a soft falling rain and went down a block to one of the few lit establishments. Though it was a brothel, he assured her they made the best meals.

It wasn't too loud inside the establishment unless you were a Telepath and could hear the thoughts of everyone, all those who had noticed her coming through the swinging doors with Edwin. Charlotte tried not to appear bothered. Her stomach kept her planted in the chair, and all the savory scents amplified her will to remain seated. Still, the telepathic whispers she heard caused her arm-hairs to stand on end. She huddled inside her new warm cloak. Although there were only two Telepaths in this establishment, the other three–who lived in town—continued to chatter about her, away from the Warden and now traveling with 'Edwin Miner.' They were all extremely curious to know why.

Edwin and Charlotte conversed very little while they waited, meanwhile watching the locals who were studying them. Once the server returned with their meals, Charlotte was quick to sample hers before doctoring it. "It's a little bland. Could use some pepper." She sprinkled a pinch of seasoning laced with her Coterie spell on hers and Edwin's plates.

"Wow!" Edwin licked his lips. "A little pepper goes a long way!" He winked at her and proceeded to put away his meal.

As they ate their chicken and biscuits heaped with gravy, Charlotte asked, "Are you going to stay the night here?"

"Not here, no."

The barkeep—a large bodied, silver-haired woman—watched Charlotte as if she were a fox in a henhouse. "Good. I don't think I like this place."

"Yes." Edwin barely looked up from his meal. "I think I will sleep in the stables tonight."

"They let you do that?"

"If you pay for enough stalls, they do."

"Thank you, Edwin, for everything."

He winked at her and took another bite. They ate among sounds of silverware clanking plates, chairs scraping floors, and murmuring conversations.

"Are you going to follow the road back to Kobiton?" He asked through a mouthful of food. "Did you pick out enough supplies to get you home?"

She hadn't a clue what purchases to make for the return trip home—what else was necessary for camping along the trail other than food? She didn't pick out any pots or pans, no tents, or bedrolls, no giant packs to carry everything. She didn't even have a horse, nor the money to purchase one. As it was, she felt indebted to Edwin for allowing her to pick out clothing on his tab.

The far door was thrown open and the mercantile owner slammed it shut as he entered the establishment. "Good evening!" He bellowed to the barkeep, "Ruthie, I'll take a plate and an ale." He looked around the saloon.

*She's in the corner.* Ruthie thought. *We've gotta get her away from Edwin Miner. It's obvious she did something to the Warden. Now she's got Edwin under her nasty grasp.*

Gavin stared at Charlotte and Edwin. *You think she killed the Warden?*

*He hasn't checked in since he called for help. So, yes, I think that Witchtress killed him!*

Another telepathic voice chimed in. *She will hear us all if she killed the Warden.*

Ruthie's voice sliced through all the telepathic chatter. *I don't care. We need to save Edwin Miner from her. Kill that Witchtress.*

*How will we do that?*

Gavin mentally murmured, *I'll take the lead. Watch me. Wait for my cue.*

Gavin grabbed his mug of ale and approached to sit with Edwin and Charlotte. He plopped down on the chair between them—a greedy grin stretched the folds of his pasty white cheeks. "Smells good! How's the meal?"

Charlotte straightened her back and tried to sit more erectly. Edwin's gaze bounded between her and the merchant. "Sorry Gavin for not inviting you to supper this time. Me and my granddaughter are tired from our journey. We just want to eat and go to sleep."

Gavin chuckled, "Oh, I get it, I get it. Sure. Of course. Of course! I'm tired too. Just thought I'd come and sit for a chat, you know. I mean, I won't be seeing ya until springtime. And we always chat."

"And play a card game or two, but not this time, Gavin, not this time."

Edwin finished his plate, pushed it away. He noticed Charlotte offering Gavin her meal. "I can't finish it all." She lied, still hungry. But she didn't trust this person and wanted to have the upper hand in case Gavin tried any telepathy on her.

He gasped and chuckled, "Can't finish ... well, I can help you with that." His looks turned sinister, but in a blink, he reverted, taking a large bite. "Yeah, Moahkai always makes the best chicken 'n biscuits, I tell ya. My favorite meal!" He inhaled the last few morsels. "Damn good." He drank down the rest of his ale. "Ruthie, another round for me and my friends!"

He didn't stop looking at Charlotte. *I'm gonna get you away from this man.*

Unlike other minds that lay open to her telepathy, the Metalists' thoughts remained sealed behind their metal-infused blood. Only through direct contact could she breach that natural ward, and even then, only fragments slipped through.

She grabbed Edwin's hand and squeezed. "Papa, I'm ready to leave."

Edwin thought, *I am ready to leave too.* His chair scraped loudly against the wood floor, and he regarded the merchant, "As always, Gavin, it was good to see you."

As Charlotte rose, Gavin grabbed her wrist apparently trying to pull her away from Edwin. She sensed it was going to happen before he acted, and right after feeling his thick sweaty fingers on her wrist, she used her powers to manipulate his belly. Gavin doubled over in pain, and a loud fart squeezed out Gavin's trousers. He let go of her. His face was at once red.

He was a large man, and it was obvious he enjoyed hearty meaty meals, and ale. One could see that he got little or no physical exercise. His body was already clogged by many things, and inflaming his esophagus and stomach only aggravated his already unhealthy body. He sputtered and gagged as though he was choking.

She heard him thinking: *I just crapped myself. Oh, fuk, I think she's killed me!*

His eyes rolled up to see her, then to the wooden beams above. He hit the floor, barely breathing. His heart had seized.

All the Telepaths in the room were frothing.

*That Witchtress just killed Gavin!*

*We need to sever her head.*

*Grab Edwin Miner. Get him away from her immediately!*

Everyone in the room swarmed them. Every patron, whether or not they knew what was going on, encircled their friend Gavin and Charlotte, meanwhile pulling Edwin away from it all. He was pushed along and outside the establishment. He looked back at her as they shut and locked the large wooden door in his face.

Edwin hustled to the window and saw Charlotte go from cowering to unconscious.

## 4

# <u>Telepathic Intrusion</u>

The bed she laid upon was dreadfully uncomfortable. Charlotte didn't know exactly how long she had been unconscious, but her sore body told her at least a day. She caught sight of Edwin's smile. A middle-aged Telepathic man stood at her head. She took in his full head of platinum hair pulled back into a ponytail, and his beady blue eyes gazing at her. The room was windowless, but the door was open. A beam of light on the far hallway wall lifted her spirits.

"They say you can go. That your story is true." Edwin offered her a hand to help her sit up, and she grabbed it.

Now she was privy to all his thoughts. *... awful mess this all is. I sure hope they allow her to leave this township—that they do not manipulate her to stay. She does not need to be around these suspicious Telepaths. Disrespectful they all are. Want to know everything about everyone.* Edwin glanced at the known Telepath; a goatee attempted to fill in the pale man's thin face. And the few teeth shown were large and crowded against thin lips.

The Telepath touched her shoulder, but his eyes remained firm on Edwin when he said, "We know what happened to you. That beast, that imposter Warden, might have been a Warden at some point, but they went rogue. We believe they were working for the Ishik regime. They were recruited, sent to find you, your half-brother H'Eirwyn, and all the others that looked like you. They had been instructed to bring you all back to Daos, to the Ishik Empire as trophies—your heads, that is—and they would be greatly rewarded."

Her jaw dropped. "I remember hearing them mutter the words Ishik Empire, but then .... Do you know why?"

"Their motives were unknown. But they exploited us." The Telepath nodded, eyes now on the wall. "All of us."

"I ... I was told that we were requested by Hakra, that we were going to Akarah City. That we were destined for greatness. But later, when we realized we weren't heading west to Akarah, they confessed that H'Eirwyn and I were children of some nobleman. Our estranged father requested we be brought to him. Something about him living in Datzar Territory. That's all I know. I was never given a name."

The middle-aged Telepath stroked his goatee. "It's possible. But with them dead, we'll never know their true motives. Though it would explain the sack of heads and why you were heading into Datzar Territory instead of Akarah, where Hakra resides. If Hakra had indeed requested your presence, that's ultimately where you would've ended up. Such a pity things happened this way."

"What a sad story indeed," Edwin's tender hand on her shoulder drew her eyes up to his.

"I was a trophy!? What a sick creature! And H'Eirwyn ...." She wept briefly.

"Do you know why he kept you alive?"

"Because I am a good cook." She wiped away the tears. "They liked my food."

"Though we don't know the reason they treated you as they did, it doesn't matter much now. They're gone. They'll never live again. Hakra will make sure of it. And of course, you're absolved of all remorse felt for any wrongdoings you had to endure. Hakra understands why you did what you did. Know that you've done nothing wrong.

"And Hakra thanks you, Edwin Miner, for your bravery. Because of you, Miss Charlotte has a second chance at life under Hakra's rule. What I mean, Miss Charlotte, is that you have a few options. You can stay here in Chinochi. Our township is kind to people like you. There are many possibilities for someone with your Talents here. And we'd be ever grateful to have you as a resident. Or you can go with Edwin Miner. He says he'll take you to Kobiton when the snow melts."

She stared at Edwin. He had groomed himself since she had last laid eyes on him. There was no cap to tame his wiry salt and peppery hair as it lifted off his balding scalp, but those locks had been brushed over. Charlotte also peered at the telepathic man in a burgundy sweater and thick corduroys leaning over her. His breath stank of alcohol and an eagerness of a kind sat in those pale blue eyes.

She received a firm telepathic order: *You want to stay here. You will stay here.*

Her mind wasn't that pliable. She knew this man, this Telepath, would try everything in his power to make her remain in Chinochi. She resolved to leave, and so she stood. Flattening her warm wool dress, she looked at everyone's feet before raising a grin.

"I'm going with Papa Edwin."

The Telepath's eyes grew large. *How dare she! If Edwin Miner wasn't here, I'd tear her mind into soft cheese.*

The other voices of Telepaths around Chinochi chimed in all at once.

*Why can't you convince her to stay?*

*He should be able to.*

*My words don't seem to work. I thought she wasn't strong with her telepathic Abilities.*

*I could really use another Erthin at the Bath House.*

*You should be able to overpower her. Do it now.*

*How can I? Edwin is here. No one can control him. And he would intervene.* The Telepath took a long moment to regain composure before moving toward the door. "Well then, may Hakra be with you always."

"May Hakra fill your soul with happiness," she called back.

The middle-aged Telepath left the room as quickly as he could, fuming. *Maybe Edwin's the one with the power over her. That can't be. He doesn't have any power other than stupidity. But she's got power. What we wouldn't do to have another person of power to milk.*

The telepathic woman from the Saloon chimed in. *I'm sure she'll return. She won't want to live with Edwin Miner. She'll want the comforts only a town can provide. I'm sure we'll see her again.*

*I hope so. She would be of great value, especially if we could breed her with another Erthin!* The Telepath's thoughts quieted the further away he traveled.

Edwin patted her shoulder, bringing Charlotte back to the room. "Is there anything we should stock up on before departing this morning? The butcher's yard is open and full of animals. I plan on purchasing two boxes of chickens and some goats. Maybe a box of rabbits too. Oh, and I also need to stop off at the mill for grain."

Joyful that she was in Edwin's custody, Charlotte's arm went around Edwin's waist, and she sang, "Let's see when we get there."

*What a sweet little lady. What have I done?*

*I agreed to take her in, take her home with me with the hope of returning her to Kobiton in the spring. Ugh. I think I bit off more than I can chew. But what can I do? Chinochi is not the place for her to end up after all of it. She deserves to go home to Kobiton.*

*I hope our home is accepting of her.*

*I hope the boys keep their heckling to a minimum.*

Charlotte thought it odd that she could hear Edwin's thoughts, but no one else when she made contact with him, and yet his thoughts were all but hidden when there was space between them.

*It must be his Powers. Somehow, Papa Edwin can ward off telepathic intrusion. Fascinating!*

"I thought I was gonna be hung when they came at me in the barroom. How'd you convince them otherwise?"

He side-eyed her, bellowed a chuckle, and dropped their contact. "I did what one is supposed to do in that type of situation. I told the truth, Sweet Miss. We both know that I am the one who killed the Warden, believing they—it—was a mountain lion bent on killing you. They looked into my memories, as I am sure they looked into yours. Afterwards they sent along a scout, a Clan-Duin, to locate the Warden's last camp. Gathering all the proof necessary to prove your innocence.

"What a bloody mess it all has been! And what that Clan-Duin brought back. That sack of heads, which—gruesome as it was—confirmed your story. They were all so angry to find a Warden was acting against Hakra's ways, taking life for sport, seeking false rewards from false gods. Disgusting it all is. I saw them—all those heads, the faces. I am so sorry you had to endure all that, Sweet Miss. I am glad I was able to rescue you."

"Thank you, again, for everything, Edwin. I owe you my life."

"Oh, I do not want your life, nor any eternal servitude you might feel obligated to bestow. No. No. All I want is to see you happy."

She bowed.

Albeit reserved, Charlotte eagerly followed Edwin from one side of Chinochi to the other. After visiting the butcher's yard, they now had a small flock of caged chickens and a box of rabbits. A herd of goats were tethered together and pulled along by Edwin's donkeys. At the mill, they secured several hundred pounds of grain and flour to the panniers.

Edwin turned to her. "This is your last chance to decide what you want to do. You can stay here until the snow melts or come and meet my family. But I will warn you, once we get to the cave, we will be bound there. There will be no access to Chinochi or anywhere else until springtime. Like I said, when we bought those chickens, there needs to be enough to get us through most of the winter. Once the goats are gone, Albert and I hunt squirrels, and that is what we eat until the snow melts."

There was no hesitation. "Of course I'm coming with you. I don't want to stay here." She tossed a last glance over her shoulder at the quaint township of Chinochi. Her smile and enthusiasm were what would keep them going their whole walk back to Edwin's humble abode.

# 5

<u>REVELATIONS</u>

They stopped to water themselves at the bottom of the ravine where they first met. Charlotte could still see the stain from her blood on the rocks below her boots. The Warden's body lay in the brambles, partially shredded. Some animals had come through and enjoyed their fill of the deceased. Neither saw the predators, and so their break was brief.

After that first leg of their journey, Edwin assured Charlotte everything else was uphill. The forest grew thick around them, shielding them from the quick winds that rattled leaves and shook loose pine needles. When they passed along an exposed outcropping, the fog and clouds greeted them. Nothing beyond a few hundred feet was truly visible. Dark and gnarly shadows of fauna played games with their eyes—was it a tree or person, or a hideous animal? It was hard to tell at times.

Their ascent was grueling. Each step, they battled against gravity and mud. Only the crunch of gravel underfoot, or the occasional cry of a distant bird parted the silence between them. The creaking of packs, drumming hoofbeats, and frequent snorts from the donkeys reminded her they were not alone.

An icy rain began and sliced through the cold air, dousing them during their hike that day.

"What is it like being an orphan?" Edwin's words startled a squirrel into hiding. "Growing up at the Abbey?"

"Hard. Every day. No one liked me."

He looked over his shoulder at her and asked, "Why?"

The sloshing of hooves and boots slapping against the moistened ground filled every silent moment.

Charlotte's sight clouded as a distant memory floated forward and out of her mouth. "I was just a tot, barely two, when it happened. I threw a tantrum and the next thing I knew; my bed was ablaze." She shook her head ruefully. "I didn't mean to. I had no clue what I was doing. But after that, it was solitary for me more often than not. Most children don't come into their powers that young, see?" She shrugged, and they kept walking.

"You had no friends?"

"I have a couple of good friends. My best friend is Miss Lori. She protected me when others wouldn't. She saw past my powers, saw me. In the kitchen, she taught me more than just cooking—she taught me to believe in myself." A deep sigh parted her lips.

"Sounds like a good person to have in your life."

"She is. I miss her dearly."

"And your friend H'Eirwyn?"

"He had a crush on me at one point. Everyone speculated we were related. And then there were rumors we were in a relationship and that our children would come out with two heads and four legs. Repulsive. Children can be cruel sometimes."

Onward they walked, breaking briefly but often for food and water. The chilly rain let up for a time, and they felt the warmth of the sun.

"I saw that book of tomes. You read?"

"It's my favorite book, out of all the tomes. It's got all the classic stories—The Red Sky; The Blue Water; Birth of Hakra; Pillars of Destruction; Revet's Making; Revet's Revenge ... But there are several new ones in this edition—Emboldened Regrets; Xudise's Exodus; Hallay the Horrible; Birth of P'Herth; The Execution; Petok Ninnith."

"Do you believe that what was written actually happened?"

"No. Oh, no. They're stories, nothing more. Though I really love reading them. Used to read to the little children before they'd go off to their dormitory at night."

"Dormitories? Is that how you lived?"

"As a child, yes. But once you graduate, move on, there're places to live. Although I never did really move on. I moved out of the dorm and was given a room on the fourth floor. That's where all the rest of us live, those of us in service to Kobiton's Abbey and Hakra. It gets hot up there during the summer moons, but I had a window. My view was of the entire city of Kobiton. I can see from tower to tower, and the mountains to the west. Always the best sunsets."

He chuckled, "Well, I can assure you our view of the west is better. We can also see to the east, watch the sunrise."

"Wow. I can't wait to see it."

Onwards they trudged. Their conversation fell silent, and they enjoyed the sweet pine scents and grand views along their way.

Soon, they stopped and made camp for the night.

"Let me make supper," Charlotte said when Edwin brought out his cooking utensils.

Charlotte hesitated before using her Erthin Abilities. Under Hakran law, powers were meant to be contained unless absolutely necessary. But here, away from Kobiton's watchful Telepaths and scrupulous PCP soldiers, she knew she was free from judgement. Immediately she made an Erthin fire appear, warm and radiating light. She then took the knife, and the food presented and started preparing that night's meal.

Papa Edwin watched her prepare the rabbit stew with beets, carrots, and several purple potatoes while setting up his small tent. His silvery eyes reflected his inquisitive thoughts; questions she couldn't hear, but she knew he had them.

The icy rain had turned into small snowflakes. They huddled around Charlotte's woodless hot Erthin fire and ate up the warm soup and fresh biscuits she made. Edwin was floored by the flavor and quantity of the food; she had made enough for a hearty breakfast that would keep them going all that next day.

· · · · ● · ● · · ·

"I should probably prepare you for meeting my family." Edwin said on the last leg of their hike toward his homestead. "There is my grandson, Albert, and his father, Jebadia. I think Albert is about your age. Though you might be a bit older. But Albert ... he has finally grown into himself, not as awkward as he once was. His voice is deeper now, and he is strong. Yes, very strong. And he can be thoughtful. When he wants to. But sometimes he just goes on and on about .... But-but he can also be quiet. And attentive. He must be, though.

"Then there is Jebadia. Prefers to be called Jeb. Now Jeb ..." Edwin inhaled deeply before admitting, "... Jeb will hate on you. But he hates on everyone, so do not take it personal. And he will try to get under your skin. Pick you apart. It is one of his things. He enjoys finding your weakness. So, I will tell you not to engage with him. In fact, if he says anything to you, you might just want to remain quiet. Oh, and sometimes he will burst with anger and from out of nowhere. He will scream and kick too."

Her jaw dropped. "That's horrible. Why does he do that?"

"Jeb has many issues. Mostly with himself, but mostly with me too. He will never say it, but I know he hates Albert. He bad mouths the boy; curses him behind the boys' back. Jeb is a mean old cuss. And he is not afraid to tell you what he thinks of you or anything else, for that matter. That man has no filter, says whatever is on his mind. Oh, and he hates being told what to do, so never do that."

She chuckled, "Lots of people don't like being told what to do."

"Well, you see, he believes he is right about everything, regardless if he is. So, unless you want to deal with his wrath, do not contradict him."

"Sounds boorish to me. Why live with him? I wouldn't put up with any of that."

Edwin paused, looked Charlotte up and down. "He is my son. Beyond the horrible attitude, he is a hard worker. He knows how to mine, knows what to do down there. Should at least," Edwin muttered, "damned fool." But then raised his voice, "I taught him everything he knows."

It became foggier as they came around a bend in the trail. They could only see a hundred feet ahead. The trees were thinning, and it was only getting colder.

They hiked a bit more before Charlotte asked, "How long have you lived up here?"

"Since before Albert was born."

"Does your family ever go to Chinochi with you?"

"No. Well, Jeb has, but that was before Albert was .... But then Albert has never visited anywhere, any town before."

"Why not?"

His silvery eyes reflected the dark green colors that surrounded them. "Telepaths."

# 6

## <u>SEEDS OF CHANGE</u>

They hiked the remaining way in silence. The snow fell and the chilly wind tugged on them from every direction. Soon the trees thinned. Flurries occluded the vista, attempted to hide the worn trail Edwin had been following. Charlotte pulled her knit cap over her cold ears and put her mittened hands in her armpits. Her steps shadowed Edwin's as he wound around boulders and further up in elevation. Between the clouds and flying flakes, it was hard to know where to go, but Edwin knew the way and suddenly they were entering the cavernous homestead.

Snow drifts hid the dark entrance until the last moment when they were drawn into the warmth and light of a campfire.

"About time you arrived, slimy old piece of salt," Jebadia shouted from across the firelight and stood up. "Where is my silver?"

They entered a circular cavern, immaculately carved yet dreary. A small coal fire provided meager warmth; its sooty scent permeated the air. Old hides were draped across stone seats around the firepit. Perfectly cut cubicles along the far arched wall served as personal sleeping quarters. The wall closest to her was oddly smooth, unmarked by tools.

Charlotte stepped further into the cavern, the chill seeping into her bones. After experiencing the vibrant chaos of Kobiton her whole life—even Chinochi's riot of colors, the constant buzz of voices and thoughts, the smell of cooking fires were warming—this cave's silence felt like death. The air here tasted of metal and stone, ancient and unchanging. Where Kobiton's buildings reached desperately for the sky, these walls curved inward, embracing an ever-present darkness. Her old home had also been a tapestry of competing powers—Erthins wielding fire and water, Clan-Duins shifting forms like quicksilver, Telepaths weaving invisible webs of thought—here there was only uncomfortable silence.

Even the light was different, as if being sucked up by the surrounding gloom. In Kobiton, sunlight painted everything in sharp relief, leaving nowhere to hide. But here, shadows danced at the edge of every torch flame, and secrets seemed to lurk in every hidden crevasse. It wasn't just a different place, Charlotte realized—it was a different way of existing entirely.

*It is so quiet. Is this what it's like to not be a Telepath? To not hear other people's musings, their worries. Regrets. It's … it's wonderful. Magical.*

*Maybe now, maybe here, I can finally be more than just my powers. I can be me.*

Charlotte remained close to the donkeys, hidden from the firelight, and watched this moment unfold as Jebadia advanced on Edwin quickly.

He stepped around the lead donkey, puffed up his chest, and stood his ground. "I spent all the silver, Jeb. But I brought back a woman."

All their eyes held a silvery glow that was unlike anything she had ever seen. Jebadia's eyes were fiery, firm on her. "You said nothing about bringing home a woman," Jebadia spat, eyes blazing with a hatred that seemed to go beyond Charlotte herself. Every word dripped with years of bitterness.

Charlotte flinched at the harsh words; maybe saw something in Jebadia's fiery gaze—a flicker of pain, quickly masked by anger. She didn't need her telepathy to know that he was a mentally disturbed man—but possibly a broken man because of past events.

"Miss Charlotte, this is Jebadia, and that is Albert." Edwin pointed at each family member; she held still in the donkeys' shadows.

Albert stood in the darkness, his lean frame taut with mingled curiosity and wariness that reminded Charlotte of a wild creature encountering humans for the first time. Dark circles ringed his eyes, speaking of sleepless nights spent mining the mountain's depths. Yet there was an intensity in his gaze that belied his hesitant posture, an intelligence that seemed to catalog every detail of her presence.

When he went to unhitch the goats, his movements were precise, practiced—a reminder that while he might be unfamiliar with the outside world, he was far from helpless. His eyes darted between Charlotte and his father, gauging reactions, measuring responses. Only when he slipped away into the familiar darkness of an adjoining chamber did his shoulders relax slightly; the weight of this unfamiliar presence in their sanctuary temporarily lifted.

Charlotte continued to study Albert, peering into the dim chamber where the animals were kept. She was sure she was several years older than the nervous young man. A pang of anxiety about this place, these people, made her fingers and toes wiggle. She wondered about being in the sooty cavern with unknown men.

Was this a good idea?

Jebadia and Edwin continued to argue.

"She is a fat fuking whore! How dare you bring another mouth into this already crowded sphere!" Jebadia shouted. "We have no need for a woman. You were sent to take the coal and bring us back food. And yet you have failed us again, stubborn old man!"

"Shut it Jeb. I do not need your heckles."

"Bah, you. Piece of shit! Maybe we cook her. She would feed us for a few days at least."

"Bah you, you rotten child. You better not touch her."

"Or what? You will kill me? You do not have the strength."

"You rotten soul. I would if I could. Be nice!"

"Fuk you, and that whore you brought. Damn fool you are!"

"Fool? You are the fool, Jeb. Your own son is better than you are, good-for-nothing miner." Their voices echoed around the chambers.

Charlotte wasn't as large as she had once been. The trek over the mountains and the Warden stealing her mind had thinned her. But she knew she would gain it all back. She had never minded being larger than most of the ladies her age. The extra fat kept her warm during the colder moons, and there were many men who enjoyed a larger woman.

She quietly stepped further into this uniquely created space and peered into the barn area. The donkeys had one large corral; the goats' space was much smaller. There were places for the chickens and rabbits, too. They had walked past the animal refuse piled at the exit—or entrance into the wintery world beyond.

"Come here, Miss Charlotte," Edwin beckoned her. She was slow to leave the donkeys, scratching the ear of the one she stood beside before stepping over to Edwin and Jebadia.

"There should have been a discussion about this, about her, before you went and did what you did."

"How was I to know she would happen?"

Jeb's reflective eyes scrutinized Charlotte. She stood two strides away. His arms were folded tight against his chest, and his dry and cracked lips puckered. "She needs to leave. We have no need for a woman. Not now. Not when we must conserve our food."

"Be nice Jeb. She will be with us until spring. I promised I would take Miss Charlotte to Kobiton once the snow melts."

"Promised. You! Bah. Kobiton? Bah! That place is full of nothing but rotten people."

"It's not full of rotten people!" Charlotte defended. "There're many good people, hardworking people who live there and have for hundreds of years. Besides, it's where I'm from. Where I was born. Where I belong. And Papa Edwin's kind enough to offer to take me back when the time comes. Until then, he assured me I could stay here."

"Assured! It is not his place to assure anyone."

She snapped back, "Papa Edwin wasn't joking when he said you're hard-headed."

"Papa Edwin. Papa Edwin." Jebadia's eyes were giant, and he snorted like a feral boar. "Bah! She cannot curry favors with me. You might permit it, you old scoundrel, but I will not!"

"She is not here to curry favors, Jeb. I promised Miss Charlotte I would take her home. And that is the end of it. Until then, you will leave her alone."

"You always make promises you cannot deliver. I would trust none of us, fat girl. You should head back to wherever my father found you. Go on. Scurry along." Jebadia's hiss echoed around the circular chamber.

Edwin hit Jeb's head with the back of his hand. "How dare you be callous towards her? She has been through much, deserves our respect. Understand?!"

"Have you gone soft, old man?! What Power does she possess? What are you, besides a fat girl?"

"She has no power over me. She is Erthin, nothing more."

"Nothing more? Bah!"

They glared at each other before Albert's grunts caught everyone's attention. He had accidentally dropped one of the bags of grain and it split open. He then kicked and cursed the sack. None of his elders came to help, so Charlotte left them to help Albert scoop up the precious grains.

*Ugh! Albert smells ... smells like rotten eggs.*

She held her breath when helping Albert sew the edge of the sack closed. He made it a quick task; the needle flew between the sack layers like a hot knife to butter, and just as quickly, it was sealed.

Their hands brushed as they finished tying the sack. Charlotte felt a small jolt, surprising her. She glanced at Albert, catching a flicker of something in his eyes before he looked away, cheeks reddening slightly.

"Thank you," Albert said softly.

Charlotte nodded, meeting his gaze. "It's nothing."

As he hurried away, Charlotte found herself watching him go, curiosity piqued by this shy, earnest young man. She then noticed the elders hovering between them and the fire. The older men were nothing more than dark shadows, their reflective silvery eyes dutiful on the youngsters' exchange.

Albert grunted some more when he placed the heavy sacks inside a small food storage room. Charlotte didn't interfere and pressed her back against the cold stone wall. She continued to assess this place and these people—all her options. For now, the snow wasn't too deep; she could traverse back to Chinochi if necessary. But then she remembered how sneaky the Telepaths were in that town.

*I know I made a good decision. I must remember that this place is better than Chinochi. And before long, I'll be back in Kobiton. I'd much rather be around Telepaths I know. I don't trust those in Chinochi. The ones in Kobiton are good, kind ... not greedy like those in Chinochi.*

*I'm sure I can trust Edwin. He's genuine. But Jebadia? Good thing I don't have to interact with him if I don't want to. And Albert. He's a shy one. Kind of sad, pathetic really. He needs a bath.*

*I must remember that I'll be alright. I've got nothing to worry about.*

Jebadia tore into Edwin again. "She must be the reason you delayed your return. We have been starving, you know! Had you not arrived, we would have gone hungry tonight."

"I set a dozen traps! Did you harvest them all?"

"We did!" Jebadia seemed ready to boil over. "And we ate all we caught. No leftovers. You better get to making us some food, old man."

Although Charlotte was across the room, hearing Jebadia's harsh words brought her back into their conversation. "I'll make supper," she chimed in. She decided on rabbit stew for dinner.

A tiny smile drew up his mostly flat lips.

"You like rabbit stew?" He blinked, and she added, "I'll make biscuits too. Where did you put all the vegetables, Albert?"

Albert hiccoughed when hearing his name. He kept looking at his elders who were suddenly quiet, once again attentive to their interactions. Albert never spoke but drew Charlotte down several well chiseled steps into a small domed-shaped cold storage room. She was impressed by this space, and how perfectly carved it was. The stone walls were as smooth as the main cavern above and kept cold by blocks of ice.

Albert had to duck when inside this room, but Charlotte could stand—her strawberry-blonde hair barely missing the ceiling. Chunks of ice left puddles at the entrance. He knelt in the wetness. She bent over while holding up her skirt. They rummaged together, pulling out a few fresh vegetables for her to cook. Albert carried them for her and followed Charlotte back to the firepit. They had no real kitchen area, no countertop to lay the produce on, nor was there a cutting board to use near the fire pit. But she was given a knife that was so sharp she accidentally cut herself—hoping no one witnessed her flesh instantly regenerate.

"What do you usually chop your meat on?" she asked.

Edwin was the one who replied, "We do not chop meat; we simply fire it or boil it. Had I known you required a chopping board, I would have bought you one at the mercantile."

She looked at the tallest flat rock alongside the firepit. "It's okay. I'll use this stone. I just don't want to dull your knife."

"Do not worry about our knives," Edwin light-heartedly assured. "Albert likes to sharpen them. Right, boy?" He ran his hand through Albert's greasy hair.

Albert squirmed away from his elder's grimy hand. His eyes dropped—as did his shoulders—once more. Charlotte quickly spoke. "Albert looks older than a boy." He peered up at her with a captivating innocence. She smiled at him. "He is a man, just like any other man I've met."

*It's sad that they keep him here. I wonder if he's ever met a woman. Edwin had said he's the only one who goes to town ... well, more than likely Albert hasn't. So sad. There're many amazing things to see and experience. He deserves to know the world.*

"A man you say." Edwin's gaze narrowed. "How many men have you had?"

"None."

Jeb stomped his foot, clapped his hands, and shouted, "Liar!"

"I do not lie! Don't ever call me a liar."

He pointed and screamed, "Liar!"

She spat, "Liars don't live long where I'm from."

"Is that why you are here? You lied to the wrong person. They sent you off to die!"

"No. That's not what happened to me."

"You should go back to Kobiton. Go home, little girl! Leave us be." Jeb's lips puckered; his silvery eyes boiled with hate.

"Just ignore him Sweet Miss. Jeb is just hungry."

Charlotte shook off their interaction and went back to making their meal.

*I don't doubt Jebadia's mouth or mind now. I must make sure to avoid him. Ugh. This'll be a long winter. I can always leave. Or I can curry Jeb's favor like I did with the Warden.*

Soon the cave was full of hot smells, of bread and percolating rabbit stew. The biscuits remained warm in their cast iron pan on one of the flat stones usually used for sitting. Meanwhile, the soup boiled in an enormous cauldron hung over the fire from a fancy metal spit. Although these men lived simplistically, she noticed bits of original flair from feathered details on the arms of the spit to perfectly chiseled stone spheres. And the cooked rabbit soup with carrots and potatoes added to the uniqueness of the room.

Jebadia greedily took the first bowl of soup. Edwin and Albert were softer about receiving their meals. They sat near the fire with Charlotte, meanwhile Jebadia crossed the room and sat on his bed. She noticed him glaring while scarfing down the meal. He went as far as licking his bowl clean before coming back to the fire and refilling it. He snagged more biscuits and returned to his bedside; those silvery eyes never left her. Once he was done with his meal, he shoved his cleaned bowl into a bucket and then slithered off to bed. Jebadia would only get up once more, before everyone else went to sleep, and that was to use their shared pisspot—a tall bucket opposite the animal refuse pile near the entrance.

Albert seemed hypnotized by Charlotte.

Edwin complimented the meal and thanked her before retiring for the night. But before laying down, he brought her a stinky bear's hide to wrap up in. He chided the adolescent miner, insisting he leave Charlotte alone. Albert wasn't doing anything other than staring. He remained alongside the fire a little longer—completely mute, but she could see his thoughts moving behind his eyes—before retiring to his cozy sleeping space. Charlotte tried her best to make a sleeping spot for herself. The ground was hard and cold.

*It's nothing like home. Oh, how I miss home. Even if that room was so damn hot during the summer, frigid in the winter ... the view made up for it. The view from up here ... it's all white .... nothing compared to home.*

She thought about her dark wood room with its narrow bed parked against the door frame. The tall peak of the dormer window made her room a long one. Not only did she have a small wardrobe, but under the tall window it was wide enough for a chair and tiny table. Often, she would open that window during a hot night to cool off. The breeze would always whistle. In the winter, there were thick red curtains to keep out drafts.

That room had been a blessing. Not by Hakra's hand, but from all her hard work and good deeds. There were many workers in Kobiton's Abbey who had much less than she and had lived in those tight accommodations longer too. Some of those rooms on that fourth floor were nothing more than slanted walls with a bed tight against the slant and hot year around.

This new place, the well chiseled cave, was wildly different. Not something she ever thought she would be in.

*It's like going back in time. This must have been how my ancestors once lived. Now I'm living it.*

*I must trust that Edwin will make good on his word ... that I'll see Kobiton once winter breaks. If not .... I don't want to kill these people.*

She found little comfort that first night with sleep or chase-filled dreams.

# 7

## <u>LOST PUPPY</u>

Albert's heart raced as he tended to the animals after Edwin and Charlotte's arrival.

A woman.

Here?

In their home!

He had never seen one up close before, only heard stories from Edwin and Jebadia. Stories that often ended in warnings about the dangers women posed.

But Charlotte did not seem dangerous. She seemed ... kind. Her smile made him feel warm inside; a feeling so foreign it almost scared him. Was this what his father had warned him about? Or was it something else entirely?

He could not help himself after she came to the rescue and helped stitch the oat bag back together. Albert wanted to interact with her, wanted to help her with anything and everything—wanted to follow her around like a lost puppy. He felt stupid for wanting to be by her side, as if under a spell. So many feelings and emotions rumbled around within him.

All evening he watched Charlotte, studying her like he would a caves' wall before attempting to bore through it. Meanwhile, he had been aware of Jebadia's annoyed scowl that sat stiff all night long. Jeb never softened, unlike how Albert and Edwin had, even after the scrumptious meal.

As he watched his father use the refuse bucket one last time before bed, he reflected.

*Is there anything that makes that old fart happy?*

Albert remained on the hard stone seat closest to Charlotte. His attention attuned to her and unwavering. That was until Edwin snapped, "It is rude to stare, child. You are done with your meal. You have placed your bowl in the bucket. It is time for bed. Time for sleep. We must allow Miss Charlotte to take her rest. She has had a long day. Leave her alone. Go on now. Get!" He shooed Albert away from the fire—away from Charlotte.

Albert sought solace in his quiet corner of the cave, his grandfather's harsh words still ringing in his ears. He always hated being told what to do, but especially now—in front of her. Moreso, he had always accepted this life, this hierarchy, without question. But Charlotte's arrival had ignited a desire for more, a belief that there could be an alternative path for him to live. For the first time in his life, Albert granted himself the ability to picture a life beyond these stone walls, and the notion of it scared and thrilled him.

As he lay in bed, Albert pored over that evening's events. He marveled at how quickly his world had changed. Just days ago, he had never known a woman's touch, never imagined the softness of Charlotte's skin or the warmth of her smile. Now, he could not fathom a life without her. Yet beneath his joy lurked a nagging fear—would she remain with them until spring? Or would she disappear like a foggy dream? Worse yet, would he be enough for her? Could he protect her from the harsh realities of their life in the caves?

Everyone else snored. Even now, he could smell Charlotte over all the other stinky odors that lived in the dank cavern they inhabited.

His heart hurt from its rampant beats.

*She called me a man,* Albert marveled. *No longer a boy to be dismissed. If they try to battle me again ....*

*She called me a man!*

*Edwin told me this day would come, though he always made it sound far off into the future. I have dreamt of this; so many curious dreams where women looked like animals and not like she does. How many times have I wondered what a woman looked like? ... smelled like. Be like. And now it has happened. She is here. Sleeping only a few feet away. She does not snore like father or grandfather even. So soft and quiet.*

*I wonder if all women are like that, or if it is just her.*

*She called me a man.*

*Why was father so venomous? Calling her fat? And a whore. What is a whore? And how can she be fat with all the clothing she wears?*

*I wonder if all women look like her. Edwin said they are like us, but different. How different? She looks like me, but then again she does not. There are things about her that make me feel ... indescribable. I want to feel this way forever. I really hope she stays.*

His eyes watered, but his mouth was dry. Albert continued to pant.

*She is everything I did not know I wanted. But I want her. Her smell. Her hair. Her skin. Her face. I just want to know .... Why did they keep her from me? How long have they known about her? Where exactly did Charlotte come from? And why could I not speak when she spoke to me? How did she render me breathless? What type of Powers does she hold? I know she is not like me, a Metalist. But she has Power.*

*Erthin ... I recall her saying Erthin. What is Erthin? It must be the ability to render me mute.*

*She is so different. Everything about her is different. Beautiful. Like the meadow on the other side of the mountain.*

*I am foolish. Shame. Horror. I cannot tell what this is I feel. My heart. My throat. My body. Go to her. I want to touch her. Lay with her. Smell her. She smells so good. I just .... No. I must be good. Father will beat me if I am not.*

*Will he?*

*I am a man. He cannot beat me anymore. This time I will beat him.*

His throat felt thick. For a moment it was hard to swallow, but then he gasped for a cool, calming breath.

*I hope she can stay. Please let her stay, father. Please. If he were gone, I know she would stay. He would not be able to banish her.*

*But why was he so angry? Why did he call her fat? She is not .... She is beautiful, like wildflowers.*

*Maybe father wants her. I saw how he was staring at her. But there was rage. I felt his magnetism radiating. He does not covet Charlotte. I think he wants her dead.*

*I will not let that happen. I must protect Charlotte, keep her safe from father. But what if ....*

Again, he had a problem swallowing.

*If he lays one finger on her, I will beat him.*

*I am a man.*

*I will be her man.*

*And she will be my woman.*

As sleep finally claimed him, Albert vowed to become the man Charlotte deserved, even if it meant defying everything he had ever known.

# 8

## <u>TUNNELS & TALES</u>

Charlotte awoke first and made porridge for everyone. Jebadia was but a moment behind her, grunting and farting as he waddled across the room to use their shared refuse bucket. Out in the open, there was no privacy amongst these men. She appreciated how quiet it was in their humble home. She didn't have to worry about mental conversations or inappropriate thoughts. But the contemptuous glares and grunts were hard to ignore.

Albert rose once his father was done. And, after inhaling a bowl full of cooked oats, he and Jebadia went off to work. On the far side of the stables was the entrance that led further into the belly of the mountain. They took a torch and two donkeys with packs and set off for the day.

Edwin awoke after they had left, complaining about his aches and pains before settling down for breakfast.

"Sorry about Jebadia's mouth last night." Edwin sighed. "Jeb was not always like this, you know. When he was young, before River ... he was different. Kinder. Full of dreams."

"What happened?" Charlotte asked softly.

"Life happened. Loss. It changes a person." Edwin's voice dropped to a whisper. "Sometimes I wonder if I failed him as a father. If I could have protected him from the harshness of this world."

He scooped up a bowl of hot porridge and took a seat.

"Is this how it is, your life here?" She asked, staring at the short flames.

Between mouthfuls, Edwin replied, "Yes, pretty much. We are simple folk who wish to live in peace. This mountain is where we belong."

"Why is that? Why do you think you belong here? Why not live somewhere else?"

"We are miners. Men of the mountains. That is why we live here and nowhere else." Edwin's eyes grew distant. "Long ago, our kind lived among others. But our

Powers made us feared—hunted. These mountains became our refuge and our prison.”

“Have you always mined?”

He nodded. “As long as I can remember, yes, I have mined.”

She settled down alongside Edwin. “What do you usually do, you know, your day-to-day tasks?”

“Well, to start, I clean up around here. That shitter can get quite gross, and dishes always need to be washed.”

“Do you ever wash your clothes, or bathe your bodies?” She immediately regretted what she said.

He laughed. “During the summer, perhaps. Yes, we do smell, but it suits us.”

She wished for a way to permanently plug her nose. Beyond the stank of rotten eggs, the men smelled of their own foulness. “Back home we bathe all the time, well not all the time, but every few days. And we wash all the children too. They can get nasty rashes if they’re not washed often.”

“There is a hidden lake. We can go there today to wash up if you want. That is where we will wash the dishes.”

She glanced at the dull beam of light coming in through the exterior entrance. The howl of wind wasn’t as loud today as it had been yesterday. “How often do you go outside?”

“I go out often, depending on the weather of course. And usually, I only go for fodder. It is only when we run out of rations that I set up traps. And knowing Albert, he forgot to bring them back, so at some point today I must traipse out and retrieve them.” He looked at their only exit. “I hope the sun shows up today.”

Once breakfast was consumed, Edwin took Charlotte on a tour of the perfectly carved cylindrical caves and corridors. Never had she ever imagined a place like this to exist. Everything was smooth to the touch. She had been told of cavern making by friends who took up that position, how they used dynamite, chisels and timbers, carving day and night, taking weeks to make a hundred-foot squarish corridor that would still be rough to the touch. This circular stony wall was soft, and it had been ground to a satin finish. There were no imperfections in the first few corridors they traveled through. Charlotte felt waves of wonderment.

“What type of tools do you use?” she asked, her hand rubbing the wall as they walked along.

“We are Metalists, and this is how we carve.”

"Metalist? But how? This looks like something an Earth Erthin would do. Is it your Power that does this?"

"We are not Erthins. We are Metalists." Edwin nodded. "We use our Power to make these corridors. Mining requires precision only achievable through joint Metalist effort. One of us senses the ore's song, the other shapes the tunnels. It is why our family must stay together—our survival demands it. Though I learned to work alone after my brother's departure. It takes twice the effort and yields half the reward.

"But all told ... this, what you see here, is how it has always been done. There is no way to explain the process other than we channel the tunnel."

"It's just .... Wow! I'm in awe of you, your family, Edwin. I won't ever tell anyone anything about you. I promise."

"Thank you, Sweet Miss, that means a lot."

"Are there any others of you? Sisters? Brothers? Aunts? Uncles? Cousins?"

Adamantly Edwin's head swiveled. "No. We are the only ones."

"What about Albert's mother?"

"Talya. She died just after childbirth."

"Oh, I'm so sorry. That must've been hard on all of you."

The old man shrugged. He seemed ambiguous about it.

Edwin took the next intersecting corridor and soon they entered an enormous cathedral of a cavern, not made by Metalist ingenuity, but by Mother Nature. It was musty and cold. The water that dripped came from a glacier that sat, slowly melting, above them. All along the Kruluver Mountain Range, there were hundreds of glaciers—Urthis was in the middle of what was being called an ice time.

High above their heads, stalactites hung like bats awaiting an invitation for flight. This place was dark indeed, but didn't smell as rank as the rest of this underground landscape. Their lantern pressed back the darkness, shedding light to the constant dripping and splashing. And then she saw the small lake hidden inside the mountains' flank, calm as a small puddle, and sparkling despite the absence of light.

"Wow!"

Red columns rose apart from the interior walls and were ringed by layers of orange, brown, and yellow sediment. Each layer had its own feel, but not as soft as the corridor the Metalists had chiseled. The sandy ground appeared to be a shade lighter than everything else, reflecting the lamplight swinging in her hand.

"This place is amazing."

"The water is ice cold. But we have a firepit over there. Extra buckets." Charlotte followed Edwin towards a set of stalagmites tethered by a rope. A few feet ahead was a stone circle that had several pieces of coal waiting to be lit. He took the lantern from her and dribbled some oil onto chunks of coal before lighting the fire.

"I usually grab a bucket of water and boil it before washing the dishes."

"I can boil the water, and without the fire's help." She took the dish bucket he carried and went to fill it with icy water.

The lake wasn't deep when she began filling the bucket, and though she could have used her Erthin Powers to do this chore, she did not. Instead, she hummed softly, considering the sublime icy waterway. She waded out until the water touched the top of her boots where she stopped and filled the bucket. Then she returned to the fire. Edwin had found a seat, fashioned a seat among the multitude of rocks. She took up a nearby stone, placing the bucket next to her feet. A little wave of her hand, and the water inside the bucket began to steam, slowly reaching a boil.

"What I would do to have your Powers, Sweet Miss. If I did, I know at the very least that I would never be cold."

"Yeah, I'm seldom cold. Which is fine. I kinda prefer it."

*Edwin's such a nice man. I wonder what his Metalistic Powers can do. I'd like to see them at work. They must be what keeps his thoughts hidden. They definitely help him channel perfect tunnels into a gravel and coal mountain.*

*I'm definitely in awe of these people, these miners.*

Soundless. Only water droplets pinging against cavern walls broke the silence.

Edwin leaned closer. "I noticed Albert has a hard time keeping his eyes off you."

"Yeah, I noticed that too. He's cute."

"You should ask him to take you on a walk this evening after supper. Get him out of his shell. Besides, there's much to discover beneath our mountain. More places to go than I can take you," he chuckled.

With a smile and nod, she replied, "I will."

• • • • •• • •• • •

That evening's supper was unnervingly quiet. Living amongst people who had thoughts—she could see them behind everyone's steely eyes—somehow the way they warded themselves from telepathic intrusion was fascinating and scary.

Jebadia scarfed down his meal. His glare on her constant.

*He doesn't like me. Remember what Edwin said. This is just the way Jeb is.*

"Albert." Edwin broke the silence and pointed his spoon at her. "You should take Miss Charlotte for a walk. Show her around this place. She will be with us for a while. You need to get used to having her around. Maybe this evening after supper."

Jebadia grumbled under his breath and glared at Edwin, but his spoon never stopped shoveling the tasty stew into his vindictive mouth.

The young man sneered at his elder without a pause. He was obviously afraid to regard Charlotte. Albert said nothing and went slower about finishing his meal. Those shy eyes of his were afraid to commit to hers, but she kept on staring at him. Every time he saw her, his cheeks puffed and reddened more. She couldn't help but smile.

*He can't be older than sixteen, maybe seventeen. He's still just a boy. I hope I've made the right decision to remain here with these grimy men. Miners they call themselves.*

*All I know is the quiet of this place makes me miss home. I want to be home.*

She closed her eyes, dredging up the bustling kitchens of the Abbey. The clatter of pots, the sizzling of meat on the grill, the chorus of voices calling out orders—it had been her world, her purpose. The memories put her there, in that moment, in all those moments. Now, in the cave's quiet, she wondered if she would ever again feel the satisfaction of feeding hundreds, of knowing her skills brought joy and sustenance to so many.

Once Jebadia was done eating, he retired to his sleeping quarters; his silvery eyes glowed as he kept an eye on the two youngsters.

Edwin sternly reminded Albert to take Charlotte for a walk, the tour he had suggested. The young man seemed flustered by it all. Even after they entered the main shaft, he kept looking back to see if Jebadia or Edwin might be watching.

They walked in comfortable silence, the rhythmic drip of water echoing around them. Charlotte was acutely aware of Albert's presence there beside her, the warmth radiating from him in the cool cavern.

"It's beautiful here," She murmured, her voice barely above a whisper.

Albert turned to her, a small smile playing on his lips. "You think so?"

Their eyes met, and for a moment, Charlotte felt as if the air between them was charged with electricity. She glanced away, her heart beating faster than usual.

They walked on for several feet. Then she asked, "How long have you lived here?"

His voice cracked. "I do not know. Since a long time ago," he ventured. Grinding pebbles beneath their feet echoed from the edges of the cavern. Before long, Albert asked, "Where do you live?"

"A place called Kobiton. It's a city. Have you ever been to a city?"

He shook his head.

"Do you know what a city is?"

Again, his head shifted, but Albert's eyes were wider now.

"Well, Kobiton is a place full of buildings. Many are four and five stories tall, as tall as the trees in the forest. Those places are, as a rule, residential homes where families live. There are many avenues lined with plum, apple, and cherry trees. They flower every year. Smell's divine. Terraced gardens—throughout the city—where many grow certain kinds of herbs or vegetables. The ones for specific reasons. Cures. There are communal bath houses, open markets, and wide parks with lots of trees and playgrounds. There're so many places to play and to just sit with friends. My favorite place is the market, and believe me, there are so many of them! Some sell meats, others fresh vegetables. Always the best food is being sold. Everything you'd ever need is in Kobiton. No reason to leave." She glanced at her hands.

"Then why did you leave?"

*What do I tell him?*

"I was taken against my will. Used as women are. But I fled into the forest. And then a wild cat found me and tried to kill me. Your Papa Edwin, he's courageous."

Shadows and light beams grew and shrank from their lantern's swing as they walked down the dark passage.

"Do you miss Kobiton?"

"Yeah. Very much so. I miss the people, and I miss the kitchens at the Abbey. They had everything: brick ovens, iron grills, so many utensils!" She realized she was jabbering. "How far down the mountain have you gone? Have you ever visited Chinochi? Or Goshee?"

His head barely shook, but his wide eyes said it all. "You've never been to either of those places, have you? That's sad. Well, not Goshee, but Chinochi's a good place to visit. I mean, there are good parts to it. Why haven't you ever visited Chinochi?"

"I am not allowed."

"Why's that?"

He shrugged and continued to lead. She knew the truth: Telepaths.

Albert brought Charlotte to a large circular room with a refuse bucket in the corner. But ahead of them and against the far arching wall, there was a pile of coal chunks. Albert looked like he felt, a strange mix of pride and shame. Pride in showing Charlotte the fruits of his labor, skills he had honed over the years. But shame too, at the simplicity of their lives compared to the wonders she had described from Kobiton.

The air was stagnant. The now familiar rotten egg smell closed in on her as they continued their stroll.

"This is where we store the coal," Albert said, his voice gruff to hide his uncertainty. He looked at Charlotte's face, searching for signs of disappointment or disgust. Instead, he saw her genuine interest. It stirred something in him, a longing for approval he had not realized he craved.

They stood there together for quite a long time.

"Why does it smell so bad?" she asked.

He shrugged and took her further into the enormous cavern where Edwin had brought her earlier. The air here smelled better, but still it was humid and stuffy.

"I never would've guessed such a world could live under the ground. This place where you live is pretty, but different from what I'm used to seeing."

"What are you used to seeing?"

"More color. Blue sky, rainbows, flowers, trees, wildlife. I miss hearing wind rattling leaves. Bird calls. Crickets and frogs. Seeing people's faces. All of it, but then again, you don't know, I'm guessing, what all that means."

"I know what bird calls sound like, and crickets. Frogs. What are frogs?"

"Well, they're green, and sound like a loud burp, kinda. They're little long-legged creatures that hop around. You'll usually find them by a pond, or creeks, around stagnated water. You wouldn't find them here, I suppose, too cold. And sometimes you can find them in trees."

He blinked. "We have wildflowers and trees. But only if you go outside. Come on. We should return to the fire. Father always says I need my sleep."

She nodded, swooping her arm forward to indicate he should continue to lead the way.

As they returned to the main cavern, Charlotte found herself reluctant to part from Albert. Their hands brushed accidentally, sending a spark of warmth through her. For a moment, their eyes met, and Charlotte saw a softness there she hadn't noticed before. The moment passed quickly but left her heart beating a little faster.

# 9

## <u>CONTROL</u>

The morning's oatmeal sat like lead in Albert's stomach, each spoonful harder to swallow than the last. He had barely slept. Charlotte's stories of the outside world fought with his father's warning. The sweet taste of sugar on his tongue mocked the bitterness rising in his throat.

Every morning, the same dance—shoulder hunched, eyes down, silent compliance. But today felt different. Today, the weight of every unasked question, every swallowed protest, pressed against his ribs like metal waiting to be shaped.

He walked half a step ahead of Jebadia, not wanting to lay eyes on him. He was trying to figure out how to say his feelings in a way that didn't give him head trauma, but he knew Jebadia would beat him nonetheless.

*Why have you kept me here, inside this mountain? Away from women? Townships and cities? Away from colors and frogs? Is it to deprive me? Is it? Because now ... I now know how deprived I am, and now ... now I want justice. Revenge. I ... I ....*

His lips moved in the angry breath he was blowing, puffing up like a dog's jowl. But before he could speak, his own fist made the first sound. And then words erupted from him like ore breaking free from stone. "How dare you keep me here! Keep me from meeting people. From women. From seeing places like cities and towns." Each syllable carried years of suppressed rage. His fists flowed, clumsy with fury. "You do not care. You never have."

That first punch connected with Jebadia's jaw, the impact jarring upward on Albert's arm. He should have felt triumphant. Instead, he felt something crack inside him—not bone, but something deeper, something more fundamental. The barrier between obedient son and rebel had shattered. He continued to hit and sometimes missed his father's face.

"Ungrateful pissant!" The words his father shouted tasted like blood in his mouth. "And you know you are!"

Jebadia absorbed the blows, his silence more damning than any shout. Then, with the swift efficiency of a lifetime's violence, he struck back. The familiar dance of abuse, but for the first time, Albert did not retreat.

"You ungrateful child. You cannot handle a woman like that. She is a Witchtress, a woman who has come to take your mind and soul. You cannot see it, but I can."

"Horseshit!"

"The stories she has told you have filled your mind with fluff. She's a soul crusher, and so is her world. You cannot handle it. Any of it! Townships or otherwise. You have no clue about the chaos that happens in those places. The singing. You cannot control it. You are naïve and stupid. Ungrateful child. Ungrateful I say!"

Albert landed an uppercut that threw Jebadia onto his back, knocking the air out of him. The young man then pounced on his father and did not let up from their fight.

"You do not trust me. That is what this is about. But I am a man now. I am a man. And I can handle you. I can handle anything." Jebadia's body went limp.

The donkeys watched with liquid eyes, silent witnesses to this long-coming explosion. How many times had these tunnel walls absorbed the sound of flesh striking flesh, of bitter words and broken promises? The animals knew, as the mountain itself did, each crack and crevice holding echoes of generations of pain.

Albert's hands trembled, speckled with his father's blood. For the first time, he understood that violence did not end things—it only transformed them into something else, something harder to heal. But he could not stop, not now. Charlotte's words about the world he lived in, but knew nothing about, rang in his ears and mixed with the thunder of his heartbeat.

Metal in the walls seemed to pulse with his rage, responding to emotions he had spent a lifetime concealing. He felt no remorse. Every time he made contact with his father's body, Albert felt victorious in his desire to finally have control.

Control. It was always about control—but what was the point of controlling power when you didn't even control your own life?

· · · · ● · ● · · · ·

Later, when Charlotte found Albert sitting alone in the dark, she did not ask about his bruised knuckles or the way he flinched at sudden movements. Instead, she settled beside him, close enough to share warmth but not touching, respecting the rough edges of his pain.

"I used to think anger made you strong," he said finally with an unusually rough voice; reflecting a newly felt determination. "That is what father always said. But it just makes everything harder to see clearly."

Charlotte's silence was patient, accepting. When she finally spoke, her words were soft but sure. "Sometimes we have to break before we can rebuild."

He looked at his hands, still trembling slightly. "I do not want to be like him."

"You're not," she said with open frankness. "You're choosing a different path."

The truth of it settled in his chest, heavy but somehow freeing. He wasn't just fighting against his father—he was fighting for something else, something better. Something that felt suspiciously like hope.

# 10

## <u>Growing Close</u>

As they walked through the winding tunnels one evening, Charlotte felt Albert's eyes on her. When she turned to meet his gaze, he glanced away, a blush creeping up his neck. The air between them crackled with an energy she couldn't name or understand.

"So," she said, breaking the silence. "What do you do for fun around here?"

Albert's shy smile made her heart skip a beat, surprising her with its intensity.

"I whittle," he muttered. "Sometimes stone, sometimes wood. Once I made a pinecone into a multi-pointed arrowhead."

The first time Charlotte used her Erthin Abilities in front of Albert—just a small thing, warming the chilly air around them—his reaction was mixed. While curiosity lit his eyes, something else rested within those silvery pools on either side of his nose. There was a war going on within the young man that she wished to understand.

· · · · ● · ● · · ·

Sometimes, in the deepest tunnels, Albert would hear something beyond the metal's song—a deeper resonance that seemed to come from the mountain's core itself. Those notes spoke of Ancient Powers, of things buried so deep they had no names. He never told Charlotte about this, about how the very stone seemed to pulse with unknowable intent.

As he stood there under Charlotte's beautiful gaze, Albert's mind drifted to a lesson that had helped him understand his own powers.

Edwin guided Albert's hand along the cave wall. "Feel it?" he asked. "Each metal has its own song. Gold whispers, silver hums, iron thunders. We keep metal within us because it is like keeping a piece of that song alive inside. Without it, we are cut off from the harmony."

"But why cannot we just carry it?" Albert asked.

"The metal in our blood does more than amplify our Power," Edwin explained. "It connects us to each other, helps us heal, keeps us strong. External metal is like looking at a fire through glass—you can see it, feel some warmth, but it is not the same as having that flame inside you. That is why cities are so dangerous for us. Too many metal voices screaming at once, trying to pull the song from our blood."

Albert nodded, understanding dawning. "That is why we stay together? The harmony?"

"Yes. Separated, our individual songs grow weak. Together, we create a symphony that makes us stronger than we could ever be alone."

· · · • · ● · ● · ● · · ·

The memory faded as Charlotte's warmth brought him back to the present. "That is different," he said slowly, feeling the warm air ripple around them. "When we ... when I work with metal, it feels like ... like awakening something that was always there. It flows like a waterfall, easy to channel. Does your Power feel the same?"

When Albert told Charlotte about himself, it was by far the most he had said to her at once, and she found herself smiling. "Kinda. Each type of Power has its own nature," she said carefully, knowing not to press about his Abilities. "Like the earth and sky—different but connected."

A ghost of a smile touched his lips. "I have never met anyone like you," he whispered.

"I've never met anyone like you either," She replied, and she meant it. Blushing, Charlotte tried to shed the awkwardness she felt. "I've never tried to whittle, but there was a class on it if one wanted to learn. I took a sewing class, though I've never been very good at it. I prefer to plant and cook, but mostly cook."

Onward, they clomped down to the underground lake.

Unlike other minds that lay open to her telepathy, the Metalists' thoughts remained sealed behind their metal-infused blood. Only through direct contact could she breach that natural guard, and even then, only fragments slipped through.

She waited for him to speak, hoping for more insight about him, his lifestyle—likes and dislikes.

After a while of walking, she asked, "Did you ever use that pinecone arrowhead?"

"No."

"Why not?"

"Father smashed it with his boot. Called it stupid."

"It didn't sound stupid to me. Kinda brilliant. I'd like to see it in use sometime. It might have worked for killing squirrels, or rabbits. I mean, the kids who whittled would make spears and arrows, bows, poles for fishing, you name it. It was a neat class to take, but was never my thing, you know."

Again, their gaze met. Charlotte giggled. Albert's face was redder now, their steps in unison echoing up and down the corridors.

Without thinking, Charlotte reached out, gently squeezing Albert's hand. "I'd love to see what you've created some day."

Albert stared at their joined hands, then back at Charlotte. The vulnerability in his silvery-gray eyes made her breath catch. Slowly, hesitantly, he interlaced his fingers with hers.

They stood like that for a long moment, neither speaking, both marveling at the simple intimacy of this gesture. But soon their hands grew sweaty, and a tender moment slipped away, yet still felt by both of them.

The constant drip of water echoed throughout the caverns, a rhythmic heartbeat of the mountain—much like the metallic songs that only a Metalist could hear.

They began their return trip home. As they walked side-by-side, Charlotte reached out with her hand and traced the cool, smooth walls, marveling at how the stone seemed to pulse with an energy she couldn't quite understand. The air tasted of minerals and secrets, hinting at depths yet unexplored.

There wasn't much more said between the two. But they both seemed to be enjoying each other's company. At the end of their walk, Charlotte and Albert said their goodbyes, retiring to their respective beds, and allowed sleep to overtake them.

· · · · • · • · • · · ·

The days fell into a good rhythm. Charlotte found comfort in the simple routine of chores with Papa Edwin. The enormous underground chamber became their sanctuary away from the soot and silence of the main cave. Here, between the washing and folding, stories were shared, and trust slowly built. She grew fond of the elder grandfather figure. Thankfully, he didn't shy away from that position.

*I never thought I would want to be part of a small family,* Charlotte thought as she folded dried clothing. *But I can see the perks of living with just a few people, opposed to living and working for an Abbey and Seminary. All those hungry children and workers. I always thought I'd miss home, Kobiton, but this place—these caves—has its own kind of charm, albeit simple, plain.*

When she became bored with the soot coated, gray walls, Charlotte would pull out her large leather-bound book. There were tomes of information about plants, stones, and recipes, some fiction, stories she would read to Edwin during cozy evening times.

"... Then Petok Ninnith granted them corporeal form, and they descended upon the land to wreak their terrible revenge. Darkness shrouded the earth, and the heavens trembled with thunder as torrents of rain turned the ground to mire. Yet the women and children were blameless, and the once-young man, now old and wise, had long carried the burden of remorse for his conquest. When at last he perished, he ascended to Hakra's embrace, his sins forgiven.

"But those who had chosen vengeance, whom Petok Ninnith had imbued with monstrous power, were cast into the fiery depths of purgatory, there to remain for all eternity."

"That is a chilling story."

"Most of them are. But there's always a lesson to be learned. Don't seek revenge or Petok Ninnith might grant it and you'll be stuck in purgatory forever."

"I have often wanted to learn to read, but I think I am too old now." Edwin said.

"You're never too old to learn to read. I can teach you. There's an alphabet at the back of the book. Easy to remember words, like mama and papa, food, drink, clothing, poop ...." She giggled.

"That would be nice. Thank you, Miss Charlotte."

"Of course, my pleasure, Edwin!" Charlotte then took the time to introduce the alphabet to Edwin. And every day thereafter, she taught him more about reading and writing—relishing this time together.

Even Albert showed a bit of interest in the stories she was reading. Though he wasn't interested in learning how to read, he enjoyed the stories. She read only a few to him, afterwards arguing the philosophy of it all. She appreciated that he felt the same way about Hakran culture. They enjoyed conversing about Hakra's reign and plight—to keep everyone safe from tyranny.

Jebadia's lips curled whenever Charlotte read out loud from her book. "Stop filling Albert's head with nonsense," he would snarl, though she caught him listening from his bed, tension visible in his shoulders. Once, she glimpsed something else in his expression—a flash of recognition, perhaps even longing—before it hardened into familiar contempt.

"Stories are dangerous things," he spat one evening after she had finished reading. "They make you want what you cannot have."

Charlotte noticed how Jebadia's gaze lingered on Albert who sat silently enthralled by the tales. Was it concern she saw there, or fear? Whatever drove Jebadia's hostility seemed rooted in something deeper than mere dislike of outsiders.

· · · · · ● · ● · · · ·

"Can you cut hair?" Albert asked Charlotte one afternoon, hat in hand.

She had been darning one of his stockings but stopped and looked up at him.

Jebadia had cut Albert's hair. She had heard him grunting while struggling to get an even cut, but she had learned early on not to pay attention to anyone's grunts.

"I've never cut anyone's hair but my own. Even then, I usually go to the Barbery to get my locks trimmed up. It's not that I couldn't do it myself, I just prefer someone who is able to see what they're doing. The last time I cut my own hair, I just kinda lopped it off and hoped for the best."

Albert's hair looked like a knife had been used to cut it; the haircut he had received wasn't even at all—there were a few nearly bald spots, hair had been pulled out; it was all very jagged. He looked up at her with dopey eyes. "Father cut my hair again, but I dislike how it feels. Do you think you can cut it better than he?"

She peered at his silvery-grayish hair in disarray. "I could probably fix it. And I can clean up your face too. Trim your beard. If you want."

"Yes. I would like that." His smile was sheepish and drew her in.

"Do you have scissors?"

"Scissors? No. I do not believe .... We-we use a knife."

"Yes, I can tell. Scissors are like shearers, but smaller." She showed the action of the scissors with her fingers. Albert just stared. "You don't know what those are, do you?" He shook his head. "Well, they are like long thin knives, but they are put together, blades facing each other, and then they cut whatever it is you're trying to sever, such as your hair. It could be clothing, or paper, fleece, or even your beard, even hair."

Edwin stirred from his bed. A pair of small scissors seemed to appear in his hands. He stepped across the cold stone floor and handed them off. He nodded at her, and in that moment of brief contact she heard his thoughts. ...*I hope she is careful with these....* And at the same time, she felt a loving warmth radiating, saw images of a few women who had been as kind as Charlotte was to Edwin and Jebadia quickly flash in her mind's eye. At least that was what the exchange felt like—he was comparing her to them, but in a loving way.

Both ladies were pale-skinned, Charlotte's age. One had brown hair, the other woman had soft strawberry-blonde hair, like Charlotte's, and a straight toothed smile. She was the only one who looked to have held amazing Elemental Powers, like Charlotte's.

*Was she Jebadia's mother? Or maybe Albert's? Or just a woman they had met in passing?*

Now that Charlotte held the scissors, those images faded. At once, the cavernous room returned to view.

"Use them well," Edwin remarked, then hustled back to the warmth of his bed.

"Thank you." Charlotte automatically replied, yet still wondered about what she had just seen. What did it mean? Did Edwin not trust her with scissors? Was he comparing her to previous women who had cut their hair?

Even after all this time spent together, she still hadn't seen the men using their Metalistic Powers, yet she shared her magical Abilities willingly (well, not all of them). She wondered if this was the right thing to do? To show her vulnerability with these mountain men? Charlotte couldn't be sure. Thankfully, she was able to manipulate the basic components of all organic food matter to create delicious meals. This gave her the upper hand, just in case something went awry. Though she was unwilling to poison them, she would if it meant saving her life.

Casting aside those petty thoughts, Charlotte tried her best to fix all the horrible cuts made to Albert's hair.

"Father likes it clean cut," Albert snarled, "but then he goes and slices my hair like this."

"I'm not sure I'd trust him to cut anything very well."

"Oh, he knows how to cut things, but he is hard-handed." He looked up at her, their eyes locked, if only for a moment. "Not soft, like you."

"Well, thank you for trusting me, Albert. It means a lot."

"Thank you for fixing my ratty hair," he chuckled.

"Of course, you're welcome."

She groomed him the best she could, although the cut ended up being shorter than he preferred. It was a handsome haircut, and after shaving his face clean, Albert looked younger and somehow taller. She patted and rubbed his face, taking a long moment before removing her hand from its softness. She felt she did a good job maintaining his appearance.

From out of nowhere, a mirror appeared in Albert's hand, and he gazed at himself before she saw his eyes staring at her in the reflection. "You did a great job."

"Thank you!"

He had a hard time pulling his eyes away from hers in the mirror.

"Well, sleep good." His dopey smile stretched his lips a moment longer before he yawned and glanced at his bedroom.

"You too," She called to Albert as he left her side for the night, a slight spring in his step.

# 11

## <u>BITTERSWEET THOUGHTS</u>

*She cut my hair better than anyone ever has.* The thought surfaced with a mix of wonder and unease. *She is good at everything she touches. Too good, maybe.*

His hand drifted to his freshly trimmed hair.

*No more of father's rough hands, his 'accidents' with the blade.*

Anger flared, hot and familiar.

*If he tries to cut my hair again ....*

The threat remained unfinished; shame followed close on anger's heels. Even in his thoughts, he could not quite stand up to Jebadia.

*But Charlotte's hands were so gentle.*

The memory of her touch lingered, stirring something both wonderful and terrifying in his chest.

*No one has ever been gentle with me before.*

A tremor ran through him—fear or excitement, he could not tell anymore. His body seemed to hum with new awareness whenever she was near. He forced his breathing to slow, trying to sort through the storm of unfamiliar emotions.

*Charlotte.*

Even her name in his thoughts made his heart skip. Her scent lingered in his memory—clean like mountain air after rain, sweet like the wildflowers in the meadow he wanted to show her once the snow melted. So different from the metallic tang that perfumed everyone else in his world.

He ran a hand through his hair again, marveling at its softness. Such a simple thing, really. But it felt like a transformation.

*She should not have to sleep on the cold ground,* he reasoned, trying to ignore how his pulse quickened at the thought of her in his bed. *It is practical, that is all. Sharing warmth is practical.*

But there was nothing practical about the way his skin tingled when she smiled at him, or how he found himself watching her hands as she worked, imagining those fingers intertwined with his own.

*What would father say?*

The thought came unbidden, unwelcome.

*She is an outsider. Different. Dangerous.*

But different did not feel dangerous anymore. Different felt like possibility, like hope. Like waking up after a lifetime of sleeping.

His heart pounded in his ears as he lay there on his bed.

*Ugh. I cannot stand these feelings any longer. I just want to touch her. Taste her. Feel her against me. Would she sleep like me?*

He sat up. The embers from the fire made it hard to see her, but he could hear her breathing just now. She, too, was still awake, but her eyes were closed.

*She sleeps on her side. Good to know. So, if she slept with me, then she should sleep here.*

He wiggled aside the center of his bed and pretended she was already there, asleep at his side. He listened as her breathing became quieter and more rhythmic. He imagined feeling her body there against his. He could smell her ... wanted to touch her soft hair and lean against her flesh. He also wanted to ....

*This is not like the animals,* he reminded himself firmly, ashamed of the crude comparison.

*Charlotte is ... Charlotte is ....*

Words failed him. How could he describe someone who had brought color into his monochrome world?

His knowledge of intimacy came from glimpses of nature, raw and unrefined. But Charlotte deserved better than that. She deserved ... what? He did not even know what he didn't know, and that terrified him almost as much as these new feelings did.

*I want to be worthy of her,* he realized. *But how can I be worthy when I barely understand myself?*

The question haunted him, mixing with sweeter thoughts until sleep claimed him. In his dreams Charlotte smiled at him, and he was someone better, someone braver, someone who knew how to love without fear.

# 12

## <u>SPECIAL PLACES</u>

Albert wiped the sweat from his brow, his arms aching from hours of mining. He had just uncovered a promising new vein of silver when Jebadia's gruff voice echoed through the tunnel.

"Boy! Get over here!"

Sighing, Albert absorbed his metal tools and made his way to his father. Jebadia stood, swaying slightly, a nearly empty flask of wine in his hand.

"What is it, Father?"

Jebadia's eyes narrowed. "Do not take that tone with me, boy. I saw you ask that whore to fix your hair. Talking. Smiling. Laughing."

Albert felt the heat rise to his face. "Her name is Charlotte, father. And yes, we were talking. She fixed my hair, cut it better than you ever have. What is wrong with that?"

"What is wrong with it? With her?" Jebadia spat, "Everything! Women are nothing but trouble. They will fill your head with nonsense, make you soft. Is that what you want? To be soft?"

"No, Father, but—"

"But nothing!" Jebadia roared, his face inches from Albert's. "You listen to me. This is our life. Mining. Surviving. There is nothing else out there for the likes of us. You would do well to remember that."

He punctuated his point by shoving Albert hard, sending him stumbling back against the smooth cave wall. Albert was dazed momentarily, but rose and went after his father. A long-winded tussle ensued. Blood splattered, grunts and the sounds of bodies hitting the walls and ground echoed around the chamber. This time, they were equally matched. Jebadia was ready to beat Albert with the same vigor as his son had done to him before. And yet Albert's ego would not back down.

When Jebadia tossed Albert into the wall, the young man's nose met a hard protrusion and knocked it sideways—breaking it. Blood soaked his lips, dripped from his chin. He spit several times, teeth now red. He looked dark, menacing, yet Jebadia matched his intensity.

"Get back to work. Now!" Jebadia shouted, pointing. "And stay away from that woman. That Witchtress. She is and will always be nothing but trouble, mark my words."

As Jebadia stumbled away, Albert stood frozen, a mixture of anger and shame burning in his chest. Then, without a word, he turned and moved to his calm hideaway in the cave, his nose throbbing. His father's spiteful words were still reverberating in his ears.

Pressing his shirtsleeve against his nose, trying to stop the bleeding, he not only found himself thinking of Charlotte, but of his father. He recalled a rare moment from his childhood—Jebadia's calloused hand guiding his as he learned to use his Metalistic Powers for mining, a gruff laugh at some childish joke. What had turned that man into the bitter, angry father he now knew? Was it Charlotte? Or something more horrific from Jebadia's past?

· · · · ● · ● · · · ·

After that tense encounter with Jebadia, Albert sought Charlotte out.

Without a word, he pulled her into a tight embrace. She felt the tension in his body, the slight tremor in his hands as they pressed against her back.

"Thank you," he whispered, his breath warm against her ear, "For being here."

In that moment, Charlotte realized that their blossoming love wasn't just about passion or attraction—it was about support, understanding, and facing life's challenges together.

"You're welcome. I'm here for you, Albert. You can tell me anything."

Albert was quiet for a long time. "I never knew the world could be so ... big," he finally said. "Your stories of Kobiton, life outside ... it is overwhelming sometimes."

Charlotte reached out, hesitantly taking his hand. "It can be scary, but it's beautiful, too. There's so much to discover."

He squeezed her hand, his eyes meeting hers. "Will you show me someday?"

"Of course," she whispered. "We'll discover it together."

As Albert's hand held hers, Charlotte felt a flutter in her chest and attempted to dismiss it as nothing other than the excitement of the unknown.

That night, as she lay in bed, Charlotte's mind swirled with conflicting emotions. Her feelings for Albert grew stronger each day, but with that came a gnawing fear.

She thought of her life in Kobiton, of the dreams she had before coming here. Was she ready to let those go? And what of her Powers? Albert knew so little of the world outside—could he truly understand and accept all of her?

Yet when she remembered the warmth of his smile, the gentleness in his touch, she felt a longing she had never experienced before.

• • • • ● • ● • • •

A few days later, on their nightly walk to the icy underground lake, Albert urged Charlotte to continue on instead of the usual stop and sit. Tonight, they followed the lake's edge as it wound around the cavern. They helped one another climb over boulders and circumnavigated past giant stalagmites, journeying to the far side of the grand chamber.

Their hands brushed as they walked side by side, sending a jolt through Charlotte. It both excited and terrified her. Love had never been part of her plan—it was too risky, too unpredictable. But here, in this isolated world, she found herself longing for connection.

She stole a glance at Albert, noticing the way his brow furrowed in concentration, the gentle strength in his hands as he helped her maneuver between and over jagged rocks. A part of her wanted to reach out, to bridge the gap between them. But another part hesitated, aware of the complexities of their situation, the potential consequences of giving in to these feelings.

*What if I'm not enough? What if once he truly knows me, he'll reject me like so many others have?*

They hiked lower, further than she had ever journeyed. The enormous cavern narrowed, and they stepped into a long passage that had not been chiseled soft like so many before it. This new chamber he took her through was rough and weathered. Soon the wind howled down its enormously long corridor.

Albert's teeth chattered. "I wish I had brought a blanket or my jacket."

Charlotte stepped in close to him and radiated her Erthin heat. She tried to remain by his side as they continued to scramble through this passage, but there were several tight spots, and the rocks and walls were ice cold. The deeper they descended, the narrower the tunnel became. Water trickled alongside, and there were many places where water pooled. But the water always chiseled this place wider, following gravity as it went. There were a few times Charlotte felt claustrophobic, but then Albert grabbed her hand and calmly led her through the tightness and further along their trek.

Ahead of them, a dull light beckoned.

Finally, they reached the mouth of the haphazard corridor and now stood at the base of a tall gap along the eastern side of the mountain. The wind howled between the protrusions, creating several boisterous notes. It wasn't very dark out, the ever-present clouds had cleared, and the half-moons' light sparkled across the snowy tundra.

It was chilly yet beautiful—everything glowed like midday.

Not too far beyond was the forest; it surrounded three sides of the open space below the giant gap. "Late spring-early summer, this becomes a colorful meadow. I come here often when I am bored, or father is disapproving of me. Which seems to be more often these days." He huffed.

"This is impressive. This view. Even in the winter. From Kobiton you can't ever see the mountain tops like you can from up here. There's no way Hakra made all of this. It's all just happenstance." She sighed, her warm breath floated out and dissipated just as quickly. "You'll have to bring me here in the spring, when all the flowers are in bloom. I betcha it's just wonderful then, huh?!"

"Yes. It is. And I will. I come here often. At least I used to. But then you arrived."

"This is nice." She took his hand and pulsated her warm air bubble to encompass him too. Instantly, she was privy to Albert's thoughts.

*—what is with her obsession with Hakra? She is always comparing ... just like father comparing Charlotte to River—a woman who was not even my mother. But he compares everyone to River.*

She cut through his mental chatter. "Thank you for sharing this place."

"We can come here to get away from them. Father and Edwin." *I hate them.* "They get on me sometimes. Ride my ass to get shit done. Constantly telling me I could do better." *Father's way is the only way.* "That their way is better than mine. It is like they hate how I do things. They never say nice things." *I cannot recall the last time they were as nice as Charlotte is.*

"That's not true, Albert. Papa Edwin's complimented you, at least to me. He always says how hard of a worker you are, that you pay attention to details and such. It's your father that's the hard ass. You do good work, Albert. I've seen it."

*Edwin has also said that I should be grateful for what I have. That he had less and for longer.* "Edwin lies! He has never liked how I do things. You have never seen it, but Edwin can be just as mean as father. Some time you will see that side of him. Just wait! It will happen."

She dropped their contact, folded her arms across her chest, and said, "I don't believe you. Papa Edwin's always been nice to me. I can't see him being like Jeb. Your father ... he's got some problems."

After a long contemplative moment, he nodded. "You are definitely correct about that."

She gawked at the amazing view of icy mountain tops glimmering in the moon's light. Soon she felt Albert's gaze heating up the side of her face. She only glanced, not knowing if she wanted to be privy to his thoughts again. Before long, he leaned his head on her shoulder.

*—so happy she is here with me. This moment is perfect. I never want her to leave.* He inhaled and his thoughts dissipated.

The howling wind cut through their silent moment.

She was also enjoying this time with Albert, not wanting it to end. Yet suddenly Albert perked up. "Well, I, ah, I just wanted to show this to you. We should get back. We will return on a better day, when it is warmer."

"I like that idea."

They remained at that wide gap in the mountainside a little longer; watching the moon move slowly across the dark and sparkly horizon before returning to the cold, damp caves and their long hike home.

# 13

## <u>Hidden Powers</u>

The depths of winter had come, and the cave's entrance to the outside world was now closed, coated in a thick layer of ice and snow. The donkeys got their exercise by walking around the long halls, often bringing heavy loads of coal. The smell of chickens and rabbits had faded. There were only two goats left and once they were consumed, Edwin and Albert would then hunt for squirrels. This was how these rugged miners lived. It was hard every winter. Edwin had confided that calculating how much forage would be consumed by the animals seemed to be an easier task than figuring out rations for the family. But with Charlotte around, the food was tasty and lasted longer than Edwin expected.

One day, he broke the silence they worked in. "If I may ask, Sweet Miss, how do you make the stew last so long? And I thought we had consumed all the apples by now. How did you make the pie?"

Charlotte shrugged. "I add more water and potatoes, mushrooms or beats and carrots to the mix."

"Ah. But the meat. It never lasts as long as it does in your stews."

She blushed. "The cauldron is large. Much of the meat stays at the bottom. Sometimes I forget to stir it before it's served. As for those apples, I found them at the bottom of the bag. They must've been overlooked. That's why I made a pie. I figured it would be a good meal. I mean, who doesn't like apple pie? Goes great with the grilled goat we'll be having tonight. Oh, and that's the other thing. I cut the meat into thin strips, you know, and that just makes it last longer."

He thought she might be lying. "You cannot make more meat from the same amount just by slicing it smaller, Sweet Miss. I know how to cook. I am calling your bluff!"

Her light greenish-gray eyes grew wide and bright.

"And I was the one who emptied those apple bags. I remember folding them up and putting them in the basket." He wagged his finger.

A deep sigh parted her lips, and her eyes dropped to her hands. Charlotte pulled an apple seed from a small pouch she kept hidden in her skirt. Placing the dark brown seed with a black spot on it in the center of one hand, she then cupped it with the other hand and looked at Edwin. Charlotte said nothing while gazing at him. But within those coupled hands, something was happening. From that tiny seed, an apple grew.

"You caught me," she said and handed him the apple.

Edwin looked the yellow apple over, smelling its sweetness, and wanted to take a bite, but then shoved it at her. "You take the first bite." He demanded, and she took three.

"These are really good apples." She said, mouth full, and handed it back to him.

Edwin took a nibble, then a bite, and suddenly half of the apple was consumed. "Indeed. I too like these apples. But how did you do it? How did you make that apple appear?"

"It takes a seed to make another fruit or vegetable. Now there won't be any seeds in this apple, but that's okay. That's why I ask for the cores when you're all done eating them. That's why I take all the eyes growing on the potatoes out of them. That's why we will never run out of food. I can replicate almost anything, just need a piece of it to ...."

"But the animals. I, ah, I have to kill them because if I don't, then you'd all have knowledge of my secret. But don't worry, I've preserved much of the meat. It's hidden, being kept frozen and out of the way. I'm sure no one knows about it. And please don't tell anyone."

It took Edwin a moment to process it all. "How do you reproduce the meat?"

"The thing is, I don't reproduce it. The mushrooms, beets and potatoes, they can take on the taste of the meat. And they're better for you than meat, anyway. But don't worry, we've enough meat to get us through the winter."

"That is an amazing gift, Sweet Miss."

"I'm sure it's the reason the Warden kept me alive. They knew what I was capable of. I've never told anyone I could do this, including Miss Lori and H'Eirwyn. And they're my friends." She blinked, feeling more honest than she ever had with any adult. "But there's something else," She whispered, not meeting his eyes. "Something I've never told anyone. Sometimes, when I touch people, I can ... take their energy. Their life force. It's how I survived on my own for so long. Why I was in solitary so often. The Warden wasn't just poisoned. I drained them first, made them weak enough for the poison to work."

Edwin sat back, taking in her confessions. "Do not worry, Sweet Miss. I will keep your secrets safe. To my grave."

"Thank you, Edwin."

They smiled and went back to washing the linens. Soon Edwin paused to say, "Your Powers are very amazing, young lady. The power of fire, water, and air, and now the ability to make food and suckle someone's life force. Are you happy to have these Powers?"

"Most of my life I've felt burdened by them, but not now. Not as an adult."

"Do you ever worry about passing on those traits?"

"I've never thought about it." Charlotte lied. She feared passing down her Powers, having been ridiculed by other children. But then, she had never seen herself having children, anyway.

His smile faded; those steely eyes stared at her—through her. "I have noticed Albert's fondness of you grow. He has the same look Jebadia had when he met his first love, River. How do you feel about him?"

She quickly admitted. "I like Albert. Though he's quite naïve about many things. But that's probably a good thing. Hakran indoctrination and all."

"Indeed. We live as we live and are not burdened by your Hakran culture."

"That's a blessing, for sure. In that, he's lucky. All of you are. What I would've done to have grown up like you have." Then Charlotte's sight drew up to the distant ceiling, with stalactites jutting toward them like a thousand sabers. She lamented, "I miss Kobiton. And my friends."

"Well, once spring arrives, we will return you to Kobiton."

"Will all of you come? Jebadia included?"

"Well, maybe not Jeb. No. He can stay here, mine by himself. Might give him some time to think." Edwin chuckled. "But maybe, perhaps, we could bring Albert with us. From here, the journey takes about seven to eight days. We must cross a river, go through a few valleys, so there will be some up and down hiking. And we enter town by the southern route, not the northern ... the route you took to get here. I have never taken Albert on the trail, well, not all the way. But it is quicker than taking the road through the pass. That direction would take you over half a moons' time, and you must go through Goshee." He stuck out his tongue.

She shivered at the thought of passing through Goshee by herself. Then she saw how lighthearted Edwin seemed about everything. "I'm so thankful you're in my life, Edwin. Albert too. I'd love to do that, travel with you and Albert, and without Jebadia! That sounds like a fun ol' time. I know you'll love Kobiton. It's the best. And if you like it, wanna stay, maybe you and Albert can move there!"

"Now, see, that might be a challenge. See we all, ah, we stay together. We must."

"Is it because of your Powers?"

He rubbed the back of his neck. "Well ... that too. We agreed not to separate. There needs to be harmony."

She chortled. "Harmony and Jebadia, ha! Yeah, good luck with that."

"He brings a type of harmony that cannot be defined by words. It is a Power thing."

"Okay. Then, I guess you'll be returning to Jebadia after taking me to Kobiton. But I know Albert will want to remain. We've already talked about it, some. I know of a few places we can live in town. My friend Miss Lori has a homestead on the south side. She rents out rooms. We could probably stay with her until we find our own place."

Edwin made a long-winded sound before replying, "Albert might prefer to live outside of town."

"I don't think so."

He blinked at her. "All I know is that you and Albert will not live far from us. You can live downslope if you prefer. But I will visit you every day. Trust me when I say I would miss you if you left."

"I'd be fine with that. Just as long as we're close to town. That way I can visit my friends too."

"We could do that, but we must live further away from town than just the outskirts."

"Why is that?"

# 14

## TRUST & TRUTH

What I am about to tell you must not leave these stony walls. But as you have probably already figured out, we, my family and I, are not from here, not from these mountains or any other place beholden to Urthis.

Born in the damp manganese mines of GnSaan, me, and my twin brother Edge were but child labor to powerfully cruel overlords who used us Metalists to extract all the precious ores we could. And at the cost of our own lives. We did not know how little we mattered. Maybe by our mothers, but not in the hearts of those who brought us there, not in the eyes of our great grandmother Baena, the woman who manipulated all of us to follow the orders of other Telepathic creatures. But they were men, and as such, died the same as any other.

I remember convincing Edge to follow me and escape the pits of the mountain for an unknown future. He had been contented with living as a servant, eating what was given, doing as ordered, never asking questions .... Never wanting to know why we were sent there in the first place. Had it not been for our elder Pakax, or the tongueless women we were forced to sleep with, I might not have fathomed escaping. But sleepless nights filled with anxious days only led me to this conclusion. Escape or die young, as all our elders had. I now know Pakax had been maybe forty years old when his heart seized. He fell over dead before us all. We did not know we could be overworked, but we were every day until our day of freedom.

But that freedom came at a harsh price.

Coming from a life where everything was handed to us, food, water, sleeping provisions, cleaning essentials, survival had a steep learning curve. But with Edge at my side, even though he had contempt, we still had our harmony. It was the one thing that would keep us linked, the one thing that made us feel safe. It is a magnetic feeling, a positive attraction, so to speak. Without it, we feel weak, like we cannot go on. Having our twin with us is essential for enjoying a peaceful life.

Peace and harmony would never be part of our life after leaving GnSaan. And neither of us knew this until just recently.

When we found the gritty city of Somper, we were clothed, housed, and found menial jobs at the wharf. Edge and I met women, wanted families, steady jobs, and found homesteads to foster these intentions. Finally, we felt a unity in our shared accomplishments. That was until my wife gave birth to a little girl and boy. Edge's wife bore only boys. We thought nothing of it. Lived our happy lives. Raised our children to know love.

Kebrii, our girl, she was a jealous little child. Early on, we noticed how she could command not only her brother, but cousins to do what she wanted. She tried to control me, but I was always firm with her. Set my boundaries, as I knew I must. My wife and I, we just thought she was a bossy little girl and would grow out of it. But then she murdered her mother. So, I had to kill her.

Edge's family was caught amid it all. Only he and I survived. But we did not. That fight cost us more than our families, it cost us our livelihoods. We were ostracized, tossed on a ship, and set sail to our doom. Or so they told us.

The thing is, seedy Telepaths always talk. They always want control. And they figured out how to control us—and in the worst of ways. Tossed around the sea like driftwood, we managed to escape if only to end up in a worser place .... A place called Nuaki Village. But do not worry, it is not there anymore. Edge and I, along with another captive named Dephen, watched that place burn to the ground. Then we helped each other escape the Jungle of Datzar. Dephen disappeared in the markets of some village, while Edge and I were hunted down by Wardens. As you already know, they are vicious creatures—can take the shape of anything, friend and foe.

But we slaughtered them all.

And once we arrived at our destiny, the Kruluver Mountain Range, we agreed to separate. Edge left. It was hard at first. That was until I met Tayla. She made me feel whole. She loved me for who I was, a monster of a man. She earnestly wanted to grow old with me, be a mother to my children. But when she bore what she bore, I had to take what was mine and slaughter the rest.

Tayla was my biggest regret. Though plain, she held a spark that I have only seen in one other person. Her name was River. She was a sweet and kind young woman who caught Jebadia's eye. She was the perfect mate for him, adoring and faithful. Jebadia was about the same age as I had been when he asked to bring her home and marry her.

It was an exciting time for all of us.

And yet I worried about the things that would happen. I worried about the love and loss that might occur. I was thankful she had a miscarriage at five moons. That was a hard time for everyone. Poor Jeb. He could not handle the grief. We left her that day. Years later, Jeb met Faith. She was a drunk and mean, a foulmouthed woman bore the same fate as every other woman our family has coupled with. It was then that I understood our curse. Though every Metalist is born with a twin, my offspring will always produce one male and one female. And female Metalists are strong, stronger than any male Metalist. The power they hold ....

The hard truth is that female Metalists hold powers we cannot control. My great grandmother Baena ... she could do more than just sense and harness metal. She could instruct any one of us to slaughter thousands with just a thought. Although the men could just harness and telepathically speak to our twin, we could only speak to our twin. Meanwhile, the females could telepathically speak to any one of us, all of us, and without being of direct relations.

All female Metalists develop this telepathic Ability. Without exception. Without limit. Their minds can reach into ours and bend our wills like soft metal.

If you ask me, it is too powerful a Talent for them to wield. It is why they are not allowed to live. Every generation, when twins are born, we must ... we must kill the girls immediately. I have seen what happens when we do not—my own daughter Kebrii grew too powerful too quickly. She murdered her mother. Sliced her into pieces. She was only three years old. I had no choice but to ....

That memory haunts me still. It is our curse; you see. The price we pay for our Powers.

·　·　·　●　·　●　·　●　·　·　·

Edwin's expression tightened almost imperceptibly. "Some stories, Swee Miss, are warnings disguised as history." He studied her with an intensity that felt different from his usual warmth. "When we tell ourselves certain truths are merely stories, we often find ourselves repeating the very tragedies we dismissed." His voice dropped over. "Trust me when I say some fears are earned through blood."

After a long pause to process everything she had just heard, Edwin admitted, "I see so much of River in you sometimes. The same kindness, the same strength. And it terrifies me."

Charlotte sat quietly, absorbing the weight of Edwin's confession. His words seemed to echo in the cave's darkness: female Metalists were too powerful to live.

"Why tell me this now?" she finally asked

Edwin's weathered face was etched with worry. "Because I see how my grandson looks at you, Sweet Miss. And I need you to understand what that could mean."

For a moment, the mask of kindly grandfather slipped. His silver eyes hardened, and his hand reflexively moved to the knife at his belt. "I have become fond of you, Charlotte. More than I should allow myself. But there are truths in our blood that even my affection cannot change." The steel in his voice matched the metal he wielded, and Charlotte understood his warnings were not hypothetical—they were promises. Then, like clouds passing from the sun, his expression softened again. "I just want you to be prepared, Sweet Miss. Knowledge is protection."

# 15

## <u>Evening Walks</u>

Winter's temptress prevented the miners from leaving their mountain. The cave was forever cold. Only the fire kept the crisp air at bay. Their existence was tiring and boring. Yet they managed through this tough time by sleeping and keeping busy.

One day, Charlotte leaned into Edwin and softly told him. "I've always wanted to have someone like you in my life, a fatherly figure who wasn't as authoritative as the priests or headmasters at Kobiton's Abbey."

"I do not mind being your fatherly figure, though it might make your relationship with Albert awkward." He chuckled at her.

She giggled, "Oh you!" and hugged the old man.

Edwin's fondness for Charlotte continued to grow, as did Albert's. Jebadia only seemed to appreciate her after meals were consumed. He never praised her, but always made noises of satisfaction. She worked as hard as they did and maintained the kitchen space and homestead as well as Edwin would. The two of them had done much to make their stark cave inviting for Charlotte. She now had a bed, padded by tree branches, lichen and moss, with a few hides tossed across for extra comfort. Kitchen cabinets and countertops, crafted from logs and secured by hemp rope, were added. To showcase her numerous herb bags, Charlotte placed them on thin granite slabs resting on wood. They were arranged in a row on one side of the flat prep surface. On the other side, the cleaned silverware, plates, and bowls were stacked neatly. Despite her spotless kitchen, she persistently pursued her hobbies of reading, sewing, and knitting, maintaining their home to the Miner's standards. Papa Edwin aided her daily in keeping up their homestead.

Charlotte continued to daydream of home, of Kobiton—her small bedroom and all its comforts. Her heart ached for her return. She tried not to think of

Lori—every day, but it happened anyway. She was becoming depressed by the dull routine of her monotonous home life.

Thankfully, every day after toiling in the mines and supper, Albert would whisk Charlotte away from her routines; and Jebadia's glower. They would talk at great lengths about their ambitions and dreams. He was blossoming into a thoughtful young man, who was earnestly interested in Charlotte. He followed her around like a lost animal, wanting to spend every waking moment with her—especially after being around his skeptical father all day.

"How was your day?" Albert asked one evening as they walked along.

The lantern swung in his hand and between the two of them. "Boring. I mean, it was good, but I just don't know how you all do it, every day like this. I miss the outside world. Fresh air. Rain. The sights and colors. People. But other than that, it was good. I'm almost done knitting that shawl. Should be done tomorrow or the next day, probably. I know it'll keep my shoulders warm when I don't want to wrap up in this cloak. How was your day?"

He shrugged. "We started a new passage. Father thinks we can angle it in such a way that it will exit the mountain, but that will take much time and calculations."

"Calculations? Like math?"

"Yes, we do math. Though, I am not very good at it. Another point of contention between father and me. I just do not understand the necessity of it if we sent out probes to find the easiest of ways."

"Probes? What are those?"

"Little pieces of metal. We push them through the rocks. Once we feel less resistance, we move that way, following the easiest course before drilling."

"Sounds complicated."

"Not really. Just time consuming. I would much rather spend my time with you."

She grinned. "Same here. With you I mean. Though Papa Edwin is pretty fun. He's got some crazy stories. The people and places he's lived and visited; it's just amazing. I mean, he's a world traveler. Have you ever wanted to travel the world?"

"No."

"Hm. Did you mine anything interesting today?"

"Yes. We brought back some coal, but mostly we chiseled. It is a boring job, but someone must do it." He chuckled at what he believed was a funny joke.

Charlotte didn't get it at first, but then laughed with him. "A boring job, that's right. I get it. It must be, huh!"

"Yes."

Their boots ground against the gravel and they walked on in silence.

After some time, Albert asked, "Do you want to travel?"

"I always thought I wanted to, but after doing it, I don't. There's a reason I decided to live in Kobiton once I grew up. It's a nice place to live. And I miss it terribly. That's why I want to go home.

"But had Hakra wanted me to cook food for him, I would've in a heartbeat! I mean, that would've been a great honor to bear. And moving to Akarah would've been part of the deal. But that city … it's amazing. I would've given shelter, food, and clothing. But there's so many things that I'd miss—like I do now. Celebrations and festivals, and friends ….

"When I was younger, and this is something every Hakran believer does at least once in their lifetime, I took the pilgrimage to Akarah. You're supposed to go when you're older than twelve, but no older than seventeen. And they happen every five years, because it takes many moons, sometimes years even, to get to Akarah from your hometown. We were guided by our ecclesiastics, who their only job is to guide the innocent to meet Hakra. Sometimes older folk will come along too, as chaperones. We all sleep outside and under the stars or clouds. At every township, there was always a place for us to rest and eat, but we would just continue along, every day, following the roads to Akarah. All roads lead there, you know.

"And just more and more people amassed. At every township, more teenagers joined the parade. Some were so innocent, having never left their mother's bosom. The orphans were less scared. We've delt with worse terrors than what met us on those roads. It's like a rite of passage for all innocents. Though you're not very innocent afterwards. And if you don't take the pilgrimage, well … you have to. It's part of Hakran ways. Indoctrination, of course. You either believe in Hakra afterwards or you don't.

"But it's crazy all the people you meet along the way. How kind and caring some of them are. And such compassion is given to those of us taking the pilgrimage. I mean, all our elders have taken this same route before. They've all been part of that historic trek. It was … it's amazing. There're prayer circles at dawn and dusk, and daily meditation. Even while we walk, we are in this type of trance, because it becomes like that. Always going forward, droning on and on, but with a purpose, a destination; to see Hakra. To deliver our faith to him, and to lay eternal dedication so that we are always with him in this life and the next.

"Even on the return we were so mindful, so one with each other and the world. Taking that pilgrimage is something that leaves you understanding yourself and your life's purpose. It's something that will be with you forever."

They walked on, Albert taking it all in. "Wow. And everyone takes the pilgrimage. I guess I would be too old to take that journey." A while back, he had admitted that he had seen at least eighteen summers. Those silvery eyes were always captivated by her. "Did anything bad happen to you?"

"Yeah." Charlotte only disclosed, "That's why we're not so innocent afterwards. That whole journey ... it changes you. Either you become complacent to it, or your soul is killed by it."

The shadows of their bodies grew and shrank as they walked side-by-side, the lantern swinging between them. Once they arrived at the cathedral, they stopped to take in the monstrous sight.

The ethereal glow of the cavern cast dancing shadows across Albert's face. Charlotte found herself mesmerized by the play of light on his features, seeing him as if for the first time. When he caught her staring, she didn't look away. Instead, she reached out, gently tracing the line of his jaw. The tenderness of the moment surprised them both.

She was thankful for this ritual of theirs; appreciated the long walk to the underground lake and back. It was a good post-supper hike; the air smelled the best in the giant chamber. Sometimes they would stand or sit, but sometimes they would pivot and return home only to retire.

· · • · • · • · • · ·

"Have you ever wondered what it'd be like to live by yourself? Or maybe with just one other person. Someone like me?" Charlotte asked during one of their many walks. "It's not that I don't like your family, but as we get older, we're not required to live with our families. That is, if we don't want to. I mean, most couples in Kobiton live together, without their families, and in small flats and lofts and such. One-bedroom dwellings, they're called. You know, a place to call our own."

"No. I have not. But I would like to. I would like to live with you. Just you." He gazed at her, his face flushed. "Okay, so maybe ... maybe I have thought about it. Fantasized about it. Just you and me. No Jeb. No Edwin. Just the two of us." He impulsively kissed her. "I never want to leave you, Charlotte. I will always be with you, always protect you."

Taken aback for that moment, Charlotte moved in and kissed him just as quickly as he had with her. They could see each other's teeth, their cheeks round and rouge.

Her swinging hand found his and their fingers intertwined. "Thank you, Albert. I never want to leave you either. You've stolen my heart. Your kindness ... and how thoughtful you can be. It's all I could ever want in a companion."

Those silvery eyes went to his boot as it crushed the gravel, but slowly they lifted to see her. "You are all I have ever wanted, Charlotte. And I did not realize I wanted anything. Especially you."

She felt a little odd in this moment, being the first female Albert had ever known. Yet how he was when around her, she knew his reactions were altruistic. And his loyalty to her, to help with whatever she needed, was beyond reproach. Such dedication helped keep her warm at night. Still, Jebadia complained about her, and her power over his only child. He never considered that Albert might have been enamored by her simply because she was the first woman he had ever met.

"I'm glad Papa Edwin brought me into your home, into your life." Charlotte then pulled Albert in close and passionately kissed him. They gasped and panted, bodies creating their own type of warmth. He held her tight, breathing her in, his wet lips remained plastered to hers.

When they pulled away, Albert gleamed. "I never want this to end."

"Neither do I."

They dove in once more, passions flourishing, hands fondling, pulling and pushing, groping and moaning. It took them a while before they could separate. When they finally left the giant cavern, their handhold remained tight until arriving back home. They pulled apart and went their separate ways. Yet glances lingered as they laid down in their own beds and tossed blankets across themselves.

· · · · ● · ● · · · ·

In the quiet moments afterward, Albert wondered at the intensity of his feelings. Were they purely his own? Or was there something more at play? His father had warned him about women's Abilities to cloud men's minds with desire. But surely Charlotte would not .... He buried these thoughts deep, ashamed of doubting her love.

# 16

# <u>FUTURE THINKING</u>

*I could kiss her all night, every night, and for as long as we live. Charlotte*
**• • •** *is amazing.*

"What are you doing, you bloody fool? Just standing there ...? Daydreaming?!"

The sting of the smack to his head made his ears ring.

Indeed, Albert had been daydreaming, recalling the previous night with Charlotte. But now he was back and in the present moment—deep within the caves.

"And wipe that smug smile off your damn face. You have nothing to smile about. Get back to probing."

"Fuk off." Albert moved away from Jebadia's flying fist and the older man's hardened hand met the wall.

Jebadia cursed loud and long. Blood coated his knuckles, dribbled down to his fingertips; the newly smoothened wall now splattered with body fluid. Though banged up, Jebadia's anger was always there on the surface and ready to burst. He attempted to throw another punch. Albert stood ready and knocked his father flat on his back.

"I am a man now! You can no longer beat me. A man!" He shouted and stormed off, but he didn't get far.

Jebadia clambered onto his feet and used his magnetism to pull for Albert's metal. Nearly eight pounds of precious ores sat deep within Albert's body; always there for him to channel. But when unrightfully extracted, it felt like an electrical jolt—throbbing throughout his body.

Jebadia had done that trick on purpose. He knew it would bring Albert back to the fight.

With fists and kicks flying, Albert exploded upon his father. "Why did you do it? Why did you keep her from me for so long? Why are you so cruel? Why do you hate me?"

"You do not know cruelty until …. She is a Witchtress, a vile Witchtress. Edwin allowed her to come in here, take your mind, pierce your heart. She will break you! Mark my words. A vile Witchtress." He spat on the ground. "You should not trust her. She is pure evil. The worst evil you will ever know."

"Fuk off, father. You are just jealous. Jealous! I know she reminds you of River and you are jealous of her. Of us. Of me!"

"Jealous! HA!"

Again, more angry throws and physical contact, more blood splatter too. The newly carved corridor was becoming tie-dyed and dirtied from the wet red matter. Soon they both ended up on the ground, heaving with breath. Their clothing soaked with each other's blood, and their own. Although their Metalistic Powers aided in healing the flesh wounds, it would not aid their stamina.

Jebadia's hand slapped the back of Albert's head again. "Damn dumb clot."

"I am the dumb clot? You are the dumb clot! You created me. If I am the dumb clot, then what does that make you?"

"You are the dumb clot!" Jebadia's rage pushed him through that winded moment. Soon he was on his feet again.

Albert was there and met him with comparable rage. "Edwin should have killed you when he had the chance."

"You would not be alive had he!"

Albert overpowered his father and threw him down—towering over him. "Stay down, you dumb clot!" He kicked his father a few times, then turned on his boot heel and huffed away.

"Yes. Go!" Jebadia spit up blood as he shouted—voice echoing, "You good for nothing. May she break your heart tenfold!"

• • • • • ● • ● • • • •

Albert raced back to the cavernous homestead. He was eager to find Charlotte. He wanted to talk to her, to vent. Neither she nor Edwin were there.

"They must be at the lake." He said to himself.

He charged off after drinking and eating several spoonfuls of stew. Just like his father, Albert could not deny the lustful taste of her food. The sauce lingered on his lips, much like her kisses, and satiated his eagerness to find her. He darted down the long corridors, hopeful not to see Jebadia. Yet as the stew's taste vanished, his desire to be angry about his father and their brutal exchange rose.

He was nearly frothing when he found Charlotte and Edwin near the lake, hanging up freshly washed clothes. They had heard his footsteps and were looking his way when Albert approached.

"I hate him."

"What happened this time?" Edwin asked.

Charlotte was at his side, pulling at his bloodied clothing. "What happened to you?" The long-sleeved tunic slipped up and over his head, and she tossed it into the dirty wash bucket. He pulled off the dirty pants, attempting to toss the wadded clothing like she had into the bucket. It landed only a few feet ahead of him.

"Damn clot." Albert grumbled at himself, picked up his pants, and threw them into the fire.

"What are you doing?" Charlotte shrieked and instantly extinguished the fire. Their only light source vanished. She then yanked the slightly charred piece of clothing out of the fire pit.

Edwin said, "He called you names again. You should know by now to ignore him."

"He called everyone here names. He is the damn dumb clot. We both know it." He looked at Edwin, then to Charlotte. "We all know it!"

She passed him freshly cleaned clothes, warmed by her powers. Once he was dressed, she placed a tender hand on his arm, sliding it up to his face. "Let's go for a walk."

"Yes, that is a good idea," insisted Edwin. "Go for a walk. Cool down."

Charlotte pulled Albert toward the backside of the enormous chamber. This was the way to the wide gap in the mountain. They walked a long way before the howling wind could be heard.

"You wanna tell me what happened?"

He did not, instead asking, "What was your day like?"

"Well, you found us washing clothing. That's always exciting. Oh, and the entrance is still sealed up tight. I was hoping to see the outside world today, but nope. I've been feeling a bit cooped up lately. Want to feel the wind, you know. And then Papa Edwin. He's been repeating the same stories, which, after a while …. But I made grilled goat stew that's full of—"

"Beets and potatoes. I wish I could cook as good as you do. Your food is always so …. Thank you for cooking, for always making such tasty meals." He snuck in a kiss and suddenly felt his worry about his father slipping away.

"Yum. I can taste it on your lips." She said after pulling away. "I'm sorry that your father's so hardheaded. Some people are … you know. You just gotta get past it, roll with it. Think of your future, what you want. Make plans for it. Think about what you can change in your life right now, so that you can have that future. You have the ability to change your life. It isn't his to live, it's yours. Regardless of what your father says, you can have what you want. He, however, he might be too stuck in his ways to change."

"Is that what you believe? Or is that something Hakra would have you believe?"

"I see it, nothing more. And I have lived it, I have changed. We all change. We're supposed to. I mean, who wants to stay the same forever?"

"How do you change?"

"Well, first you've gotta think about what you want. Envision it, that future. Is it to live with me in some loft in Kobiton? Or to stay here wishing for a better life?"

He smiled, replied, "No. I mean, how did you change? What were you like before?"

"I was young and naïve once, with lofty dreams. But my Powers meant I had to adjust my ambitions. Becoming a head cook was my way of proving myself, of showing I could be trusted despite my Abilities. I mean, they don't grant businesses to people like me, like us, unless you establish that altruism—that trust they need to see."

"They?"

She was hesitant to reply. "Telepaths."

He nodded, and they slunk between rocky formations and followed the narrow passageway down to the wide gap.

"I know what I want." He smiled and reached for her hand. "I want you."

"You already have me, silly. What do you really want?"

"For us to be together, and without them."

"We can have that. When we go to Kobiton, we can look for something that suits us. I know my friend Miss Lori will let us stay with her until we find something. She always has extra rooms."

"And I want to work for myself. Not for that dumb clot … that asshole."

"Why can't you do that now?"

"It is not safe. There should always be two of us. We are stronger together."

"Can't Papa Edwin help you?"

"He says he gave it up. But he probably would if …." He huffed and shrugged. "But I do not know."

"It's okay. We just gotta think positively. We can have what we want. We'll just have to work for it."

"I am fine with that." Albert led the last few steps before they encountered the usually giant gap in the mountain. The ice and snow were trying to seal them in from the east side of the mountain, but there was still a cool wind, a howling breeze they stood in the presence of until it was too deafening.

"Thank you, Charlotte."

"For what?"

"For everything. For being in my life. For helping me change."

# 17

## <u>Warmth In Stone</u>

"**I** want to show you something, Charlotte." Albert appeared anxious, but happy throughout supper time. He pulled her away from the fireside immediately after their meal, encouraging their post-supper walk to happen now and not after her evening chores were done.

*I hope she likes it. I really hope she likes it. I hope it does not scare her.* Kept repeating in Albert's mind. He pulled her on until his hand became uncomfortably sweaty. Then yanked it away to wipe it clean.

He took her deep into the belly of the mountain. "This is what we carved today." He reached for her once more, but she grabbed her skirt instead and picked it up to look down at the freshly smoothened circular corridor. Charlotte then knelt and felt the unbroken surface from bottom to top, though on tiptoes.

"Holy Hakra! This is impressive."

He had stepped down the corridor. "This isn't it. Come along." He came back for her and grabbed her hand once more.

*I wonder what she is going to say. What will she think of it? What will she think of me?*

She could feel his body quivering. "Are you gonna be okay, Albert? You seem nervous." This time, she wiped his sweat clean from her hand.

"Yes. It is just …. Come here." He yanked her on and then pressed her towards a large seam of silver stuck in the wall.

"You should have seen Jeb when he found my claim. He could hear it, but I found it first. It is mine. He tried to claim it as his own, but it is mine. This whole seam. Mine. I mean ours."

"Wow, this is …." She walked along the thirty-foot chunk of exposed silver, a giant plate of it. Her hand moved along the changes between ore and rock, how it all felt both soft and hard. "How do you … How are you gonna extract this?"

His dirty teeth glistened in the light of their lantern. "I am not supposed to take much of it—promised Jeb I would not speak of it—but ...." Albert extended a finger and summoned a small stream of the metal from the wall into his flesh. "This is a large seam, and there is more, both up and down, and that way too. But we must assess the spaces before we can extract it all. Would not want to collapse the cave on us."

The metal swirled across his flesh before he made a ring appear in the middle of his right palm. Silver swirled in his eyes, and his gaze remained vigilant on her.

"I want to give this to you. I have wanted to give you something ever since I met you. But I have had very little silver until now. This is all my silver. And I want to share it with you."

There was a pulse of energy she had never felt from him before—a confidence she had yearned to see in him. Albert pushed his hand toward her. The silver ring glistened, and the exterior transformed into a braided motif. On one side sat a falcon with wings raised, as if catching the breeze. He picked it up and then grabbed her right hand to slide the large ring on her middle finger.

As the ring slid onto her finger, Charlotte felt a surge of emotion. It wasn't just the beauty of the gift, but what it represented—Albert's love, his commitment to her. For a moment, all her doubts and fears faded away, replaced by a certainty that together they could face anything.

"I love you, Charlotte, today and everyday hereafter," Albert said, his voice thick with emotion.

She blinked, her heart swelled. This man, so different from anyone she had known, had become her whole world.

"Albert," she breathed, "I never expected to find love here, in this cave. But you ... You've shown me a different kind of freedom. A different kind of home."

The ring shrank under his power, fitting her finger perfectly—snug enough to stay, loose enough to twirl. Just like their love, she thought. Secure, yet free.

Charlotte traced the intricate design of the ring, marveling at its beauty. "Albert. This is .... I've never had anything like this."

He took her hand, his thumb gently caressing her knuckles. "I wanted to give you something as unique as you are," he whispered.

Tears pricked Charlotte's eyes. She leaned forward, resting her forehead against his. They stayed like that, breathing each other in, the world around them fading away.

Their eyes locked. She beamed, "Thank you, Albert. For this, for every-thing. I love you too. More than I ever thought possible."

They embraced for what seemed like an eternity, gasping for breath and giggling with glee.

"I love you Albert, today and everyday hereafter."

He then made another ring appear, encircling his finger, with matching knotted pattern and falcon embellishment. They enjoyed another long em-brace, followed by gasping. They were drunk on each other, on love and emotional vulnerability.

Right there, on the smooth floor, they fell into a heap, kissing and gasping. Before long, they revealed their flesh to one another and reveled in their passions.

· · · · ● · ● · · · ·

*I cannot believe we did what we did. She seemed to like it.*

*It was so amazing!*

*Father is an ass. He has never known actual love. Not like what Charlotte and I have. He is just jealous.*

*What of his words about River?*

*Fuk River. She was not my mother. Just a whore he compares everyone else to. I know River is nothing like Charlotte. Nothing like her. Charlotte is better in every way. Every way!*

*And we ... we are committed to each other. Our rings! She loves me. And I love her. How could this not be the best thing ever?*

It felt weird having a piece of metal snug on his finger, yet it was deeply symbolic of their love and dedication to each other. He was relieved to know she felt the same way about him. He knew this was what love felt like—this was unlike any other sensation felt to date.

*Father is going to lose his mind over this, over her sleeping in my bed.* He looked at Charlotte, asleep by his side and in his stinky bed. *But is that not what they want? Well, Edwin seems to want this. But father ... he will continue his hate—now and forever.*

*Bah. He is an asshole. He has never had the love I have for Charlotte.*

*He will be so angry.* He snickered, but then reality set in. *I hope he does not hurt her after this. If he does .... I must kill him before he can do that. But how?*

*His hate and anger toward her is beyond menacing. It is scary. Could Charlotte defend against Jebadia? I do not think she would meet Death quick. She would put up a fight. I wonder if Charlotte could kill father. Her powers are …. I wonder if she is powerful enough. All I know is I would love to see him dead.*

Charlotte adjusted the covers around her body and snuggled further into Albert's side. For a long moment, he was afraid to move, afraid to breathe. He did not want to wake Charlotte. Having her sleeping next to him in his bed, for real, was exquisite. He breathed in her scent and closed his eyes.

*Thank you, Papa Edwin, for bringing Charlotte into my life. We will find our way together. Maybe in Kobiton. Maybe somewhere else. No matter, we will build a home. Charlotte will have all the food she can cook, and there will be children abound. And we will do it all without Jebadia.*

*If Papa Edwin wants to come, I am alright with that. He is not that bad … not as bad as Jebadia.*

• • • ● • ● • ● • • •

The next night, Albert watched Charlotte as she prepared their evening meal. She pulled seeds from her pouch, and with a simple touch, fresh vegetables sprouted in her palms. The Power was both beautiful and terrifying. His father's words echoed in his mind: "Women with Power will strip everything from you."

But when Charlotte smiled at him, eyes bright with love, as she handed him a perfectly ripe tomato, those fears seemed foolish.

Still, in the quiet moments before sleep claimed him, he would catch himself wondering—was this all too good to be true? What if father was right? He pushed the thoughts away, but they lingered like shadows in the corners of his mind.

• • • ● • ● • ● • • •

Albert wasted no time inviting Charlotte to his bed every night now. They said it was for warmth, but they were sure Edwin knew the real truth. And though they enjoyed each other's embrace, Albert was afraid to ask Charlotte things he felt he should already know. So he went to Edwin, who was unprepared for the inquisition.

Albert leaned in with large, curious eyes. "So then, how long does it take?"

"Does what take?"

"For the baby to hatch?"

"First off, babies are not hatched, they are birthed, like how the goats and donkeys do it. And it takes at least three quarters of a year."

Albert counted on his fingers. "Nine moons?"

"Yes. Have you coupled with her, Albert?"

"Yes. And it was so much fun."

"Have you asked her if she is with child?"

"No?"

"Why not?"

"I am afraid."

"Well, I am sure that when she is with child, she will tell you first."

They both saw Charlotte watching them. Most likely, she had overheard their conversation—or a slightly muffled version of it. Albert approached her, hand extended. She gladly took it. And then they both moved away from the homestead cave and took their after supper walk.

· · • • • • • • • ·

It was a charming time for the two young people. Their fondness for each other had turned to love and everyone but Jebadia was alright with it. He wasn't afraid to express his feelings about the two, whether or not they were in earshot.

"She is going to lure him away," Jebadia grumbled. "Always talking about Kobiton this ... Kobiton that."

"She will not lure him away."

"Bah you! Yes, she will. She is a Witchtress. She has taken your mind and will have his next—if not already. I want her gone. Damn you! She needs to leave and without Albert."

"Why? She cooks and cleans and is lovely company compared to you. You want to know what I think? I think you only want her to go because she reminds you of River. Just as soft and caring. And I think you want her to want you and not Albert—"

Jebadia lunged at Edwin, fists and spit flying. The old man was spry enough to miss the fist, but his face was now wet. He hit his adult son, and both men ended up on the stone ground.

"I cannot help your jealousy, Jeb. The least you can do is not show it when the boy is around."

"Fuk off, old man."

Again, their fists flew, welts occurred, and before long, they were winded and red in the face. "You let them be, Jeb. Let them be. Albert deserves her. He needs her."

"He does not know what he needs. And you ... you fill his head full of dreams and fluff. It will be your fault if she breaks his heart." Jebadia's finger extended, tapping Edwin's chest. The aged men glared at each other.

The love-struck adolescents scurried away from the fight.

Meanwhile, Jebadia recoiled and went back to his area. Those beady silver eyes continued to watch the room, and everything that happened thereafter.

· · • • · • · • • · ·

The miners moved through their dark world with the sure-footedness of cats, every sense attuned to the mountain's rhythms. Charlotte struggled to adapt to their ways—the perpetual chill that no fire seemed to touch, the metallic twang that coated her tongue, the way sound behaved differently in these stone chambers.

Yet there were unexpected moments of beauty. The way certain crystals caught their lamplight, scattering rainbow patterns across the walls. The deep resonant hum of the mountain itself, a sound felt more than heard. And increasingly, the soft catch in Albert's breath whenever their hands brushed in the darkness, a sound that sent warmth coursing through her despite the cave's endless chill.

Albert's transformation around Charlotte was like watching a flower slowly turning toward the sun. Yet sometimes, when she used her powers, he would catch himself wondering about their true extent. His father's stories of manipulative women with hidden Abilities would surface unbidden. But Charlotte's warmth and genuine care always seemed to chase these dark thoughts away—at least for a while.

In private moments, his smile would break free—bright and unguarded, meant for her alone. But at the first echo of Jebadia's footsteps, that light would dim, the weight of generations of secrecy and fear descending once more.

"Tell me about the sky again," he would whisper during their walks, voice hungry for knowledge of the world beyond their cave. Yet whenever she suggested viewing it firsthand the terror would flash across his face.

"Father says ..." He would begin, then fall silent, caught between longing and duty.

The rare times Jebadia caught them in these moments of vulnerability, his rage would explode like a storm, words sharp as metal shards.

"You will destroy everything we have built!" He would roar. "Everything we have sacrificed to keep safe!"

Each time, Albert would shrink back into himself, that precious smile vanishing like mist. But later, when they thought they were alone, Charlotte would catch him practicing her gestures, mouthing the words to her stories. His rebellion, quiet but persistent as water wearing away stone.

Despite the harshness of their surroundings, moments like these reminded her why she had chosen this life. She reached for his hand, their fingers inter-twining naturally. In that brief touch, she felt a connection that transcended words—a promise of a future together, no matter the challenges they faced.

Another day came and went.

Another argument endured.

Once again, Jebadia had retreated to his bed, yet remained within earshot of the lovebirds.

She kept quiet and wiped away a few tears. "I was never treated this harshly at the Abbey. I miss Kobiton. That man's beyond abusive. I don't know why anyone would want to live with that. Yes, I've tried to curry his favor by making him superb meals and cleaning his stinky clothing 'n such. But I didn't have to..."

Charlotte recalled how Jebadia's hand would drift to his knife whenever she entered a room, how his eyes followed her with increasing malice. He would position himself to keep a maximum distance from her, as if her very presence was a contamination. The hatred that started as words was becoming something more dangerous.

"...I don't have to do anything for that disgusting pig if I don't want to, neither should you. You're a grown man, Albert. You deserve to be treated as such and not like an eight-year-old."

"It is okay. I am used to it. But father does like your food and all you do; he just does not know how to say it. And you are correct, he is an asshole. But this is all he knows. And he learned it all from Edwin. Sometime soon you will see that side of Edwin."

She ignored his warning, nodding with satisfaction when saying, "So, Jebadia does like me. I thought so. He just doesn't know how to show it. You know what that means?" He appeared aloof. "Then that means we've got nothing to worry about," and she leaned in to kiss him.

"Not here." He noticed Jebadia eyeballing them from his bed and pulled her away from view.

"He's seen us in your bed together. He's seen me naked when exiting your bed. What are you worried—"

"Yes. But. I just ...."

She leaned into his ear and nearly inaudibly said, "I can be quiet."

His eyes grew, and he grabbed her wrist. "But I do not want you to be quiet."

She glanced back and noticed Edwin's elderly gaze following them into the coal mines, away from the fire. They went to the underground pool and listened to the water raining down. Winter's grip was receding. There were far more dripping sounds now. And the daylight was growing longer. Soon, the entrance to the cavernous abode would open. Until then, the two enjoyed each other's company in the dark depths of the mountain.

She lit the firepit using her Erthin Abilities, and they sat arm in arm. She leaned her head on his shoulder and sighed. She could hear his inner turmoil. He wanted to follow her to Kobiton, to see what a town, a city, looked like. Yet Albert was afraid to leave his father. He was also afraid of leaving the only home he had ever known. But there was much excitement too, of the unknown and doing it all with her.

"I'm glad I ended up here." She told him and leaned in for a kiss.

One thing led to another and ....

# 18

## <u>FEAR & JOY</u>

Charlotte's predictable cycle served as a calendar in the timeless mountain caverns. Three cycles had passed since her arrival, each marking the slow progression of her new life. During those days, she stole away and only came back when the blood was gone.

She would retreat to the enormous cavern with the cold pool. It was there that she made a camp far from the water and spot of cavern the miners had claimed to clean their wares and hang their clothing to dry. She had a bed, layered with donkey hides, and a small fire pit circled by stones that she had built. That was where she stored her belongings, spending her days reading, knitting, or sleeping. It was a nice place to go to be alone. It was also the place where she and Albert would steal away for moments of closeness. Yet she missed being there, being quiet. Her cycle seemed much longer than usual—she knew what was going on inside her abdomen.

Charlotte's hand trembled as it rested on her still-flat stomach.

A child.

Her child.

Fear and joy percolated. She had never imagined herself as a mother—her powers had always seemed too dangerous, too unpredictable to risk passing on. But now, feeling the tiny life growing inside her, she was filled with fierce protectiveness.

"I'll do better," she vowed silently. "I'll give this child the love and acceptance I never had."

She knew the risks of being pregnant. During her lifetime at the orphanage, Charlotte learned much about babies and rough pregnancies. As it was, they were far removed from a healer—if the need arose. And Charlotte didn't believe that these men were prepared to aid in the birthing process.

*Well, maybe Edwin, but not the other two.*

Her mind swirled, emotions boiled. She tried to keep herself contained, her thoughts about any of it restrained. She hoped she was just fatigued, tired from the constant use of her power and from worrying about their dwindling food supplies. Yet Edwin's confessions of his life, the women left behind, and the children he had murdered echoed in her thoughts too. She knew the risk of being pregnant with a Metalist's child. Charlotte was fearful for her life and the baby, or babies, she now carried. She kept this knowledge hidden from the men until it was too hard to keep silent.

Her body was expanding. Her gut, breasts, all of it ached. And the fluttering she felt never subsided. When morning sickness accompanied the flutter, she knew it was time to confess. Who should she tell first? Albert? Edwin? Her emotions rolled like stormy ocean waves. One moment she found the gumption to confess what was going on, the next she bit her tongue and kept her lips still. She wasn't sure if she was afraid to be pregnant, or afraid to confess it. It took until she was violently ill before she told Albert.

He held back her strawberry-blonde hair as she leaned against a rock. Charlotte was shaking. Albert's concern for her wrought his boyish face. "You can tell me anything."

She took a deep breath before telling him, "I'm pregnant."

He stared at her, still holding her soft hair. She felt his grip tighten before her long locks fell across her back. His eyes grew wide, and Albert sat down at the base of the rock, right next to where she got sick.

"You alright?" She looked at him.

"Are you sure you are pregnant?"

"I don't think it's anything else. All the signs are present. Anxious feelings. Feeling tired and sickly. Even the smell of garlic and onions, one of my favorite scents, repulses me now. It's been ... it's been really hard to cook lately. All the smells make me want to get sick."

"Is there anything I can do?"

"No. I wish you could, but there's nothing you can do except support me, help me out when I ask. Let me rest when I need it."

He nodded, looked so innocent when asking, "What is it like? Being pregnant?"

"I don't know. This is my first time. Though I've known many a pregnant lady. Well, I've only met them when they're a day or two away from giving birth. By that point in any pregnancy, they're ready to give birth. But it's different for everyone, and every pregnancy is different too. I mean, we all experience some of the same stuff, but not every woman has the same issues. Some love being pregnant, do it multiple times."

"How many times can you give birth?"

"I've met women who have had children who are less than a year apart in age. It's like they got pregnant the moment their babies popped out. There was this one family with thirteen children."

"Thirteen? All at once?"

"Oh no... no, no. Oh ouch, no!" She laughed. "Most women give birth to one or two, but every so often someone gives birth to three children—that's usually a Clan-Duin woman. They're known to have litters, multiple babies at a time. But usually, women are pregnant with only one child."

"I was told there is always a twin." His eyes shifted to the underground lake. "Though mine did not make it."

His eyes grew distant for a moment. She squeezed his hand, overheard his thoughts. *Father says I should forget that I ever had a twin. She was a blight, a curse. I never knew her, but I have often wondered about her, a face I will never ....*

The dripping sounds from the lakeside cavern cut through their eerie silence.

"Look, Albert, for now we can assume there's at least one baby growing inside of me. If there're twins, that'll be found out later, like the second trimester. I'll wanna see a doctor, you know, a healer when we go to Kobiton. Have me, have us all checked out. Make sure everyone is doing well, that we'll all survive."

"Sure. Whatever you need. You know what you need."

She rubbed her belly as she sat next to him, their hands touching—once again privy to Albert's mental turmoil.

*—going to be a father. I do not ... how to be ... father. What ... should I ...? Father will be angry.*

*Will he?*

*Edwin ... he will be happy. This is what he wanted. But is this what I want? I am scared for her. For the babies.* His breaths were short, eyes large, heartbeat rampant.

"Can you feel it?"

"No. Not yet. I believe it's at the beginning of the third trimester that you start to feel the baby moving."

"What is it like?"

"I don't know." Their eyes locked, both scared—both innocent in the ways of raising another life. Charlotte suddenly realized her breaths mimicked Albert's.

"But we've got each other." She squeezed his hand. "We'll get through this to-gether."

*I love her. She is amazing. Does not seem scared at all,* Albert thought—but Charlotte was maybe more fearful of this moment, of her future than he. "Yes. Together," He reiterated, his gaze firm on her. *Now we have more of a reason to move away. I do not want Jeb around our children. I do not trust him.* "I guess we should probably start plotting the trip to Kobiton."

"Yeah, that sounds good! Let's do that. I don't want to give birth so far away from town and a competent healer—they're worth their weight in gold, I tell ya!"

"Okay, yes."

"So, you're okay with us moving?"

"Yes. It would be best for all of us. Then father cannot bother you. And we can live in peace and happiness."

Albert's hand lingered on Charlotte's swelling belly, a mix of wonder and fear in his eyes. "What if …." He stared, then shook his head, unable to voice his darkest thoughts.

"It's gonna be okay, Albert." Although the taste of her mouth wasn't the best, she leaned in to kiss him. "I love you, Albert, until the end of time."

"I love you too, Charlotte."

• • • ● • ● • • •

The last of winter's chill left the air and gave way to the first tentative signs of spring. Charlotte and Albert spent more time sitting in the giant gape on the mountain's east side. Side by side they watched the clouds drift by, listened to the snow melt, noticed the first few persistent pieces of grass pushing through the still frigid terrain. There was also more rain now, but also an occasional warm breeze.

One lazy afternoon, Charlotte pointed at the spotted blue sky. "What shape do you see in that cloud?"

Albert squinted, "A … a rabbit."

She laughed. "I see a wyvern."

He turned to her, curiosity in his eyes. "Tell me about wyverns."

And so she did, weaving tales of mythical beasts and brave heroes written about in the Tomes book. As she spoke, Albert's hand found hers, their fingers intertwining.

"Your world is full of wonders," he murmured.

Charlotte rolled onto her side, facing him. "Our world, Albert. It's ours to explore together."

The kiss that followed was soft, tender, full of promise.

• • • • • • • • • • •

By mid-spring, the lower mountain slopes were lush with greenery, the valleys below were bright with flowering trees and grassy meadows—the memory of winter's snow long gone. The morning sickness had lessened, but the heartburn hadn't. Charlotte's belly felt firm now. She estimated her pregnancy to be three moons along, assuring Albert everything she felt was normal.

The changes in Charlotte fascinated and frightened the young man. Her Power seemed to grow with her belly, and sometimes he caught himself watching her too closely, searching for signs of manipulation that his father insisted must certainly be there. The conflict between his love and his ingrained fears wore on him. Yet there was light at the end of this tunnel—hope that they might find something better, together, and away from the mountaintops. But first they had to prepare for the trip to Kobiton.

Once the trail to Chinochi melted enough for his travels Edwin made sure to buy all the necessities they would need for their upcoming journey. Every time he visited that quaint township, he brought more materials back, knowing that they would use it all on their trek to Kobiton.

Unfortunately, on his last return from the township, Edwin slipped and injured his left leg from ankle to hip. He was sad, disappointed that he would not be able to make the trip to Kobiton with the youngsters.

Edwin assured them that the trail to Kobiton, the shortcut he had sketched a map of, would be easier to travel than going up and over the mountain pass. Although the old Metalist had said he would take her, he seemed glad to hand that responsibility to Albert. The young man had grown up much under Charlotte's guidance, and this made Edwin glow. He believed that under her direction Albert would do fine in the city—so long that he didn't keep metal under his skin.

# 19

## CITY LIGHTS

Anticipation and excitement for their joint adventure percolated.

Today was the day they would leave.

There was no trace of snow below the passes, and the torrential downpours that happened during mid springtime were long gone. Their journey to the bustling city should be an easy trek.

As Charlotte packed her meager belongings, anxiety gnawed at her. Kobiton had once been home, but would it still feel that way? She had changed so much—would her old friends even recognize her? And what if Albert hated it? What if this journey destroyed the fragile happiness they had built?

*We have to try;* she reminded herself, *for our baby, for our future.*

Charlotte watched Albert pack, his excitement palpable. Her heart swelled with affection, but a tendril of doubt curled in her stomach.

She loved him—of that she was certain. But as they prepared to enter her world, she couldn't help but worry. Would he still look at her the same way when he saw all she had left behind?

"Are you ready?" Albert asked, breathing into her thoughts.

Charlotte forced a smile, pushing down her fears. "As ready as I'll ever be," she replied, taking his hand.

She then noticed Jebadia watching their exchange, his face a mask of indifference. But as Albert shouldered his bag, she caught a flicker of something in Jebadia's eyes—was it pride? Fear? For a moment, she saw not the harsh, abusive man she had come to know, but a father watching his son taking his first steps into an unknown world.

It was obvious Edwin didn't want to see them go, but he said nothing beyond, "I hope to see you two soon."

Meanwhile, Jebadia kept muttering. "This should not happen. You need to stay here, Albert. You are weak without us. We are stronger together. You must stay here, with your family." He glared at her and pointed at the ground between his boots. Even still, Jebadia didn't seem ready to stop their departure either.

"Charlotte is family too, father." Albert stood, chest puffed out, at her side. "She is just as strong as us. I know she will keep me safe."

Jebadia looked ready to rebuke—disgusted by that assertion. But after studying Charlotte, holding tight to Albert, he wavered and left them for the depths of the dank and dreary mines.

Charlotte knew they would return. Secretly, she had no desire to. She wanted to steal Albert away from his family, but didn't want to disappoint Edwin.

As they prepared the leave, Charlotte's heart felt torn. Part of her longed for the freedom of a life away from the oppressive cave, just her and Albert. But another part clung to the sense of family she had found, especially with Edwin. She wondered if it was possible to have both—the excitement of a new life with Albert and the comfort of the family they would leave behind. The conflict gnawed at her, a constant reminder of the complexities of her new life.

Neither had much to pack, but they took three donkeys to carry what little supplies they had. The animals were familiar with the steep mountain terrain. Charlotte appreciated Albert's confidence when crossing chasms. His steadiness and strength reassured her. This time spent together on their own adventure, slowly descending the often-jagged hillsides, was what they needed to stoke their passions. Albert's confidence shined, and she knew they were meant to be together.

• • • • • • • • • •

Albert was tender with Charlotte; made sure there was always a roof over their heads, and she provided a comfortable bed. Their days fell into a gentle rhythm, each small kindness building trust between them. Albert watched Charlotte's hands as she prepared their meals, fascinated by how she wielded fire and herbs with the same careful precision he used with metal. In return, he shared his knowledge of the wilderness's hidden bounty—the sweetest springs, the caves where mushrooms grew in abundance.

At night, when the chilly air attempted to breach their cozy lair, their bodies found each other naturally, like ore seeking lodestone. The simple comfort of shared warmth became something precious, a defiance of the isolation that had defined Albert's life.

"Tell me about the stars," he whispered one dark evening after supper.

Charlotte painted pictures with words of constellations he had never known the names of. Her voice spinning stories of worlds beyond the stone walls he had grown up behind.

Each touch was a negotiation between desire and fear. Albert's hands trembled as they traced the curve of Charlotte's cheek, his heart thundering against his ribs. He had never learned gentleness—had never seen it demonstrated in his harsh world of stone and metal. Yet with her, his calloused fingers found a new purpose, creating territories of tenderness he hadn't known existed.

Her warmth reached deeper than skin, than bone, touching something in him that had been frozen for so long he had forgotten it could thaw. When she smiled against his lips, he felt the walls he had built around his heart crack like spring ice.

"I wish my father had been a better person, a better example of how to be a good father," he confessed one night, voice rough with vulnerability.

"I think you're doing a great job." She whispered back. "You're a good person, Albert. And you'll be an excellent father. Remember, you're nothing like your father. You're better than him."

"Thanks. I know you will be a good mother."

Her sigh was ragged, filled with fear. "I hope so."

The simple truth—that she, too, was finding her way—somehow made everything easier. They were not just sharing warmth anymore; they were creating something new, something entirely their own.

· · • · ● · ● · • · ·

The luscious landscape they traversed through, much like their blossoming relationship, seemed untamed. Still, they covered a lot of ground. Every night and morning, she made warm meals and hot tea. And every day he kissed her and showed such adoration that made her constantly warm and without the use of her Erthin Powers.

In these quiet moments, with Albert's arms around her and his heartbeat steady against her ear, Charlotte felt a sense of peace she had never known before. The world outside their embrace ceased to exist, and she allowed herself to dream of a future filled with his warmth, his love.

During this time, their love for each other was amplified. They felt equally balanced, always complimenting, seldom condescending. This throbbing energy kept them going when the light rain turned into a downpour, and when the animal traps came up empty.

At least they had each other.

"I hope you like Kobiton. I hope it's not too busy for you. There're lots of things to see and do, lots of things always happening."

"Like what?"

She paused, trying to recall, "Well, there're readings at this one cafe on leaf day. They always have free tea and cookies. Then, during the busy days, the markets have different auctions going on. We should stop past and see about acquiring some chickens and goats."

"What is an auction?"

"Where people place bids on animals slated for slaughter. The highest bid wins. Some people, farmers mostly, take the animals home, some keep them for later, some slaughter before taking them home. Locals usually just go to their local butcher and buy whatever meat they want there. When I was a cook for the Abbey and seminary, I'd go to the auctions often, bring back boxes of chickens and dozens of goats. Occasionally I'd get a bull, but I wouldn't kill them. I'd let the butcher do that job, then take the meat back to the kitchens and have my way with it."

She sensed his nervousness. "We can take it easy when we get there. It's still a couple days away per the map Edwin made us. I'm looking forward to you meeting Head Mistress Aluyelian. She oversees the Abbey, which houses nearly a hundred orphans, and the Seminary school that teaches to over a thousand children every day, except leaf day. It's always so busy there, but I'm sure she'll want to see us, meet you."

"What type of person is she?"

"She's logical, methodical. Seems to know about everything all the time, eyes in the back of her head type of person," Charlotte chuckled.

"No, I mean—"

"Oh. She's a Telepath. She can be stern. Prefers order to chaos ... but then she's trying to manage an orphanage and a school—there's always chaos.

"And depending on how that meeting goes, we can either ask to stay at the Abbey, they always have extra beds, but they're laid out in this giant hall, not much privacy, or we can stay with my friend, Miss Lori. She usually has an extra room or two. I hope. But if that fails, there are inns we can stay at. And we'll miss out on my meals, but there's so many good places to eat around town. My favorite serves an icy-creamy berry thing, mix, like yogurt, but better."

Albert wrung his hands. "What's yogurt?"

"It's a sourish cream that's made from cow's milk. It's usually served during the summer, not a treat you can get any other time of the year. Another reason to like Kobiton. Like I said, there's always something going on." She then pondered, "I wonder if the summer fair will be happening? They usually time it around the midsummer moon, the one that turns orange and is always large. I know you've seen it from home."

He seemed to shrink under her presumptuousness.

"You alright Albert?"

"I do not know. It seems overwhelming, that is all."

"Don't worry. It's not. I mean, if the celebration's happening, we don't have to be there the whole time."

Now he felt rigid. *I do not know if I want to do this anymore. Maybe father was correct. I am afraid Kobiton will wreck me. All the weird people, people with Powers, and the metal they carry.*

She pulled him to a stop. "It's alright Albert. We can go slow."

Seeing his fear, Charlotte tried to help him understand what they would face.

"In Kobiton, people with Power follow strict lines," Charlotte explained to Albert. "Telepaths govern because they claim direct communion with Hakra. Clan-Duins serve as their eyes and ears. Erthins like me keep the city running. Those without special Abilities do what they must, help where they can. But Metalists..." She hesitated. "The Telepaths fear what they can't control. That's why your people hide."

"And yet you married one," Albert whispered.

"Love doesn't follow their rules," she replied, but they both knew it wasn't that simple.

*I hope she is correct,* Albert thought, trying to swallow his fear.

"I won't let anything happen to you." Her soft lips were tender against his.

He closed his eyes, swallowed and thought, *I am doing this for Charlotte. She will keep me safe. I have nothing to worry about.*

# 20

## <u>HAZY TELEPATHY</u>

The slopes of the Kruluver Mountain Range had softened, the scent of pine and flowering fruit trees strong in the warm breeze. They now followed a well-worn path, possibly an animal trail; most definitely a trail worn by people. There were a few intersecting paths along their journey that day. They often held hands but usually walked along narrow trails single file and with Charlotte in the lead. They would always walk at her pace; the donkeys appreciated it.

A storm of emotions raged within Albert. Excitement at the prospect of seeing the world beyond their mountain battled against his fear of the unknown. He thought of his father's warnings, of Edwin's cautionary tales. But then he looked at Charlotte, her light green eyes bright with anticipation, and felt a surge of courage.

*I can do this,* he thought. *For her, for our children. I can be brave.* Yet a small voice in the back of his mind whispered doubts, echoes of his father's harsh lessons.

· · • · • · • · ·

Along their way, Charlotte plucked flowers and wove them into her hair. Her face was rounder now. Her belly was growing daily.

"I'm so glad Edwin brought me to you." She said joyously after they had found the graveled roadway to Kobiton. "This has been the best time of my life. I never knew I could be so ... so smitten," she rubbed his bearded face. "You're the best," and placed a kiss on his lips.

But even in these moments of joy, she couldn't forget witnessing Jebadia move with the certainty of a man who had been waiting for something. There was no hesitation in his stride when he pulled Albert aside for private conversations, no doubt in his eyes when he watched Charlotte's influence over his son grow—only cold purpose.

There was a spring in her step. They were finally on the last leg of their eight-day journey away from their cavernous homestead. They were glad it hadn't taken longer, but knew the walk back would be a trek. That's not to say their travels weren't without delay. There were several moments where they huddled together for warmth as hail or rain burst sideways, flooding the already fragile landscape. During these moments, they reminded each other that this was an adventure of a lifetime. And it was. It was a marvelous time that would forever solidify their eternal bond.

"You are amazing too. I love you, Charlotte. I cannot imagine my life without you in it." He had said those three magical words only a dozen times, but every time Albert said 'I love you' with fervent passion—every time he told her was like the first time. She reveled in his adoration, enjoyed every kiss, every physical embrace. He placed a hand on her belly bulge. "And I love our children. I want to spend eternity with you." Again, he kissed her, and they continued onward.

Soon the two-story tall stone wall that encircled the city of Kobiton came into view. This piece of civilization had been built on a west-facing slope and stretched toward an open plateau. The main roadway went east to west, and hundreds of buildings fit neatly along its path. Every avenue and dead-end street were precisely mapped out. Wood, brick, large granite stones and thick mortar had been used throughout the city's structures. Bright red slated roofs offset the giant and often dark green trees growing in courtyards and along the avenues. Many of the buildings were painted light, but often white, colors and had dark brown and black accents around the openings, along the edges. A variety of complimentary colors and patterns hung in open windows and fluttered in the breeze. It was a warm and beautiful summer day for the city of Kobiton.

As they approached the protective lookout and stone wall, Charlotte noticed Albert's hands shaking slightly.

"Are you nervous?" she asked gently.

He nodded, unable to meet her eyes. "What if … what if I am not good enough for your world?"

Charlotte cupped his face, turning it towards her. "Albert, listen to me. You are more than good enough. Your kindness, your strength—that's what matters. Not where you come from or what you know."

"But I know so little," He whispered.

"Then we'll learn together," she said firmly. "Every day with you is an adventure, Albert. Kobiton will just be another one."

His smile, slow but genuine, warmed her heart. "Together," he repeated, pulling her close.

Along the southern side of the city were pastures of livestock slated for auction. Most would end up at the slaughterhouse. Small plots of crops were being attended by many of the locals. As they walked along, Charlotte held the biggest smile. But Albert's enthusiasm and smile waned. He slowed, as did his donkeys. She had taken several steps ahead of him before noticing his absence from her side.

"Are you alright Albert?"

He squinted, shaking his head, before blinking several times. She came to him in a flash. Her warm hand touched his clammy face. "What's going on?" She wouldn't telepathically pry unless he didn't confess. But Albert was obviously in pain.

"I am fine."

"No, you're not. I can tell you're in pain. Is there something I can do?"

"It is ...." His voice faltered.

She felt his back tighten. "It's alright, Albert. Remember what Papa Edwin said. Contain no metal. Take deep breaths. We can go slow. I'm sorry for walking ahead of you. I should've known better." She took up his sweaty hand, squeezed it, and finally his eyes lifted. They were silver filled. "Are you gonna be alright?"

"Yes." He gritted and blinked away the swirling silver, showing off his dark gray, almost black, eyes. "Everything is intense right now. The sounds mostly. Kobiton looks huge. I am not sure I should enter."

"Don't worry Albert. You'll be alright. I'm right here. I'll never leave you."

She leaned in and kissed his cheek. A trickle of sweat met her lips. She sensed his aversion to being around all the metal. They weren't even in town, but there were many things to be seen over the two-story tall wall.

When she touched him, Charlotte could hear the resonating sounds. It sounded chaotic. And loud. And the closer they came to the towering entrance, those notes turned sour.

"You've let go all your metal, right?"

"Yes. Of course."

Charlotte refused to stop. They were so close. She had wanted this day to come. She yearned to be inside Kobiton but knew all of it would be hard on Albert.

Although she hadn't confessed to any of the miners about her telepathic Abilities, this moment called for her to use it. So, she did what she thought was best and said with influential words, "Let me help you. I will turn it off. The sounds." She peered into his dark, fearful eyes.

Albert gave a small nod and shut his eyelids tight.

. . . . . ● . ● . . .

*What is she going to do?*

*I'm calming the melodies, that is all.*

He shivered, feeling her here ... in his mind. *What is going on?*

*Telepathy. I'm telepathic.*

*Telepathic? Have you done this before, used this Power on me before now?*

*No.*

Her touch was soft and calmed the metal's song like nothing else. Albert was both grateful and uneasy. The constant chorus that had been his companion since childhood faded to a whisper under her influence.

But doubt crept in, insidious as rust. *How come you have never told me of this Power?*

She replied. *It's never mattered 'til now. I don't like to use it. And since I started living at your home, I've forgotten I have it. Which is kinda nice. Especially since I can't hear your thoughts.*

*You can hear thoughts?*

*Not your family's. I believe it's your Metalistic Power that makes it so. It makes you immune to telepathy, unless I'm touching you.*

He wanted to jerk away from her contact, but she persisted with her spell.

*Father says women with Power cannot be trusted. Says they will strip away everything that makes you who you are.*

*Do you really believe that?*

He watched Charlotte through his thick eyelashes, and thought, *No.* Yet his emotional attachment to his father's suggestion about women being evil was felt between them.

She flinched. *I've never said or done anything contrary to who I am. Albert, please trust that I'm not out to hurt you with my Power. I don't want to take anything from you. I just want to help you.*

The metal in his blood hummed, responding to his turmoil. It would be so easy to reject her help, to retreat into the familiar pain of isolation. Yet something in him rebelled against that path. *She has soothed the melodies. Wants to help me. I love her.*

He relaxed, finally, and the spell engulfed him like a swift moving squall.

## 21

## <u>KOBITON</u>

Charlotte did what needed to be done. Her warm hands pressed against his temples. She closed her eyes and telepathically laced his mind with a spell that would soothe his aches and bring comfort.

When his eyes opened, Albert looked intoxicated. And he was. She had numbed him to his desire to harness the metals and make their chorus align. Charlotte's spell allowed him to forget all about the melodies that flew at him from every direction once they entered the bustling cityscape of Kobiton.

Kobiton wasn't just a city; it was a tapestry of cultures and powers. Erthin-crafted fountains danced with ever-changing colors, while Clan-Duin shapeshifters performed street shows that defied imagination. The air hummed with the constant chatter of Telepaths, their silent conversations as vital to the city's function as the spoken word. Charlotte had missed this vibrant chaos, so different from the stark silence of the caves.

Yet, Charlotte winced as another telepathic voice pierced her mind. She had learned at a young age to create mental barriers, like silk curtains that muffled the constant chatter of thoughts around her. The same technique she now used on Albert—not to control, but to shield him from the overwhelming chorus of metal that assaulted his senses.

"I wish I could do more," she whispered to herself, remembering her failed attempts to manipulate the Warden's mind. Yet they had been trained to combat most telepathic spells. Charlotte knew her telepathy was weak compared to her other Abilities; she could influence but never truly command. Her real power lay in more subtle arts—in the way she could coax life from a seed or turn sustenance to poison with a thought.

As they walked on, she could tell Albert felt uneasy.

She had calmed the melodies—reached into his mind. It was both wondrous and terrifying for him. What else could she do that he didn't know about? What other secrets lay behind those loving eyes? He pushed the thought away, but it settled somewhere deep, a tiny seed of doubt taking root. "Are there other Powers you have that I don't know about?" he asked suddenly.

Charlotte hesitated just a fraction too long. "Nothing important," she said with a smile that didn't quite reach her eyes. "Nothing that changes anything between us."

He nodded, wanting desperately to believe her. But something had shifted, subtle as a shadow at dusk.

She kept him close. Down the main roadway through Kobiton they walked, hand in hand. Seeing all the people, bright colors, intoxicating smells, and familiar faces revitalized her soul. She wanted to wander around and reconnect with everyone she knew. But first, Charlotte needed to return home. She wanted to see the people she missed the most. From where they stood, she could see the bright yellow buildings of the seminary school and Abbey. They were all interconnected with dark covered hallways and stone courtyards. The dark openings of that long ago lifecycle beckoned her, and she pulled Albert along. A slender bell tower up on the hillside was their beacon. It was a short hike up the hill to those familiar grounds.

They passed through a wide opening in a stout brick wall. The barnyard fluttered with livestock, chickens mostly. Several goats bleated and came to meet the donkeys, who loyally followed behind Albert. Beyond the stable yard and between all the buildings was a large green meadow where trees grew in clusters. At that moment, it was full of children yelling and giggling while playing kickball.

Suddenly, the tower's bell rang loudly. It startled both of them.

The children's screams stopped, and they all started running toward the school building. Their padded pig-skinned balls lay idle on the trampled grass. Classes would now resume, time for more play would happen later.

Charlotte retained a firm grasp on his hand. But Albert's attention was now on the bell, swinging and ringing. "Stay strong." She squeezed his hand. "For me, please."

Finally, his attention fell upon Charlotte. He smiled. And then he was back in a dazed state.

"Miss Charlotte?!" An elderly man called to her from the shadows of the stable. "Miss Charlotte? Is that you?" He hobbled as he eagerly approached.

"Master Ikyrus!" She left Albert and the donkeys to embrace the stable manager.

"I thought you were off serving Hakra?" He touched her belly and whispered. "They decide to breed you instead?"

"No. No." Although it wasn't very convincing, Charlotte had forgotten the lie she had concocted. "I ... ah ... it didn't work out." No one needed to know what happened to the Warden—to H'Eirwyn.

Master Ikyrus was a dark-skinned, short, and skinny Clan-Duin man who always wore a bright yellow robe. He was always friendly to the children, but especially to the many women who worked and lived in the compound. They were all bound to serve Hakra in some capacity.

"Didn't work out? You can't be serious. Someone with your cooking abilities ...! Hakra should be ashamed." He must have noticed how sharp his opinion was and softened immediately. "Oh, darlin', I'm sorry to hear that. I figured you'd be cookin' Hakra some superb meals. Why else would he have asked for you?"

She returned to Albert's side, leaned into him. "Master Ikyrus, this is my mate, Albert Miner."

"Good day Albert Miner. Good to meet you. I'm glad to see that Miss Charlotte, pardon me, M'Lady Charlotte Albert Miner, found someone who will take good care of her." Ikyrus reached up to embrace Albert. It was an awkward moment for both men. Ikyrus shook it off by touching Charlotte's slightly swollen belly. "Oh, darlin'." He gave her another hug. "Well, I'm glad you're back, Miss Charlotte. I've missed your food, darlin'. We've all missed it."

"I've missed everyone too. Can you take care of our donkeys for the next few nights? I'm sure you'll give them the best of care."

"Of course, darlin'. It'd be my honor to do so. Are you gonna see Head Mistress Aluyelian?"

Every muscle in her body tightened under his dark Clan-Duin gaze. She refrained from explaining her reason for returning to Kobiton. Everyone had been so thrilled, possibly jealous of her invitation to meet Hakra and serve Urthis's living god. Even Mistress Aluyelian expressed earnest enthusiasm; though truly, any emotion that woman exuded was usually short-lived. Still, Charlotte worried about the questions that would surely be asked, and the answers she would have to give. All at once Charlotte felt afraid, a fraud in that moment.

"I will. Though, right now, I need new clothing. And it's the busy time of day for her. I don't want to bother her right now. I'll probably see her later this evening. Or maybe tomorrow morning after breakfast's been served. Maybe I'll go to the market with her, or something. For now, Albert and I just want to get a room and a meal and some rest. It's been a long trek for us."

"You've always a place here, darlin'. There's always an extra bed and extra food for you."

She glanced up at the bell tower, now silent, but it would resonate a few more times and into the night, and then first thing tomorrow. Her gaze dropped to Albert. He looked ready for a nap. The spell she had woven was thick and kept his mind quiet. She missed hearing his thoughts, missed seeing his adoration. But she worried about the bell's effect on him.

"I think we'll be staying at Miss Lori's place. It's been such a long time since I've seen her. And her manor is out of the way, nice and quiet. Just how we like it.

"But oh, how I've missed Kobiton. I brought Albert here so he could see what a city looked like. He's from Chinochi, a small town in comparison. For now, I just want to walk around and reacquaint myself, you know, see my friends. Make some purchases and such, you know. We'll be back, though. It'll be later, of course, maybe even tomorrow. Who knows? But don't worry, you'll be seeing us soon."

They took their few possessions and passed the donkeys' lead-lines to Master Ikyrus. Charlotte then pulled Albert along. He stumbled and tried to keep pace. They were both dirty from their long walk to town. His mining trousers were muddy and worn, with holes and rips on his knees and rump. She wanted to purchase new clothing for them both.

Off towards the market, they marched with a brief stop at a bakery. They bought strawberry muffins and found a bench outside, under an awning, to eat them. As they sat there, she stared at him. He didn't notice. Charlotte didn't like that Albert wasn't himself. She didn't like how he looked or acted when under her telepathy. Yet if she were to allow him more control, the ringing from the copious amounts of metal would rattle his brain. She lessened the impact of her hazy spell. This gave Albert the mental space to think—to be himself once more.

He watched people pass by, studying the storefronts across the quiet roadway.

"Is this place always like this?" He asked.

"Like what?"

A squeaky wagon rolled past. Two medium-sized donkeys pulled the heavy merchandise along. The driver noticed them gawking at him.

Albert muttered. "It is loud."

She nodded. "It'll be quieter near Miss Lori's manor. I promise. She lives on the downslope end of town. There's an old stand of oak trees that separates her home and a bunch of others from town. Don't worry. You'll like it there." She rubbed his forearm.

She had nearly inhaled her muffin, while Albert had only consumed half of his. They sat there until he was done, enjoying the momentarily quiet cityscape.

Soon Charlotte pulled Albert along. They went into a woman's clothing store. He stood aside the thick door quietly while she found three dresses. Two were embroidered with flowers and vines, the third was made of pink and purple strips of material sewn into a summer-style gown. They were all made to expand with her growing belly. Albert paid for those purchases, and they moved on. A few doors down was a man's clothing shop, and she pushed him into it.

They found attire that matched one of Charlotte's new dresses and purchased a few other high-end items. By the time they were done shopping, Albert didn't look like a miner. She had him change and packaged up his dirty clothing. After that store, they paused at a cobbler's shop and found Charlotte a new pair of boots and stockings. She knew her blistered feet would thank her later.

· · • · • · • · • · · ·

They were exhausted by the time they passed through the grove of oak trees. Their shade was a blessing as the late day sun had been bright in their eyes. "I think you'll like Miss Lori. They call women Miss until they take a man. Lori's older than me. And she's never been interested in men. I know she'll never take a man as a partner."

"Why is that?"

Charlotte blushed and took a moment before she explained. "Miss Lori's always been very independent. I mean. Well, we used to work in the Abbey's kitchen together. She taught me everything she knew. And once I grew old enough to take that position .... She had wanted to move on since forever ago. So, she fixed up a dilapidated cottage. Now she rents out rooms, keeps the place clean.

"She's handy with everything: ironwork, carpentry, pottery, gardening, you name it! She's so smart too. I just know you'll like her."

"What type of person is she?"

"Lori's smart, like book smart and street smart. She knows a lot about everything, at least enough to keep herself out of trouble."

"No. What I meant was, is she like you?"

"Like me meaning?"

"Her Powers. What are they?"

Charlotte paused. "She's Erthin and Clan-Duin. But don't worry. We're not allowed to use our Powers outside of work. At least that's what we're told, but sometimes we do it anyway, because it makes life easier ... sometimes. And since Lori's Erthin, she can use any excuse as to why she's using her Powers, especially because she has rooms for rent. Usually, she's not questioned. Most people aren't."

"I can't wait to see her—miss talking to her. I wanna see how she's doing. You've nothing to worry about." Albert didn't soften. "Don't worry. I love you, remember that." She grabbed his hand and pulled Albert up to the front door of Miss Lori's manor.

Suddenly, the door opened, and Miss Lori appeared. She had long, vibrant auburn-red hair, a lightly freckled brown face, and amber eyes. She wore her usual garb, a sleeveless purple tunic with tan leather pants and tall boots. An empty bag hung diagonally across her chest. She tossed it off and threw a gleeful embrace around Charlotte, and briefly they kissed.

"You're back! You're back. Oh, Hakra, I'm so glad you're back. Oh, and you've gotten fat ... full ... pregnant?! And I see you've brought a friend." Lori saw Albert and wrinkled her nose. He avoided looking at the two women.

"I missed you too." Charlotte could tell Lori was hypnotized by this moment, taking all of her in. They both blushed. "And yes, this is Albert. Albert Miner."

When he glanced at Lori, his breath quickened. Albert's voice was barely above a whisper. "Hi." Once more, his eyes fell to the entryway's floor.

"You're quiet." Lori commented before regarding Charlotte, "I was just heading up to the bakery. You wanna come?"

"Actually, we're kinda tired of walking."

"Oh, sure. Yeah, of course." Lori remained transfixed by Charlotte. "You must have a story to tell. I never thought ...." Lori flushed and blew out a large burst of air. "But of course, yeah, there's a room on the second floor, third door. No wait. It's on the third floor, second door." She blinked a few times, then dramatically waved her hand. "Just go in, find a room. If the door's shut, or the room looks used, just keep on going. I've got a chicken almost done. Potatoes are in the oven alongside. You know what I'm making. Nothing like what you make, of course.

But comparable." Lori reached in and hugged Charlotte again. "Mm, you're so round. I'm so happy you're back in town. You'll have to tell me all about it when I return. I'll be back soon. Just to the bakery."

"Just to the bakery." Charlotte laughed. There was a story behind that saying, and only they knew about it.

The story was about how they kept running into each other at the same bakery every day and for numerous moons. This was a few years after Lori had left the Abbey and became a landlord, right after Charlotte had graduated and remained at the Abbey as a resident cook.

Sometimes after meeting up at the bakery, they would go on to the markets, or stop at another store, giggling and chatting—spending much time together. They would have long and meaningful conversations about Hakra and life. Lori believed every woman should be independent before taking on a mate, if they chose, but especially with decisions and life paths. Charlotte could not help but idolize Lori's abilities and aptitude for everything.

"See you soon Lori." Charlotte's heart skipped a few beats, happy to be here and with her best friend. She watched her friend's vibrant red hair fly like a cape as she raced to the markets. She didn't realize how much she had missed this person.

Once Miss Lori was gone from sight, they entered the cool residence. Charlotte knew Lori used her Erthin Powers to maintain the ambient heat of her homestead. Roasting chicken filled their nostrils and the entire home. Charlotte insisted Albert follow, but he was hypnotized by the colorful décor in this space. Not one thing was like another, but everything was bright and whimsical, like a colorful clothing display at the market.

The open bedroom was indeed on the third floor. They met a few of the other residents; an old man who had no front teeth and sat in his room reading a book. Two middle-aged women played a game of cards on the landing of the third floor, right in front of an open window. The breeze felt wonderful, as the upper floor was stuffy.

"Good day." They said when seeing Charlotte and Albert take the last step.

"Yes, it is a good day," Charlotte said brightly.

"You two movin' in?"

She was out of breath and glanced back at Albert when she replied, "We're just staying the night."

"Staying the night." The ladies echoed and glanced at one another.

"You two travelers?"

Charlotte was hot and ready to get off her swollen feet. All at once, she felt uncomfortable. "Yes," She snapped. "I'm sorry. So sorry. I'm just tired. We've been walking a long time."

"You'll be at the supper table, correct?"

"Yes, mam."

"You have any stories to share?"

"Zira, be kind to the young lady. She and her man need time to recover," her friend scolded. "We'll see you two at supper." She waved, and then the one named Zira mimicked.

"See you two then!"

Charlotte hustled over to the second door, opened ajar. The room was warm, filled with stale air. The window and its curtain were closed. Immediately, she opened it. A breeze blasted through and found the doorway to exit. Soon the sounds and smell of Kobiton overtook the room. Charlotte stood there, taking it all in.

From behind her, Albert groaned. He tossed their belongings aside the bed and flopped on top of the covers. "I am tired."

"I am too."

He reached for her. "Come. Rest with me."

"I will." She surveyed the nearby treetops, across the sea of red rooftops and occasional green crowns protruding. She had missed this view; missed Kobiton. A deep breath turned into a yawn and Charlotte lay alongside Albert, then snuggled into his side. Immediately privy to all his thoughts.

*—stand why everyone touches everyone around here. This place is … is not for me. And why did she kiss Lori? Charlotte should only kiss me. No one else! She is mine, not Lori's. And how Lori looked at me, she does not like me. That is okay. I dislike her too.*

Albert yawned. *I should ask Charlotte why everyone touches everyone. Is it a custom or something? Does everyone everywhere do that? Hug and show affection?*

*I am glad we are not that way at home. Disgusting it is … like they all want to fuk each other or something.* He yawned again. *At least the bed is … is ….* And suddenly his mind went quiet.

Albert fell asleep within moments. Charlotte's mind swirled. She needed to nap. Her eyes wanted to rest, but her mind wouldn't.

# 22

## <u>CHICKEN & CHATTER</u>

Charlotte had forgotten about the mealtime bell that would ring.

On every floor of Miss Lori's tall homestead, there was a bell tied to a master string located in the ground floor kitchen. Albeit tiny, those bells were loud enough to catch the attention of hungry occupants.

Albert jolted out of bed faster than Charlotte could grab him. Yet she managed to stop him before he made it to the door.

"It's okay Albert, that was just the suppertime bell." His hard breath stank. Charlotte wouldn't let go of Albert until he calmed down. "Relax."

*I cannot relax, not with all the metallic songs coming at me. I did not know it would be like this. Papa Edwin, nor father told me ... well, father did. He will say I told you so, too. Asshole.*

*Though the bed is very comfortable, I am ready to go home. All the songs, all the metal. I want to summon it all!*

His jaw was tight, eyes swirling with silver.

"You know, I never realized how many bells there are in Kobiton. I mean, they never bothered me. I thought they were quite pretty, how they ring out at different parts of the day—let you know what time it is. I'm sorry that they're wrecking you, Albert. Never thought, never knew much about how the metal influenced you until now." She stared at him lovingly. Meanwhile, Albert winced. "You know, Papa Edwin told me a lot about your Powers. What all you can do? And you both have shown me .... He also told me about the ringing and how he wards from his mind. The way he does it is by shedding his metal. All of it. That's not to say you can't keep it near you, like in a pouch or a dagger tucked into your belt. Did you shed all your metal before we came here, Albert? You said you did but ...."

To a Metalist, the ores they kept, hidden deep within his flesh and floating in his blood, were what sustained their livelihood. It helped mend their flesh; it maintained a harmonious energy that was hard to shed. Albert had never shed all his metal, not since the first day he could harness it. He was six years old at that time.

Charlotte glanced at her ring, then pointed at the one he wore that matched. She would wear hers forever. He sometimes absorbed his.

"It's okay, Albert." She rubbed his forearm. "Like I said, you can wear your metal, or keep it in a pouch, but not inside of you. I think that'll help."

"I-I do not want to."

"It's okay, Albert. I understand your aversion to letting go of it. But trust me when I say it will help. Papa Edwin would tell you to do so. It works for him."

"Father says we cannot live without it. And Edwin always holds some within him. I know it! I feel it!"

She believed he was lying. "Does he do it all the time?" Albert blinked, and she continued to press, "Well, does he?"

"I am not giving up all my metal." He stomped.

"Albert. Don't be like this. It's not going to hurt you to not have it inside of you. You'll still have it with you. It can be on you, just not in you," she pointed at the ring. "You can wear a necklace or more rings or just have it in a pouch of coins." She went to retrieve one from their baggage. Inside that small brown sack, she found rocks of silver.

"But I have seven pounds in me. I am not going to carry all seven pounds of metal on me."

"We're not going anywhere but downstairs. You can leave most of it here. If you need to bring some, make it into a blade or something. I mean, you can make it into anything you want with just a thought." She stared at him. "Just make it work. Okay?"

He gritted. "Okay."

She hated being hard on him. Charlotte was realizing why Albert's family had such an aversion to living inside any township. The metal chorus would make them crazed.

Her touch was warm and soft. "Thank you, Albert. I don't want you to be without your mind. I want you to be you, to experience things without a haze."

He didn't appear convinced. "I said yes."

She stepped back, and he shed all seven pounds of metal contained within his body. Almost immediately, his skin tone warmed. And at once his hair appeared more gray than silver. But his frown deepened. Albert made a dagger and put the remaining metal into orbs that clanked in the pouch affixed to his hip.

He grumbled, "Happy?"

She wasn't, but she kept that knowledge to herself. Charlotte changed out of her heavier dress and into the recently purchased one with flowers. Her soft strawberry-blonde hair cascaded around her face. Her cheeks were rosy, light green eyes were bright like her smile.

• • • ● • ● • ● • •

Charlotte left the room first. Albert was two steps behind. They descended the stairs and came into the dining room, already filled with the residents. Lori had reserved the seats nearest to her for Charlotte and Albert. She encouraged them to sit and passed a bowl of sourdough rolls, still steaming, to Charlotte.

"So, tell me everything. How'd you two meet? How far along are you in your pregnancy? I want details!" Lori was persistent. Her residents had their own questions too.

Charlotte offered only half-truths, admitting only that the Warden left her in Chinochi—said he was called away for some secretive mission. Took H'Eirwyn with him. And she had been on the road, returning to Kobiton when a mountain lion tried to kill her. That's when Albert's grandfather, Edwin, came into her life, saving her from the mountain lions' fangs. She spoke about her savior in great length, the catacomb caves they lived in, the chilly nights and busy days—avoiding all questions relating to the Warden.

Albert barely looked up from his plate. He ate everything on it and didn't make a sound other than the chomping of food and gulping of wine.

"You're a quiet man, Albert." Lori tried to engage him a few times. It was only after the meal that he parted his lips for conversation.

"Thank you for the meal. It was good."

"But not as good as what Charlotte would make, I bet. And thank you. It was the captain who requested roasted chicken."

All eyes fell on the older telepathic Clan-Duin man, with no front teeth. He was bald save for a well-kempt goatee. He had been eyeballing Albert all night, as if he looked familiar somehow.

From the corner of his eye, Albert noticed the dubious captain and snapped. "What is your problem?"

Sticking his chin out, the former Captain looked ready to say something. He peered at Albert, then at Charlotte. Instead of speaking his mind, the captain stood. The chair rattled across the wooden floor. He regarded Lori with a quick gesture, went into the front room and out the door—later confessing it was time for his evening walk.

The air in the dining room was warm, stiff. Miss Lori stood from her seat and took up empty plates. Almost immediately, Charlotte did the same, helping clear the table. She sensed the contention in the room. Wanting to do something about it, but wasn't sure what.

· · · ● · ● · ● · ·

Albert glared at his mostly drunk glass of wine. The noise, the smells, the constant press of people—it all overwhelmed him. He felt exposed, vulnerable in a way he never had in the quiet of their cave. Part of him longed for the simplicity of home, for the predictable rhythms of mining and survival.

But when he looked at Charlotte, saw her joy at being back among her people, he felt a pang of guilt for his discomfort. He wanted to be better, to be the man she deserved. But years of isolation and his father's bitter lessons were hard to overcome.

*I am trying*, he thought, meeting Charlotte's gaze. *I swear I am trying.*

· · · ● · ● · · · ·

She put a hand on his shoulder when passing him by with her other hand full of empty dining wear. "I'll be right back." Charlotte followed Lori into the kitchen.

Over to a giant washbasin, the women crowded. Lori whispered, "What type of Power does he yield?"

"He doesn't have a Power."

"Don't lie, Charlotte. My nose knows he's something other than Mortal. At first, I thought maybe he was just unwashed, but then he smelled fine at supper until just now. He changed, like a skunk letting out their stink."

"What are you talking about?"

"He's bad Charlotte. Smells of Death."

"He's not bad, Lori!"

Lori grabbed Charlotte's arms and stared deep into her. "And you're pregnant with his child. Death's child. What ... what were you thinking?"

"I don't—"

"I thought you said you never saw yourself mating with a man. That you would dedicate yourself to Hakra and do what you needed to succeed. I know you never wanted children!"

"It's just ...."

"What happened to you, Charlotte? What made you give in to a man like him?"

Charlotte might have been older than Albert, but she was many years younger than Lori. She had idolized the older woman long before befriending her as an adult. "He loves me."

"Really? That's the reason."

With a shrug Charlotte said, "I don't ... I .... What do you want me to say? I'm sorry?"

"If you truly love him, don't be sorry. It's just, I didn't expect this from you. But it's okay, I still love you." Lori pulled Charlotte in for a hug. "Damn, that's a solid belly. And you say you're only four moons along?"

She nodded. "We didn't start our trek down here until I stopped feeling sick. I'm thankful to have more energy now."

Lori looked down at Charlotte's protrusion. "You must've twins growing."

"Twins." A sob parted Charlotte's rosy lips. Her palms flew to her face. "That's what I feared. I don't want to raise twins. It'll be so much work. And they never help. They want me to do it all. I mean ..." She was pulled back into Lori's embrace. "... Papa Edwin helps. He's the nicest out of the three of them. That's not to say that Albert isn't nice. He is, but he's got a temper sometimes."

"He hasn't hit you, has he?"

Charlotte reflected on a recent conversation with Albert after reading the tomes to him. They had argued about the semantics of a story—it described a woman's place was to always be by her partner's side, to listen and obey, to create a loving homestead for every family member, where food and clothing and shelter would always be readily available. She argued that women don't always have to dedicate themselves in such a way that women could be more than a complacent housewife, that they too could hunt and gather. Women could work the fields, or mines, that they could build fortresses, or own a business and use Miss Lori's situation as an example. Charlotte knew men could cook, clean, and sew, as Papa Edwin had done until she arrived in their life.

At that time, Albert didn't care about the argument itself, he just wanted to be correct. That quarrel was the first time Charlotte had witnessed Albert's anger; the only time he brought up his hand and hit her. He had been forever apologetic after the incident.

"No. He's never like that. But sometimes he yells ... but only because he thinks no one's listening to him. His father, Jebadia, doesn't listen. He's a piece of shit. Hates everything and everyone. Like a hard rock that you can't chisel, no matter how many tasty treats you give 'em." She refused to leave Lori's arms.

"I thought you were going to live with me when the time came. I thought we were going to grow old—bake together forever. But then Hakra took you away. And now ...."

Charlotte looked into Lori's amber eyes. "I really want you to come with us. Live with us."

Lori cackled. "There's no way. I just got full control over this place. It's finally in my name! There's no way I would just .... I can't give this up now! No way. I've worked hard for years now. I've contested against people twice my age for this residence. I've earned this place. This is what I've wanted. Oh, Charlotte ...." Lori tucked a stray strand of Charlotte's hair behind her ear. "You would've gotten your freedom had you just .... But those Powers of yours doomed you from the start. I feel so bad for you, Charlotte." They hugged. "Makes me glad I'm just a Clan-Duin Erthin. I wish. I wish things could've been different."

"Same here." She grabbed Lori's hand. "Maybe I can convince him to live closer to town. Though him being here has been hard on him. He's not used to all the sounds and lights and such. I mean, we've been living in a cave! Everything's more colorful out here."

Lori brushed Charlotte's face. "Why do I feel like this'll be the last time I'll ever see you?"

Charlotte grabbed Lori's hand. "It's not. After the children are born, we'll come and visit. I prom—"

"Don't say you'll promise. You've already broken a few of those with me."

Charlotte knew her shame, but Lori was one to forgive. "I thought I'd never see you again. And now I'm here and fat as a pig."

"You're not that fat. Not yet."

It was here in the safety of the kitchen that Charlotte felt able to confess her deepest, darkest fear. At once, her eyes became wet. "I don't know if I wanna be pregnant."

"Do you love him?"

"Yes."

"Did he force you?"

"No. But I ... I might've forced him. I mean ... he was showing me a pretty find in the cave and gave me this ring, and then one thing led to another, and ... and .... But then again, we've done it many times since then."

"And that's how you get pregnant."

"Had I any herbs I would've .... But now, it's too late. I'm hoping to see one of the Doctors at the Abbey."

"You haven't done that yet?"

"No."

"That would've been my first stop. I mean, you're large for only being four moons along. I hope it's not triplets!"

"Oh Hakra no. Please, no. But that's my nightmare."

They both sensed someone had entered the kitchen and turned to see Albert in the doorway. He glared at Charlotte. "My head hurts."

Charlotte acknowledged Albert. "Yes. Of course." Water glistened on her eyelashes when she turned back to Lori. "We're going to bed now."

Lori's mouth hung open. She watched them leave the kitchen. Charlotte glanced back but followed Albert through the dining room and front area, over to and up the stairs. They retired to their room right at dusk. Albert's mind ached, and Charlotte soothed it with her telepathic spell.

"Thank you for trying, Albert." Charlotte told him after they were under the quilt.

He grunted and turned away from her. She rolled onto her shoulder and grabbed his torso. "We will start our return trip tomorrow, after visiting the markets. I'm sorry. I wish this had worked out, but it didn't. So sorry."

Albert's mind was a whirlwind of emotion. *Maybe Chinochi would be a better place than here. I cannot stand Kobiton. This place. The people. I wish we never came. And all the smells. I hate it ... hate it all. And that bald man. He was disrespectful. If I had my way, I would have ... I would have slaughtered him.*

She recoiled from him, his vicious thoughts. Charlotte turned her back on Albert and tried not to regret her decisions. But did.

# 23
# <u>EXPOSURE</u>

They awoke early. So had Lori. There were bowls full of moist and dried fruits and nuts on the communal dining room table. Albert sat at one of the many vacant seats. Charlotte poked her head into the warm kitchen. Lori was busy painting a glaze on a large loaf of sweet bread that had just breached the oven. It smelled of peaches and honey.

"Good morning." Lori said, without looking up. "How'd you two sleep?"

Charlotte stepped into the room. The kitchen door swung closed and hit the back of her heel. "Decent. I mean good. We slept well. Well, Albert tossed and turned, but when he started to snore, I knew he'd get through the night."

Lori nodded.

The moment was awkward for both.

"Look Lori, about last night I-ugh—"

"How long have you kept him like that?"

"Like what?"

Miss Lori placed the brush down; the glaze was finished. The room smelled wonderful. "Look, Charlotte, the captain had to leave because of his smell last night. On his way out he muttered something about noticing a telepathic haze, a shrouding spell across Albert's mind—wasn't interested in being part of it. I know what you're doing to him. But why?"

"I had to do it for the safety of this whole place. He's been under assault from all the ..." She had to think about what she could disclose. "... colors and people." She knew not to say anything about Albert's Metalist Powers. She had promised Edwin. "He's not used to it ... any of it."

"Then stay another night. I can be more accommodating."

"I don't think we can." Tears clung at the corners of her eyes.

"What aren't you telling me, Charlotte?"

She huffed, exacerbated by it all. Her head shook back and forth violently. "I can't."

"Who would I tell? I never gossip."

"Yeah. I know. You're far too smart for that." There were too many things she had to hide. Beyond the fact that Albert could yield metal, Charlotte knew Edwin was a wanted man. And if anyone were to know about the Metalists .... "That's why I love you. Please! Come with us."

"I can't. If I leave and have to return .... We both know what type of work I'll be doing. I don't wanna be a wash maid."

"But you won't. You can be with me. And we can live in the mountains and off the land. We don't have to go back to the cave."

"Is this your idea? Or Albert's?"

"Mine."

"Ha. Didn't think he'd be that type of person who'd want to share his woman with anyone else."

She bit her lip, glanced at the closed door. "He might." Charlotte knew Albert wouldn't want to share her with anyone, including Papa Edwin.

Lori stared at Charlotte. "It's not what I want. Besides, I don't like how he smells. He's not a good person, Charlotte. Can't you see it?"

"You don't like how he smells so you're gonna judge him based on that?! Come on Lori, little miss scholar, who knows just enough about everything. You shouldn't judge someone on their smell, nor how they look. Out of any-one, you should know that!"

"I didn't want to say anything, but you both looked outlandish with those matching outfits yesterday. I mean, who are you? You don't like matching anything. You're like me in that you like whimsical things. Or at least you used to."

Charlotte staggered, caught herself on the nearby counter. "I still do. What's gotten into you, Lori? I thought we were friends."

"We are. And that allows us to be honest with our feelings. And to be honest, I think he's a terrible choice for you."

Charlotte scoffed. "Are you judging me ...? What I've endured?"

"Maybe. But your story wasn't very convincing—lacked detail. And you're always into details. So, what're you withholding?"

She felt like an animal caught in a trap. "The mountain lion was the Warden."

"Papa Edwin killed the Warden?"

"Yeah. But that only happened because I tried and failed to kill them. But I tried! You should've seen me, Lori. I almost killed a Warden. Little ol' me!" She shook recalling that moment and now felt better about telling the truth. Charlotte had wanted to tell Lori the truth last night at the dinner table, but wouldn't disclose such brutality in front of Lori's residents.

"So, the Warden didn't leave you in Chinochi?" She gasped, then whispered, "What happened? Wardens are practically immortal. How'd you do it?"

"I poisoned them."

"Poisoned! Wow!"

"It was crazy! The Warden kept me against my will for many days. I don't know how long I was under their spell. Well, long enough to get me across the pass and into Datzar Territory. But I don't remember much. They kept my mind stilled most of the time. But I do remember them taking H'Eirwyn's head off. Slicing it clean off his shoulders and right in front of me. Then they told me we were both children of some nobleman who went around fornicating with every pretty flower. That they had been sent to find all of us. That's why they had the bag of heads. Serious, I don't know why they didn't take my head off too.

"Though it might have been because of my cooking. But maybe for the companionship. I'm not really sure. And that sack of heads. There were over a dozen. That's where they put H'Eirwyn—stuffed his head inside, right before my eyes. Said my head would be next if I didn't comply. It's obvious that Warden had gone rogue, turned into a hell-bent bounty hunter, somehow stopped working for Hakra—somehow became corrupt. I thought they were smarter than that, trained not to be .... It's so messed up, I tell ya. And he didn't let me eat for days yet made me cook for him. Said he liked my cooking. So messed up!"

Lori's mouth was as wide as her amber eyes.

"So, then, when I had my chance, the one time they let me have my mind, I tried to kill them. I thought they were dead. Well, I hoped they were. But then that Warden survived and came after me. The wild cat. Pounced right on me, knocking me unconscious. But then Papa Edwin arrived and took off their head. Had he not been there at that moment, I wouldn't be alive at all."

"Wow!"

"Not gonna lie. I felt indebted for what he did. Even though he said he would take me back to Kobiton, I felt I should do something for him."

"Does that mean you're not really in love with his grandson?"

"I-I love Albert. He's awkward, I know. Takes a while to shine on you, but when he does .... And he's never been inside a town or city, especially one as big as Kobiton. This was his first time leaving his home."

"Why didn't you tell me that?"

"I didn't want to embarrass him. Don't worry. It's okay. He's just ... He's good. And kind. Thoughtful. It's all been really hard on him. Not used to any of this."

"He better be good to you."

Charlotte returned to her story. "But what's even crazier is what I learned after Papa Edwin saved me. I still can't wrap my head around it all, but I guess the Warden had been hired by the Ishik Empire, sent to find my father's estranged children. All of us. We were all wanted, wanted dead. That sick fuk took our heads as trophies for the Ishik Empire. I mean, we know from history class that the Ishik Empire is all inbred, but how crazed can one country be? The Warden probably would've been paid handsomely for all our heads."

"That's just disgusting."

"I'm guessing my father was ... was a horrible man. Somehow wronged the wrong person, so we—all his offspring—were hunted down. It's despicable. I still can't forget seeing .... It changed everything, Lori." Charlotte's voice broke. "Watching them kill H'Eirwyn—my only family. I'll never be the same person I was before that moment!" Charlotte sobbed, recalling the blood, H'Eirwyn's eyes looking up at her from between her feet, and her shrill cry—that moment would be forever etched in her mind's eye. "It was brutal, Lori. Absolutely the worst moment of my life! And then ... then the Warden just looked at me, cold and calculating. They said something about me being 'valuable cargo' and 'changing plans.' I didn't understand then, but now I wonder if there's more to this than just a rogue Warden working for the Ishik Empire. I think it's something bigger, something more dangerous."

"I'm so sorry you had to witness that, Charlotte. Damn. That is brutal. All of it!" Lori cackled, "But, ha-ha, you're cooking ... you're cooking saved your ass!" She came and kissed Charlotte's cheek.

"It did. It really did." She wiped away her tears as they laughed.

• • • ● • ● • ● • • •

Albert watched Charlotte leave him in the dining room for the kitchen. He sat down and took an apple from the bowl of fruit placed in the center of the table.

He studied the apple, turning it over in his hands, feeling it, then setting it on the tabletop between his fingers—a flat expression on his pale face. Soon, his eyes rose to see the captain enter the room. The old man's freshly shaven head glowing in the morning light and candles. He was hypnotized by it all, as if in a drunken stupor.

The captain glanced at the closed kitchen door before taking a seat opposite Albert. His blue eyes were firm on the young man, who didn't seem to notice his stare. After a while of listening to the women's murmurs from the other room, the captain placed his wrinkly pale hand on Albert's hairy forearm.

An energy flushed throughout Albert; the fog occluding his mind had lifted. It was then that he felt the elderly man's hand on his arm—saw those telepathic blue eyes staring at him.

"You alright, young man?"

Albert studied the hand gripping his arm.

"That woman you're with; she's got you under a spell. Did you know? Can you tell?" He looked around, as if inside Albert's head.

"She is keeping me from using my Powers."

"What?!" The captain's blue eyes grew brighter. "She's keepin' you from your Powers. That's not right. Not at all. She's not allowed to do that! Not here in Kobiton."

"No," Albert said, not too sure of himself. "It is not like that, she is—"

The captain leaned forward. "She's got you all sedated. Doin' what she's done, it's just not right. You should be free, not sedate. Not in Kobiton, not under Hakran rule. Do you understand what I'm sayin'?"

Albert flexed his arm, attempting to pull away. He grumbled, "Take your hand off me!"

"If I do, she'll have you again. Is that what you want?"

Everything felt completely off. The dining room had been dull and drab, but now all the colors came to life: from the short curtains framing the two windows to the tablecloth and stack of embroidered napkins, the pictures on the walls of distant cityscapes, marketplaces, and a captivating sunset at a beach were also bright and bold.

And then he noticed the Telepaths intense stare. Those keen blue eyes made Albert's heart race. He continued to squirm, trying to pull out of the hard grasp. "Let go of me."

"She's a Witchtress if she's keepin' you like this. But I can keep you safe from her. I'll warn the soldiers, have them come an' take her away."

"What? No. Charlotte would never ...." He continued to struggle against the hard grasp. The captain did not back down.

"But she's keepin' you sedated, young man. And for her own reasons, that's easy to see."

"What? No! Let me go!" And with a burst of energy, Albert finally yanked free and stood. A blade appeared in his right hand, and he brought that dagger down and into the middle of the captain's hand, all the way through to the table.

The captain screamed, "What the fuk's wrong with you?! I was tryin' to save ya! You-you deathly smellin' whoreson!"

· · · · · ● · · ● · · · ·

Charlotte and Lori charged out of the kitchen. Albert stood back from the table, away from the bald captain. A knife protruded from the back of the captain's hand. Blood pooled on the tablecloth. Charlotte rushed to Albert. Lori went to the captain.

Charlotte snapped at Albert to retract his metal. Lori scolded the captain for provoking. He was the type of Telepath who would. And Albert was the type of man who didn't back down.

Immediately, Lori healed the captain's wounds. They both watched Charlotte pull Albert from the dining area. She kept her hand on his back, pushing him towards the stairs.

*Damn manipulators,* Albert thought, his glower firm on the older Telepath as they exited the ground floor for their bedroom. *I hate to believe Charlotte is one of them too. But that asshole captain says she is. Called her a Witchtress, just like father has. Could they be telling the truth? Charlotte has hazed my mind, took away my Metalistic desires. And I dislike it.*

His thoughts caught her off guard. She wanted to know, "What happened with the captain, Albert?"

"He touched me. Took your spell away. That is all."

"When we get back to the room, I'll replace it."

*Has Charlotte been manipulating me from the beginning?*

*I have let Charlotte into my mind and heart, every time, but should I?*

He glanced over his shoulder at her. *We are going to have a family together. Babies. Children who are like her. Children who can manipulate the mind. How did I let this happen?*

*Everything I have ever felt, all of it, was cultivated by Charlotte. This is all her fault. I should have ....* He did not know what he should have done, only what he could not face: Charlotte.

*Father has tried to warn me. And now the man named Captain echoes father's words. Has father known all along about these manipulators and not told me? These Telepaths ... despicable creatures they are.*

*Was River one of them? Is that why he cannot forget her?*

He huffed loudly. *I would hate to believe that father was correct about Charlotte this whole time and I am the dumb clot.*

Charlotte pulled her hand off his back, not wanting to listen in on his angry thoughts anymore. She was glad none of the other residents were there to witness Albert's anger. But most likely, they would hear about it later.

Once they returned to their room, he snapped, "Are you a Witchtress? Have you been manipulating me since the beginning? Since we first met?"

"What? No." She tore into him. "And you shouldn't have done that. Expose yourself like you did. He's a retired captain of the PCP and a Telepath. He'll tell the Hall about you. And that's a bad thing. Papa Edwin .... You shouldn't have .... Everyone will know about you and your family now. Didn't Jebadia, or Edwin, ever tell you never to be like that? To never reveal yourself in public!"

"Fuk him! Fuk you. Fuk all of ya!'

"Don't be like this, Albert. I've never wronged you. I've only wanted to help."

"No, all you have wanted was to come back to Kobiton."

He opened his arms wide and looked to the window. "Here you are."

"What do you mean?"

"You can stay."

She had never seen him like this, this venomous—like Jebadia would've been. "You can't mean that. I love you. And you love me."

"Do I? Or have you made me feel love?"

"No." She placed a hand on his heart. "Everything you've ever felt was yours. Not something I influenced. We have love." Her hand fell to her belly. "And a family."

The heat in his eyes flickered. "Are you a Witchtress?"

"I'm no Witchtress. I'm not evil. I've never been evil."

"I am not sure I believe you."

Charlotte was ready to cry. "Albert! I haven't done anything other than soothe the sounds. That spell was just that. And I have never manipulated you. Not ever. Not your heart, not your head. Everything you've ever felt about me is real."

He snorted. "I do not believe you."

"I've never lied to you. You know this, Albert. You know I'm a good person. I've always been there for you, helped you. You deserve all the good, and none of this horseshit! Please don't twist me into the person your father wishes I was."

"But the captain—"

"He's just an old man, retired from his job, but still on patrol. Once a soldier, always a soldier, they say. But you know I'm not evil. I've never been evil. Your father, however, has. If you want to know evil, he is the essence of it. He beats you, berates you, he's never cared. But I care, Albert. I care about you, and what happens to us. I love you."

His hands pumped in and out of fist formations. "But how do I know you are telling the truth? You could have manipulated us all."

She pulled her hand away from him and scoffed. "Are you fooling me?! I'm not that type of Telepath. I hate those types of Telepaths. I could never hurt you, Albert. But you look like you want to hurt me. Almost like you want to kill me. Do you want to hurt me? Hurt our child, our children?"

Albert had been shaking with rage, but then he blinked dramatically several times and suddenly all that anger fell flat. "What, no, I-I could never kill you, Charlotte. You are my sunshine. You lift me up when I feel like shit. I am sorry. I overreacted, I guess." His withered posture grew once more. "But after he called you a Witchtress, he called me Death, or said I smell like Death. He's an asshole and deserves to be cut into pieces."

"Let it go, Albert. He's just an old man. A bitter old man. And he will die soon. He's not young. Hakra will then take him and reincarnate him into the next generation of devout followers. And there's no way I'm a Witchtress. I'd have to be evil as fuk to be a Witchtress. You know I'm not." They stared at each other. "Now, please, can you just drop the conversation?"

He snorted; the fire rekindled in his eyes. Albert looked ready to say more.

Charlotte went to grab his hands, but he pulled away from her. "Please, Albert, don't be this way."

He spit, "I wish we never came here. I am ready to go home. Now!"

She couldn't keep up this hope, this wish that maybe something more could have happened here and now. She wanted nothing more than to live in Kobiton and be among the people who she cared for the most. And though Albert had hinted that she could stay, her love for him and their unborn children trumped her desires. Instead, she was bound to this moment in time, to her decisions—to this person who became explosive when around too much metal. She feared for her future if they stayed there, but more so for the further future, when she was giving birth without a healer or doula by her side.

"Is it okay if I place that spell on your mind again?"

His silvery eyes looked like daggers. "No. I want to go home. Now."

"Yes. I know. But you won't be able to navigate the city without my help. Please let me help!" It was a long moment of contemplation for Albert. But then slowly he bowed his head, flinching when her icy hands touched his temples. "Once we're gone from Kobiton, I'll remove it."

"You better."

# 24

# <u>SHATTERED DREAMS</u>

They hadn't unpacked their belongings.

Within a few moments, Albert and Charlotte appeared at the base of the stairs. The captain was gone. Lori too. The older women were now at the table, wide smiles, savoring the sweet peach bread. They watched Charlotte pull Albert into the kitchen.

Lori was cleaning the countertop. She stopped when the door swung shut. "I'm glad you two stopped past." She forced a happy façade. Charlotte knew this look. Yet they embraced with no further provocation. "Any time you're in town and need a place of respite, please come here. I'll always put you two up, no matter how big your family becomes." Lori squeezed Charlotte extra hard. It was obvious to Charlotte that Lori didn't want to let go.

Lori thought at Charlotte. *Stay with me. I will take care of you and your children. He's no good for you. Please stay.*

Charlotte kissed Lori's cheek. "I love you, Lori. You'll always be my best friend." She whispered; a tear fell from her face.

She would have remained only if she felt she could handle the children growing in her belly and their amazing Powers. She knew Lori couldn't foster a Metalist's growth. Only another Metalist could. It was best for Charlotte to stay with Albert, Papa Edwin, and Jebadia—even if the thought of living her life as a recluse pained her. She told herself she would return to Kobiton, to her friends, even if she didn't really believe it would ever happen. Charlotte had to hold on to hope that her life wasn't slowly fading into the mountain breeze. She missed the importance of her work, feeding hundreds of people without families, and the pride it brought, even though it was extremely exhausting. And yet, this new life wasn't without merit. It had given her a new perspective on old daydreams of having, living with a family—taking care of just a few people, as opposed to dozens of dozens of orphans. The more Charlotte reflected, the more she realized she preferred this new life. Even if she didn't feel it brought her greater meaning. But maybe, when the babies came, things would be different.

As she and Albert made their way out of the peach-smelling homestead and down the charming avenue, Charlotte thought about the rest of her life with Albert and what it would be like.

They would return to the cave, and the summer would creep past. Their ideas of making a homestead apart from Albert's family would remain a fantasy. Her belly would swell as would her feet and breasts. Her body would ache all over.

She didn't see Albert giving her much reprieve. He was demanding, sometimes uncaring, and his ability to tend to someone other than himself was primitive at best. And if it hadn't been for her telepathic intervention before they entered Kobiton yesterday, she knew something catastrophic would've occurred. The power, the fury that raged just below Albert's skin, was reminiscent of Jebadia's anger. Because of that fact, and the musings in Albert's mind, she wasn't sure he would take good care of their children—afraid he might kill both babies (accidentally, of course). As it was, the child-rearing responsibilities would be her burden. Yes, Papa Edwin said he would be there to help, but he was old. She was amazed he was still alive after confessing what all he had lived through. Those tales still haunted her. Especially the stories of the female Metalists being born—murdered the moment after exiting the womb. The heartache and devastation of that knowledge lit her fears.

Yet if Charlotte bore twin boys, they would live under her rule until they were old enough to yield their Powers. Once her boys came into possession of their Metalist Abilities, they would then follow Albert into the dark depths of the mountain. They would mine ore and grow up, just as their father had. She wanted more for them, options of different employment, but mining ore was their destiny.

Meanwhile, Charlotte would continue to keep the cavern looking like a humble home. She would care for their children, attend to their laundry, and make amazing meals. And she would daydream of another time, an earlier time in her life, when she lived for herself, had close friends and saw them every day. These whimsical moments would make her want to return to Kobiton as often as they could.

But cruel reality slapped her.

She was hesitant to breathe. *They'll never be able to come to Kobiton.*

If anyone went, it would be Edwin or Jebadia, maybe Albert, but never her. Charlotte would be forever bound to the heartless mountains. She would long for, but wouldn't be able to share all the splendors Kobiton offered with her children, and that knowledge spun her mind—depressed her soul.

Inside their cavernous homestead, Charlotte would remain. Tears would be shed every time she thought of Kobiton. She would dream of returning, but that's all that would ever come, daydreams. And if she were to return, sometime much later in her life, Charlotte would be afraid to see anyone who brought her joy—who reminded her of what she had wanted before the Warden had taken her away; before this new life was thrust upon her.

It was possible that she would have more than just two children, but if any girls were born, there would be great mourning. It saddened Charlotte to know that she would be the only female in the family. She would either grow old from watching her children grow up, or maybe die in childbirth.

At the same time, Albert would grow old by her side, or maybe he would die from a cave-in.

The grim possibilities were endless when living inside a mountain.

In a flash, that rabbit-hole view of her life was gone. And Charlotte's mind returned to the avenue they were walking.

• • • ● • ● • • • •

They climbed upslope toward Kobiton's Abbey and Seminary School. The tower and its bell were in view. She knew it would ring soon. Children from families, also heading to the seminary, joined them as they charged uphill. The school bell would chime once, wait fifteen minutes, then chime again to let those few straggler students know they were late to first class.

Master Ikyrus greeted them at the barn's entrance. "M'Lady Charlotte, and your Master, how good it is to see you two. I spoke to Head Mistress Aluyelian last evening. She was surprised she hadn't seen you yet. You were gonna visit her, weren't ya?"

"Oh, yeah, I, uh, I was just going to do that." Charlotte turned to Albert. "Can you get everything ready without me? I shouldn't be long."

He stared through her, appeared to not be listening, but then Albert nodded and lowered his eyes. "I promise I won't be long." Immediately, she bit her lip. "Master Ikyrus, please don't bother Albert. He likes the quiet."

They looked at one another. Master Ikyrus was Clan-Duin. He wasn't the smartest animal in the barn, but he knew when quiet was called for. She knew Master Ikyrus also appreciated quietness. The older man went back to his morning chores, leaving Albert to ready the donkeys while Charlotte darted off and into the abbey's kitchens. She was sure that's where Head Mistress Aluyelian would be.

The kitchens were not busy now. Half of the staff were down at the markets getting fresh food for lunch, supper, and tomorrow morning's meals. The few people that were present didn't look up to see Charlotte step inside the always warm room; those remaining were washing dishes or stacking dry ones. One person was scrubbing an oven, two more were kneading dough and chattering quietly. A few others were getting snacks for the youngest children, who would require a meal between now and lunch.

Head mistress Aluyelian wasn't there.

Charlotte went to the far doorway that led to a dark hallway along the back side of the kitchen. It was a secret passage, of sorts, that allowed the cooks and abbey's staff to come and go without disturbing the children, or anyone else. It was also a great place for the chefs to take a moment away from the heat of the kitchens.

She pulled back the door and peered into the dimly lit corridor. It was long, and with just a few doors that led to other rooms or hallways. At the far end was a flourish of clothing and conversation.

"Mistress Aluyelian. Miss Aly!" She knew not to call her superiors by their shortened names, but Charlotte was no longer indebted to this place, these people.

Head Mistress Aluyelian was a blonde-haired, middle-aged Telepath, wearing a lovely form fitting indigo dress with red embellishments along the cufflink and neck. Small red flower buttons cascaded down the front of her dress—looked like blood drops. She only wore this dress when some dignitary was to arrive. She and two much younger attendants, wearing plain gray dresses, stopped and turned to see Charlotte at the other end of the hallway.

"Oh. There you are." *Finally.* "Come, walk with me."

Charlotte charged forward and met up with her former employer. They entered a stone courtyard open to the sky, yet the temperature was Erthin controlled. It was here in this rectangular space where she, and a few other students, learned about their Succubus Powers. It was here where they were taught how to use it on one another, defend against each other.

Charlotte shuddered at the memory of her first time using her Succubus Power on another. Although there had been an instructor, all the students had been wary of using their amazingly deadly Power. She never enjoyed touching that channel of destruction, knowing what would happen if she took a life—that soul would be with her forever; or so their teacher had said (and she believed it). The fear of those lessons struck Charlotte hard just now. She recalled nearly killing another student during a training session, drawing out their life force before she understood what was happening. Had their instructor not intervened ....

She recalled how hard it was to turn off the Power once it came on. It was why she had spent so much time in solitary—not just for her protection, but for others. Since then, she vowed never to use it unless warranted.

The shadows from the above floors kept this place cool most of the day, as did the Erthin spells placed here. Head Mistress Aluyelian didn't stop her hustle past the dozen columns that supported the upper floors. Charlotte knew they would turn right and then go upstairs.

"What's going on?"

The Head Mistress gave Charlotte a sideways glance, "Hm. I should ask the same of you. What are you doing here, Charlotte? I thought you'd be cooking up meals for Hakra by now."

"No, Miss, um. It seems the Warden wasn't really a Warden. That he ... they, um, they had a bag of heads, Mam. And they took my mind, forced me to do Hakra-knows-what! It's believed they were sent by the Ishik Empire, searching for children of some by-blow-bastard that fuked every flower he found, if only to kill us for a fat cash prize." She was amazed that she admitted the truth, slapped her hand over her mouth.

Head Mistress Aluyelian stopped mid stride. "Oh yes, I heard about that." Her eyes then fell to Charlotte's belly bulge. "Did they impregnate you?"

"No."

Head Mistress Aluyelian began walking again. She had something important to do, that was obvious. "Hm. How'd you get away?"

"I-I was saved by a miner. He, ah, he took off the Warden's head."

"A miner took off the Warden's head. Hm."

"Yes mam. He used a sword. Sliced it clean off his shoulders."

"Hm. Was he the one who impregnated you?"

"No, mam, it was his grandson."

"Ah. I thought you wanted to serve Hakra ... that you didn't want children." Charlotte noticed the side eye, bright blue, searching for something. "What does this man do for you that Hakra couldn't?"

"I would've gone to Akarah, mam, I would've. I have dedicated myself to Hakra. It's all I've ever wanted is to serve him."

"But you got pregnant. That must be what Hakra wants for you, to be a mother, not a dedicated server of his divinity."

"Mam, I could—"

"No, you can't. You cannot serve Hakra in any capacity now. Not until you're free of your burdens."

"Yes, mam, I know." Charlotte wanted to raise her voice, to speak her mind. She kept moistening her lips.

"Have you something to say?"

"No, mam."

"Hm. Do you wish for the Doctor to view you?"

Her lip was swollen from all her biting of it. "Yes, mam."

They had come to Head Mistress Aluyelian's office. One of her attendants had already opened the door, the other remained by the older woman's side. "Doctor Feendy will be available soon. I have a meeting that I must be ready for." With a quick nod, Head Mistress Aluyelian left Charlotte in the hallway. Her attendant shut the door in her face.

• • • • ● • ● • • • •

She went straight to the Doctor's office and waited in a hard-backed chair for over an hour before the doctor arrived.

Doctor Feendy was a lanky Elementalist woman who always appeared manly. She never wore dresses, always clean-cut indigo slacks and a short-sleeved blouse, which was maroon today, and bore a bright smile everywhere they went. "Sorry it took me so long, Miss Charlotte. Mistress Aluyelian requested I meet you, but I was already in a meeting." She chuckled, "It's good to see you again." Doctor Feendy's bouncy red hair led them into their medical office. "How've you been?"

"Well. I've been mostly well. Just got done with feeling that sickness everyone gets when pregnant."

"Oh, good. No one ever enjoys feeling that way. Sit down, please." The doctor gestured toward a taller, padded couch. "And how long ago was that?"

"About a moon's time."

"And you're already this big!"

"Yes."

"You've twins. I can feel their heartbeats. I believe you're further along than expected," Doctor Feendy said, hands gentle on Charlotte's swollen belly. "You should know that twins often come early—their combined growth puts strain on the mother. And with your unique Abilities ..." She paused, choosing her words carefully. "Powers like yours can affect pregnancy in unpredictable ways. We should prepare for an early arrival."

Charlotte nodded, trying to hide her fear. "How early?"

"Perhaps a moon cycle, maybe more. It's hard to say with ..." Doctor Feendy gestured vaguely, "your particular situation. But everything seems to be progressing well. The babies feel healthy and are growing well."

"Can you tell me if they're boys or girls?" It was suddenly hard to swallow.

"Unfortunately, I can't. Not yet. They'd need to be bigger, older. Think of the third trimester. That's when we should see each other again."

Doctor Feendy reached for a mug, and immediately it was full of water. They handed it over to Charlotte. "What's the father like?" There was a long pause before they added, "Powers, that is. What are his Powers? Or is he Mortal?"

Charlotte drank the mug dry. "Thank you. Not very. He's not very Talented. Mostly Mortal, with a little bit of Erthin." She nodded as if to convince herself too.

"Should be a good fit. Mixed with your Abilities, the babies should be healthy throughout your pregnancy."

"Good. That's good to know." Charlotte looked at her hands.

"Is there anything else you want to ask? Any concerns?"

"No. I know what comes next, what's supposed to happen."

"Have you any unusual cravings?"

"Pine nuts. Craving some now. I plan on buying a few bags of them."

They stared at each other. "Well, unless you've other questions."

"No."

"Then I'll want to see you around the time the autumn fair happens. You should be in your third trimester by then. At that point I'll be able to discern the babies' sexes."

Charlotte felt numb. "Okay. I can do that." She wasn't sure she would return before the babies were born. But she was happy to know that they were doing well and healthy.

"Thank you, Doctor Feendy."

"Have a good day, Charlotte."

"You too."

She stumbled out of the room and looked around the Abbey and its immense complex. Over a dozen buildings interconnected the cathedral, orphanage, and schoolhouse. There were many memories, most of them weren't good, but this place she would miss.

• • • • ● • ● • • •

Charlotte didn't realize she had been gone most of the morning, and arrived back at the stables right before the lunchtime bell rang. Albert had fallen asleep in the stall; the donkeys were tacked up and ready to move. He jumped up, the metal within his body flushed across his skin, and she was quick to subdue his urges to manipulate the bell and all the rest of the metal within the stable yard—of which there were many pounds.

"Where have you been?" He snarled.

"I'm sorry. Let's go," she said, tossing a glance back to see where the stable-yard master was. Though she wanted to say goodbye to Master Ikyrus, she didn't want to wait long for the old man.

"Goodbye Master Ikyrus," she called down the stable aisleway. There was no response. With a shrug, she led Albert away without another backward glance.

As they hustled away from her childhood home, Charlotte mentally reviewed her shopping list. Kobiton's vast markets would provide everything they needed to create a home for their children. As they navigated the bustling city, she maintained a light telepathic hold on Albert, wincing at the cacophony of metal melodies assaulting them both. She hoped the other Telepaths wouldn't notice her spell as they made their last pass through the city of Kobiton before taking the long journey home.

# 25

## MISGUIDED INTENTIONS

The packs on the donkeys were stuffed with everything they would need to start a new life together.

As they walked through the bustling streets, Albert found himself thinking of his father. Would Jebadia have marveled at these sights, once upon a time? Or had he always been contented with the solitude of their mountain home? Albert realized with a start that he knew almost nothing about his father's past, the experiences that had shaped him.

It was midafternoon by the time they departed the city of Kobiton. The southern roadway lured them away from the busy cityscape, passing through pastures full of animals, acres of orchards and expansive fields of wheat. Once they were far enough from the orchestra of metal, Charlotte let go of her spell and Albert became himself at once.

"I never want to return to this place," he grumbled.

She walked along his side; the donkeys towed behind them. "We could always find a place to live that's close to Chinochi, if you want."

"Is Chinochi anything like Kobiton?"

"No. It's much smaller. What I remember is there're only a few places to buy things. The thing is, I like options. Chinochi is only a few blocks large, opposed to Kobiton, which takes up the whole hillside."

He grunted every time his left foot hit the ground. "Why would you want to live so close to a place like this?"

"Markets. And friends. I mean .... It was nice to see Miss Lori and walk through the halls of the Abbey. To see all the familiar faces." A smile lifted Charlotte's expressionless face.

They walked on further.

"Why do you all hug and kiss each other?" said Albert. "I thought that type of affection was only shared between a man and a woman." She blinked at him, and he shriveled slightly. "That is what I was told, at least."

"Because they're my family. All those people are my family, for better or worse. I kiss and hug them, and you, to show my love and appreciation. That's what family does. At least that's what we do. Sharing affection lets every one of us know that we're wanted in this life, even if our parents didn't, or couldn't. It's nice to know that we're missed when we're away.

"Growing up without parents is hard, as you know—your mother an' all. The people who live in the Abbey ... Head Mistress Aluyelian and all the cooks, even Master Ikyrus—although he's very handsy sometimes—we're all family. Just like you and your fathers, but you don't really show that type of affection. Which is sad.

"Living at the Abbey has made me appreciate those friends I have and the connections I've made with so many people in the community. Maybe that's why I like Kobiton so much, because the whole place is my family, from the butcher down in the markets to the Head Mistress Aluyelian. Yeah, she can be uncaring sometimes, but she's got so much to take care of every day. Like constantly putting out fires, metaphorically speaking, of course."

"Why did you leave me for so long?"

"Oh, yeah. I, ah, I went to the Doctor. We've a resident doctor, and several in training, but they don't train without the doctor present." She realized she was rambling.

He stopped her. "You did?" Albert then placed a hand on her belly bulge. "What did he say?"

"They said both babies are healthy."

He held his breath. "Are they boys?"

"The doctor cannot tell what sex they are now. But they assured me that both babies are healthy, growing well."

"They better be boys." He looked excited. "Is that what you took so long? I should have been there with you. Why did you not bring me with you? Why *did* you leave me behind?"

"I didn't know I was going to see the Doctor. Mistress Aluyelian said I should. I'm sorry I didn't come and get you. I walked all the way across the compound while she talked. She didn't have time to stand around and converse—had important business to attend to."

"You should have taken me," He snarled. "Besides, that Ikyrus man was an ass. He was rude. So much like my father. I saw him take one of those children from the playing field. Well, actually, they came to take a piss, but he grabbed them, covered their mouths, and took them into the back stall. I heard him. It was just like what Jebadia has done to me. So fuked up!" Silver now occluded his iris, swirling.

She gasped, "He did what to that child?"

"Do not worry. He will never do it again ... made sure of it. He was weak, unlike father. I was glad he could not stop me. Do not worry. I made sure he would not hurt another child ever again."

She grabbed him. "Albert. What did you do? Did you kill him?"

"Yes. Of course I did. He was raping a child!"

"You whaaaa ...." Charlotte's breath escaped her.

"Do not worry. He got what he deserved. It felt good to do it too! I am glad I did it. I have always wanted to do it to father. For years. Always wondered what it would feel like to kill someone. And you know, it felt great."

She kept gasping, eyes wide with fear. "You killed Master Ikyrus! That's .... What were you thinking, Albert? We don't kill people. That's one of Hakra's commandments."

"But he deserved it!" There was that fiery lust in Albert's metallic swirling eyes.

Charlotte took a step back. "Maybe he deserved it, but Hakra would've taken care of him. What ... what about the child? They didn't see your wrath, did they? Please tell me no one else saw your Powers."

"The child saw me. But I rescued them. So, everything is okay. And I made them promise not to speak of it to anyone. I told them I would cut them if they did. So, I think we are okay."

Her breath quickened; Charlotte felt like swooning. "You what!? That's not .... Never do that again! Wait for me, please. Just sit and wait. Next time let me know before you just ... that way we can tell .... Master Ikyrus would've been chastised. I know it. He would've—"

"A man like him does not deserve to live. He was as bad as Jebadia. Deserved what was coming. I wish I could kill Jebadia that easily. I have dreamed about it. I tried it only once. He beat me senseless for it. That is why ...." He stepped towards Charlotte, hand extended. "We do not have to return home. I do not trust my father. Not around you, nor our children. And Edwin is just as bad. I know you have not seen it yet but—"

"Papa Edwin?" She was quick to rebuke. "He's not that type of man. I mean, I can see your father doing many hurtful things. That's the reason I don't want to go back and live with him. But are you saying that Papa Edwin's just as bad for children too?"

"He yells and slaps. Berates. Uses sticks occasionally. He is not a good person, Charlotte. I am impressed that he has not shown that side of himself to you yet. But I guarantee, sometime soon, he will show his truths. I know it!"

With her hands firmly attached to her hips, Charlotte retorted, "I don't believe you. Papa Edwin's never been angry or abusive to me. I think you're lying."

"I am not lying. And I know he will reveal himself to you. He was like that with me. Horrible just like father. He will do it to you too. And soon. I know it."

"I think you are lying."

"I speak the truth, Charlotte. Who are you going to believe? Me or Papa Edwin?"

"Saying it doesn't make it true. Papa Edwin's a changed man. Everyone can change if they put forth the effort."

"Now that is a lie."

"No, it isn't. It's a fact. If you put forth the effort, you can do anything, change anything about yourself that you don't like."

Albert sneered. "I do not believe you."

"Believe what you want, but I've seen you change. So, you can't tell me that Papa Edwin can't change."

"I have not changed."

"Yes, you have! You've changed so much since I first met you. You've grown up, taken much responsibility for yourself and me. And you're more handsome now. Maybe even taller than you were. I know you've changed, in so many ways. And I'm proud of all your accomplishments."

He softened. A dopey smile lifted his face. "I am sure father would never change—too stubborn to."

"You're right. Your father's suffered from many afflictions and let them fester opposed to learning from them. Yeah, he's definitely not alright in the head. But then again, Papa Edwin admitted to dropping him on his head a few times—not meaning too, of course, but it would explain a few things."

"I have heard his stories. The people Edwin left father with were just as bad as he."

"No, they were worse. But you're not like that. And I don't believe Papa Edwin is like that either. He's just been misguided, but a good person, just like you."

"How am I misguided?"

"I didn't say that."

"Yes, you did. You just said it!"

"Not about you. I was saying you're a good person, Albert. You've a good heart. You care about me and our babies. I just want you to be kind to others. You don't have to take it upon yourself to smite all the bad people. Besides, there's a PCP Hall and a high court system put in place to penalize mean and malicious people like Master Ikyrus. You shouldn't have killed him."

"Would the PCP kill him?"

"Possibly. But then again, he might've lived the rest of his days in the Hall as a courtyard sitter. He's Clan-Duin. That's one of the ways they penalize male Clan-Duins. They take their mind, turn them into guard dogs, and chain them up for the rest of their days."

"They meaning ...?"

"Telepaths."

He blinked. "Is that what all Telepaths do? Take minds and manipulate them for whatever reason?" Charlotte shook her head, looked ready to rebuke, but Albert boldly stated, "Killing that man was the Just way. Taking his mind and manipulating him is not justice. It is wrong. Killing people like him is the only way!"

Charlotte was slow to nod. "Just promise me you won't do it again."

He stared at her before taking off once again. His footfalls were faster than she or the donkeys wanted to take, but they caught up regardless.

# 26

## <u>RETURN TO SHADOW</u>

*How could I have been so blind? She held Power over minds this whole time, kept it secret from me, from all of us. Even now, thinking of her smile makes my chest ache. But was any of it real?*

The captain's words tangled with his father's warnings in Albert's mind. His hands shook as he touched the metal at his core—the one thing Charlotte couldn't take from him. Or had she already? Even his love for it felt different now, tainted by doubt. When he looked at her, his chest still ached with wanting, but now that wanting felt like poison.

*They saw what I could not—or would not. She led me away from my family, made me doubt father's wisdom. Made me feel things I had never ....*

*Her food always tasted like heaven itself. Was that real? Or just another trick? The way she reads stories, tends the fire, makes our cave feel like ... like home. Could magic fake all that?*

*And now she carries our children. My children. Unless that too is a lie. How can I trust anything anymore?*

*Father would say I am weak for these doubts. A real man would not question. But I see her sleeping sometimes, her hand on her swollen belly, and I want to believe ....*

*No. Father was correct. As was the captain man. All this talk of love and future and happiness is just whimsical words laced with her magic. They are words never used in my house until she arrived. All false, just magic. Words that mean nothing in the real world.*

*But then why does my heart feel like it is being crushed when I think of her as my enemy?*

His feet continued at their fast pace, letting the physical exertion dull the storm in his mind. Charlotte lagged behind with the donkeys, the lead lines pulled taut between them.

*She must have manipulated me countless times. Every moment we shared could be a lie. Yet part of me still wants to turn around, take her hand, beg her to tell me it was all real ....*

*The twins she carries—our children—they are the only truth I can cling to now. I will be a better father than Jebadia. I will protect them from ....*

He wiped furiously at his eyes, angry at the moisture gathering there.

*She made me soft. Made me dream of impossible things. A life beyond the caves. A family built on more than duty. Now I know better. Now I understand why father is the way he is.*

Albert watched the dust drift around his boots as he walked, each step taking him further into his doubts.

*We had plans. A home of our own. Children racing through caverns filled with her laughter. All those nights talking about our future, while she ... while she what? Wove spells around my mind? Made me see things that were not there?*

*The way she touches me, it always feels like ... warmth. Like sunlight breaking through clouds. But maybe that is just what telepathy feels like. Maybe that is how they trap you.*

He paused, lungs burning from the warm air and bitter emotions.

*But her tears when she talks about home—those seem real. The way she holds those knitting needles like they are precious things, how she hums while cooking ... could someone fake all that? For so long?*

*And Edwin—he trusts her. Or is she controlling him too? Making him soft like she made me soft? The Edwin I knew would never let a woman ....*

The wind picked up, driving pollen and dust against his face. He welcomed the smells—it was cleaner than the pain in his chest.

*I should have known when she started talking about moving away from father. That must have been her working her magic on me. But then why do I still want what we had, what I felt?*

*None of that matters now. All that matters is our babies. They will be here soon. I must be strong for them. Must protect them from ... from ....*

His thoughts scattered like the flock of crows overhead. He could not finish that sentence, could not name what he was protecting them from. Their mother? His love? His fear?

*Father says all women with Power are dangerous. That they will strip everything from you until there is nothing left. But I already feel stripped bare, and it is not from her magic—it is from fighting against everything I feel when I look at her.*

He heard Charlotte's labored breathing behind him, knowing she was struggling to keep up. Once he would have turned back, offered his arm, shared his warmth. Now he pushed ahead, afraid of what might happen if he met her eyes.

*The twins are what matters now. They are real. They have to be real. Everything else can just fade away.*

That night, as they camped on their journey home, Albert lay awake, staring at the stars. "Why did you withhold?" he asked suddenly. "The thing you did to my mind. Dulling the metal songs."

Charlotte turned to face him in the darkness. "I didn't think it mattered," she said softly. "It's just something I can do."

"What else can you do that you have not told me about?"

She was quiet for a long moment. "Albert, I'm still the same person."

"Are you?" The question surprised even him with its sharpness.

Charlotte reached for his hand, but he turned away, pretending to sleep. In truth, he was remembering his father's warnings about women with Power. For the first time, those words didn't seem so farfetched.

And yet, when he watched Charlotte sleep, her hand resting on her swollen belly, she looked exactly as she had that first day—beautiful, warm, full of promise. His fingers itched to touch her hair, even as his father's warnings screamed in his head. The truth was there in the space between them: he didn't know what was real anymore—his love or his fear.

· · · ● · ● · · ·

Their journey back to the cave was a grueling ascent, each step a battle against gravity and growing tension. For days the silken quiet between them stretched like a living thing, broken only by the crunch of leaves, twigs, or gravel underfoot and the occasional cry of a distant bird. Albert's eyes darted constantly, never quite meeting Charlotte's gaze. His fingers twitched, as if ready to summon his metal at a moment's notice. She felt the weight of his suspicions like a physical thing.

"I need to rest," she ventured, as the sun started to dip below the jagged peaks. "Just for a moment."

Albert grunted, noncommittal, but slowed his pace. As they settled on a rocky outcrop, Charlotte fought the urge to reach out, to soothe his fears with her Power. Instead, she forced a smile, offering him a strip of dried meat from their provisions.

"How close do you want to live to your father and Papa Edwin?" She asked softly, hoping conversation might bridge the chasm between them. "Would you want to live in a cave? Or a log cabin? Or maybe something in between?"

As Albert hesitantly began to speak, Charlotte listened intently, determined to understand this man and the life he wanted to live—without the use of her Abilities.

"I want what we already have. My family's cave is the best place to live. I am not sure if I want to live anywhere else. And it is already built. The bedrooms. Your kitchen. I do not understand why you want to live apart from my family. We are stronger together. Father says that all the time. And now I know it is true. All this time away from home has made me aware of how much I would miss living there. I do not think I would want to live anywhere else."

"But I thought we'd—"

He snapped, "What I say goes, Charlotte. Understand! And we are going home."

Charlotte recoiled. She felt the same bitter pang when they had left her childhood home. This was not what she wanted at all. She wanted love and understanding, not bitterness and withholding.

In Kobiton, power flowed like water—visible, controlled, celebrated. But in the caves, power was like the metal in the walls—hidden, dangerous, waiting to be shaped. Charlotte found herself caught between these worlds, belonging fully to neither.

Yet she knew this would happen.

Albert's admission saddened her deeper than she knew, but she understood the familiarity of it all. Even Charlotte longed for the pristine views and crisp water—for a jolly story from Papa Edwin. Still, tears clung to her eyelashes and wishes sat in the crevasse of her trembling lips.

Nothing would ever be the same.

• • • • • • • • • •

During their time together, there were a few moments when Albert's inhibitions vanished and his altruism shown bright, but those times were short-lived. And yet, his belief that Charlotte held ulterior motives was firm and strained through his manifested shield. Now all Charlotte saw was the volatile side of Albert—a replica of Jebadia.

At any point Charlotte could have left, Lori had said she would help raise the twins growing inside. But Charlotte loved Albert and hoped that soon these grotesque arguments would vanish. They had been around each other nonstop for many days now. He missed his time in the caves, mining. She missed the solitude that the mountains brought, and her conversations with Papa Edwin. She was positive he would know how to handle Albert.

Their trek back to their cavernous homestead took nearly twice as long as their descent to Kobiton. By the time they arrived home, the field below the wide gap was in full bloom with all the colors of the rainbow. Wildflowers pat against their calves and knees as they made their final approach home.

The familiarness of it all was inviting. The cool depths of the cavern would be a welcome reprieve from the warm winds and blazing sun that accompanied them the last three days of their trek.

Albert led the donkeys, and they went around the mountain to the main entrance. It was there, only a few feet before their cavernous homestead, when Papa Edwin greeted them. He was hiking back from the tree line, a sack full of dead squirrels across his shoulder.

"There they are! My glorious world travelers," cried Edwin. "I cannot wait to hear your tales. Come, let us go inside and sit down. Rest your feet." He eagerly followed them inside. "So how was it? How was Kobiton?"

Charlotte rang out, "It was amazing!"

"I hated it. Never want to return." Albert spat.

Jebadia had been lying on his bed, but perked up when he heard his son. "Ha! Told you so."

"Yes, father, you were right. Damn old shit for brains." Albert took the donkeys into the corral and began unpacking them. Charlotte came to Albert's aid, and he snarled, "Go cook something."

She reached for Albert's hand, but he pulled away, his eyes fixed on her growing belly. The silence between them stretched, filled with unspoken fears.

Slowly Charlotte backed away, went and took the sack of dead squirrels from Edwin.

"Did you have fun? Did you get to see your friend, Miss Lori?"

"It was okay. Um, yeah, she put us up for the night. But I don't think I'll be returning anytime soon." She found a knife and began skinning the squirrels.

"What about that Head Mistress person?"

"Yeah, I saw Mistress Aluyelian too. She was busy, but I saw the Doctor. They said the babies are doing good, nice and strong."

Papa Edwin moved closer. "Everything go alright, Sweet Miss? Did Albert behave?"

"He was good, yes. Though he didn't want to shed his metal when I asked." Edwin glanced toward his grandson, but she grabbed his forearm to keep him from pestering Albert. "Don't worry, he made it into coins, carried it around that way. We did good. He did good. It was all very good."

How Papa Edwin looked at her made her want to speak more about it all, but she returned to preparing supper.

Charlotte added, "We got a bunch of things for the babies: rocking bassinets with cushions, wool blankets and some softer material, lots of cloth swatches, and spindles of yarn, leather pieces and such. I'm hoping to knit a bunch, make some soft blankets and whatnot. Hoping to sit out in the field, you know, draw up some inspiration from all those flowers. They sure smelled great walking through them. How've you two been?"

"Oh, well … my hip still has a hitch. I cannot seem to un-clunk it." He chuckled. "And Jeb has been … he has been, well, you know how he has been."

"Shut it you, old man," Jebadia shouted from his bed across the room.

Papa Edwin leaned in, his chin hairs twitching. "Did you two find a place to live?"

"No," a saddened sigh parted her lips. "Not yet."

The blade slipped between fur and flesh easily. The squirrels were at once ready to skewer. She didn't feel like making stew with all the vegetables. Charlotte wanted to be off her feet and maybe take a nap.

A yawn burst out of her lips.

"Maybe you go lay down until this is cooked," said Edwin.

Charlotte nodded and slunk off to her and Albert's bed. She found sleep quickly. But soon Albert woke her, insisting she boil some potatoes or make muffins from them. He had become accustomed to eating vegetables, especially during their journey to Kobiton and back. Potato muffins had been their midday meal, every day during their arduous hike there and back.

Slowly Charlotte slunk from their bed and performed her cooking duties, if only to return to the bed without eating a bite. Fatigue from all their hiking had taken over, begging for her to succumb to rest—to recharge her depleted body.

**27**

# <u>Echoes Of Fear</u>

Albert had missed the mines, the coolness they brought on sweltering summer days. Missed being encircled by the bleak chambers—dark like his aspirations. Being in Kobiton, around all the madness of every noise, made him realize what he loved the most about the mountains: quiet solitude. Yes, the wind howled, but nothing like the people jabbering and the metallic resonance of the city.

Going back to work, chiseling and harnessing his Metalist Power, Albert finally felt his shoulders soften. He had missed these circular caverns, the dankness of it all, but not the smell. Amid his work, Albert longed to feel the mid-summer breeze, warm and sweet with flowers and pine. There would never be a breeze in these corridors. At least, here he felt at peace; the fast-paced world beyond the mountaintops was almost forgotten.

Yet his thoughts about it all, and what Charlotte had done to him, weighed heavily on his mind. Maybe it too was pulling down his shoulders. He could not help his sourness toward her for lying to him, not telling him of her telepathic Powers.

*We mated. She is growing our babies. Will they have her Powers? Or mine? Or will they be combined to make some worse type of creature?*

Albert kept glaring at Jebadia, a knot of disillusionment at the base of his gut.

"How did you know?" Albert finally burst, "How did you know she was a Witchtress? Was River one too? Is that how you knew what Charlotte would do to me?"

Jebadia's face darkened. "I saw it from the beginning—the way she bent minds with her sweetness, her food, her stories. Just like River did. Women with Power cannot be trusted. They strip everything from you until there is nothing left."

"But why did you not warm me sooner?"

"Why I … I tried you dumb clot. I tried. But you … you were already under her spell." Jebadia spat. "Now you see—every smile, every kiss was manipulation. The sooner you accept that, the sooner you will be free."

"Your warnings were nothing more than stupid stories about a whore of a woman."

"River was not a whore. She was a seamstress who twisted minds and hearts. I told you!"

Albert's hand flexed, wanting to tighten into a ball, wanting to feel Jebadia's flesh smashed against it. Yet he refrained. "Why did you allow Charlotte to live if you knew of such deception?"

"Because you would have defended her. Edwin would have defended her too. Then I would have had to kill you both."

"I would have killed you first."

"That Witchtress has had Edwin under her teeth this whole time. That was how she came to be here. She saw an opportunity to use us, our powers."

"I did not think she used us like that."

"It is true. Ever since the moment she laid eyes on you, you were ensnared in her trap. Dumb clot. I knew this would happen, had to let it happen. You never would have learned this lesson otherwise. Surely did not listen to anything I had to say, acted like you knew more. That is how I know you are the dumbest of all the clots."

Albert snarled, "Had you framed your stories in a better way, I might have listened better."

Jebadia slapped Albert with his open hand. The finger marks were hot on the young man's face. He did not rebuke, only cowered.

"You would not have listened to any of my stories, no matter how they were said. You never listen to me!" Again, his hand struck Albert. "Ungrateful child. You always have been, always will be."

Albert's hair covered his sullen eyes. "I feel such shame, father. I should have known you were trying to steer me right. It is just …."

Jebadia grinned menacingly. "You should always listen to me. I know more than you ever will."

Albert looked at his father, hoping he would share his knowledge, finally ready to receive his elder's musings. But the old man went back to working his blade, rotating it further into the newly carved cavern, trying to make smooth the walls and ceiling.

"What type of woman would you have picked for me?"

Jebadia grunted, not offering his opinion for once. "Do you still love her? Or should we kill the cunt and find a woman more worthy of you, of us?"

The knot in his stomach was now traveling deeper into his gut, twisting harder as it went. Albert still loved Charlotte, although it was muddy love. Had she not been pregnant, it might have been easier to cast aside his feelings for her, but she was carrying their children. For better or worse, he wanted to expand the family, wanted to know what it was like to be a father.

"Ah," Jebadia broke Albert's momentary solace. "You should stab that pain you feel for her because it is not your feeling. She planted it there, trying to deter your mind, corrupt you into believing her and not me, not your family—your own flesh and blood. She wants to destroy all that we have created here. That was her plan all along, but you were too stupid to realize it. She has had you ever since the beginning, and until she is dead, she will continue to have you, to haunt you ... taunt you. I say we kill the cunt and throw her bloated body to the wolves. You know, her children will be just like her; nothing like you."

"No!" emotions swinging like a pendulum, Albert came at his father.

Jebadia knew it would happen and moved out of the way, tripping Albert. The young man slipped and fell onto his chin, scraping it. Blood clung to his meager chin-hairs. He wiped away the gravels, but the red liquid streaked his arm. He looked at his bloody arm, angered by the outcome.

One hard slap, and then five more came at him, knocking him back down. "Until you understand her spell, you will never be free from it."

Albert accidentally bit his lip, spit out that blood, glared up at his father, hovering over him. "How? How do I break it, break her spell?"

"Kill her. You must kill her to be rid of her spell."

The idea shocked him. He did not want to be so cruel to Charlotte, maybe banishing her once the children were out, but outright murdering her .... It just seemed wrong. She had been kind and caring, soft and helpful. Was it so wrong of him to want a different outcome for Charlotte?

"If you cannot kill her, I will."

"No," his breath escaped him. "I will kill her." Albert's shoulders tightened once more. He could not imagine himself killing Charlotte. Yes, she had taken his mind and heart, and corrupted every part of him, but was she so worthy of death?

It was here, now, when Albert wished he had left Charlotte in Kobiton, but then how would he have claimed his children? How would he raise them without her?

Albert, swept away by a torrent of feelings, pondered just how manipulative she had been. Perhaps she was sincere in everything she did. All the talk about emotions, a sense of belonging, empathy, love, and equal partnership might have been real. Their shared dream of living separate from his family, yet staying close, could have been their future.

*No. What I feel, everything I have ever wanted, all of it, was cultivated by Charlotte. I am sure of it. This is all her fault. I should have ....* He did not know what he should have done, only what he couldn't face: Charlotte.

Albert's voice barely rose above a whisper. "Do you think our children will have her Powers?"

"Of course they will, unless our Powers are stronger than hers. That is why your mother was Mortal. After River, I knew better. I warned you not to. But she wanted this, that Witchtress wanted you, used you. Took everything from you. From us. All this was contrived, and just as she wanted. I bet she wanted to take you away from us, use you, to steal more of your seed, milk you of your livelihood until you were dead. That cunt knew what you were capable of and still wants to exploit you." Jebadia spat. "I am disappointed that you did not see her spells. One can only hope our Power wins out, conquers her sabotage of you. Until then, you must stand next to her until she has birthed what is ours. Once that happens—"

His head hung more after hearing Jebadia's venomous words.

"Are all women like that?"

"Yes," Jebadia replied. "All of them."

"Then why couple with them?"

"Two men cannot create life; it takes a woman and a man to do so. Had she been meeker, more ... more Mortal, you would not have to do what you must when the time comes."

"What do you mean?"

"Once she is done being a host to your children ...." The look in Jebadia's silvery reflective eyes said it all. He was not afraid of killing a woman and taking what was rightfully theirs.

"Edwin said nothing about killing the mothers, only the female Metalist babies, if there are any."

Jebadia's head swiveled from side to side almost too fast. His face flushed, and those menacing teeth jutted out. "Women are not good for anything other than reproduction. Once we have what we want, we cut them out of our lives. One way or another. You understand? They are no good."

He tried to understand Jebadia's rage. "But you did not kill River. Edwin said you left her."

"Indeed. She was not worthy enough to contain our offspring. She got what she deserved."

"But you left her. Why did you not kill her? Why must I kill Charlotte?"

Albert saw Jebadia flinch.

"River was already ruined. She did not need my help. Her life was doomed. She was a whore, got what she deserved."

He was trying to understand. "But you said she was a seamstress, a Witchtress. Now she is a whore?"

Jebadia's lips twisted tighter than before. "River got what she deserved. Now get back to work!"

Again, Albert was hit. He lowered his brow, kept his eyes on the floor or the cavern walls, and refused to meet his father's glower. Confusion rattled around in his mind, along with rage and sadness. Once they were done with their daily toils, instead of returning home to eat the warm meal presented, Albert slipped away from his family. He was afraid to shed what little bit of love he still had for Charlotte. It was hard for him to comprehend how easy it had been for Jebadia to toss away someone who he had loved, who had loved him. Adamantly, Albert didn't want to turn his back on Charlotte, but had to get through the quagmire of thoughts and feelings that he was drowning in.

# 28

# <u>BREAKING POINT</u>

After supper one evening, Charlotte came to Albert's side. He held his empty bowl, staring vacantly at her warm Erthin fire. Jebadia had retired already, Edwin too.

"Are you done?" Her sweet voice seemed to wake him up.

Albert grunted, "Yeah." He then looked up at her as she rescued the dish and spoon from his grasp and placed them in a bucket. Surveying the mostly quiet room, he stood and bounced over to her, grabbing her arm and pulling Charlotte out of their cavernous homestead, ushering her outside and into the cooling nighttime air.

"Why did you pick me to manipulate?"

"Manipulate? What are you ... I don't manipulate, Albert."

"Horseshit. You have manipulated me since the beginning. Edwin too. And somehow only my father can see it. How did you do it without ...? How come I cannot see your power of influence?"

She was taken aback. "You're still angry that I had to keep your impulses silent, that I kept you from erupting in Kobiton!"

"You have manipulated me all along. Using words like; love, happiness, fondness ... hope. I never knew those words until you came, and I am sure they are myths, stories like everything else you have told me about. Has everything I have ever felt been of your doing?"

"What, how could I ...? It's bullshit and you know it, Albert. I've not manipulated you. Love. Happiness. Fondness. They are all words, emotions, we both experienced because of each other. They are true feelings, not fake words, not something I conjured for you to feel. Everything you've felt inside was already there. You'd just never felt it before. And the only time I've used my Powers on you was in Kobiton; and only to keep the harmonies from wrecking you. Why are you behaving like this?"

"Yes, you have. You have twisted my mind and heart with your words, your spells. On top of it all, you took my seed. All for your amusement."

She gasped. "I've done none of that. Is that what you believe? That I've manipulated you this whole time."

"I know it is true. You took Edwin the moment you touched him. And you did the same thing to me too."

She cackled, "If anyone's manipulated you, it's your father, not me."

"All the things I have felt were all implemented by you."

"Holy Hakra! You really should stop listening to your father. He knows nothing about love or happiness. He's trying to twist my words, shake up your mind. He's never liked me, and you know it. You should be mad at him for keeping you from knowing about the world."

He pointed at her. "This is all your fault. Everything is your fault."

"Culpable much?"

"What does that mean?"

She waved her hand in his face. "You're naïve Albert. You'll always be naïve. That's how your family wants you to be. They don't want you to question them, question everything. They just want you to follow, do as told. It's all horseshit, and you know it."

"You have manipulated me far too long, Charlotte. And this ... this is the last time."

Hands on her hips, her glare was as firm as her stance. "What happened to us? To you? I didn't think you'd ever be this way with me."

For a moment, Albert's resolve wavered. Looking at her face—the face he had once thought more beautiful than the sunrise—he saw flashes of their happiness together. The walks by the underground lake, her laughter echoing off the stones, the gentle way she had taught him about the world beyond their cave. A part of him wanted to reach for her, to apologize, to believe her.

Then he remembered the hazy sensation in Kobiton, the fog over his mind that she had put there. He remembered the captain's words, his father's warnings. The captain had seen it immediately—what had taken Albert months to realize.

"I trusted you," he said, his voice breaking. "I gave you everything I had to give. And all this time, you were ...." He couldn't finish the thought.

"Albert, please," Charlotte whispered, reaching for him. "What we had—what we have—it's real."

But as he looked at her, all he could think was: *how would I know?*

"I've always been honest with you, open to you. You're the one who wants to be limited, to be shut off from everything, everyone. Jebadia and Edwin did you no good service by keeping you away from the rest of the world. Shielding you from the things that make us all human. Why don't you accept the things I've done for you? Why don't you remember what all we've done, what we are when we're together? Do you really hate me? Or is this all your father's revenge? Because I ... I still love you, Albert. I love you with all my heart and soul and you're trying to stunt that, shun it because it doesn't feel right, that the words are foreign to you. Of course, it's not something you've ever felt before. You'd never feel those feelings because of your family.

"But what we have ... it's real. Everything you've ever felt in my presence wasn't made from my desires, but from your own desires ... from your want to experience something different than what you've been taught. Why won't you accept that fact? Or has your father manipulated you beyond recognition?"

"Because everything you have done was all for you! You never thought about me, about what I wanted." She cackled loudly; it echoed down to the treetops. Albert snarled, "Why do you laugh at me? I should cut you and leave you for dead."

Charlotte took a step back. "Do you really feel that way? Do you want to kill me before our children have a chance to live? Do you really want to get rid of me that much? Cauterize all the feelings we've had for one another and throw me away like I'm a used rag?" He flinched. "You don't want to do that. I can see it."

"Stop telling me what I want, what I should feel. I am done with it all. You have had your way with me far too long, Charlotte. When those children are born, I am taking what is mine, leaving you with nothing."

She looked ready to cry. "How did this happen? Why do you let your father's attitude, his reflection of the world, corrupt what you see, what you feel? He was abused and neglected as a child. Papa Edwin told me what happened to your father, how he was abused by the people who he had been left with. Your father's view of the world is shit. But that doesn't mean yours must be too." She reached out to him, yet seemed afraid to touch him. "Please Albert, don't be this way. I still love you. I want to be with you. Just you. Not Papa Edwin, and definitely not your father. What happened to our ideas for a future together? You know I don't want to be here with them, with your family. I just want to be here with you. They don't understand our love. Maybe they're jealous. But it really doesn't matter to me. What matters is that we love each other, like we did. Unconditionally. At least we …. Please, Albert."

"You have corrupted me for too long," he shouted and remained beyond an arm's length from her.

"Corrupted …? If anything, your father's corrupted you. He wants you to be bitter and lonely, like he is. Don't fall for it." Her fingers wiggled. "If I had corrupted you, we wouldn't be here. We would be in Kobiton, and you wouldn't know any different. But I'm not like that. Never have been. I want you to be you, Albert, the same you that you were when we first met." She huffed. "I hate this. It's like everything that's happened since Kobiton has been corrupted by … by, I don't know what. But probably the influence of your father's negativity. All the things you think I've been doing are all falsely based. I haven't manipulated you to feel or do anything you don't want to. If anything, I've taught you about who you could become if you weren't …. Everything you've felt originated from within you, not from anything I've done. Do you understand? I'm not that type of person."

"Horseshit! You've manipulated me since I first laid eyes on you."

"Oh, really! How?" Her green eyes were bright and curious.

He kept breathing hard, like an overworked horse. Steam flew out of his nostrils, dissipating into the nighttime sky.

"You don't believe what you say. You're only repeating the stupid shit your father told you." She shook. "You should really stop listening to that old coot. He's done nothing but turn you into an angry ball of energy ready to explode."

His lips puckered; his dark eyebrows looked like a straight line across his pained face.

"See. Even now you just want to explode." She huffed, glanced down the rocky slope. "I don't know why we returned here. We could've made a home in the forest. Something close to town. But you wanted to be around your people who you believe have kept you strong. It's not true. They've kept you weak, barren of hope and happiness. Why would you want to be here, stay here in this place, be influenced by these people, especially your father?"

"You … you do not see it, but you are a Witchtress, through and through."

Again, she laughed at him, louder and longer than before. Albert slapped Charlotte.

"You are a vile Witchtress and deserve what is coming."

She licked the blood off her lips. "May Hakra doom you—"

Albert would not allow her anymore words and struck her again. "You shut up. Keep your lips closed tight, and your hands away from me. You hear me!"

She stood tall, almost as tall as he was. Her fingers wiggled, angrily. He sensed an unknown yet powerful energy fluttering around her fingertips. The look in her eyes told Albert that he might have overstepped boundaries.

She looked ready to end his life—could have easily stolen it using her Succubus Power. Yet, in that moment, Charlotte faltered. Her love for him kept her from using her deadly power, from taking his life.

He sensed her change and made his expression even more menacing. He wanted her to know that he was in charge and would always be. He wanted her to cower; yearned to see her on her knees and begging forgiveness. Her chin dropped; her soft hair occluded her face. Her hands went up to her eyes.

A sob parted her lips. "I don't want us to be like this, Albert. Please. Think of our children. Our babies need both of us. Please, I don't want .... I'm sorry. I don't know what I can do, what I must say to .... Please, I just want us to be how we were. I'm sorry I had to dull you, kept you from .... Please, forgive me."

Watching her crumple wrenched his gut. He hit his stomach before hitting her. "Stop making me feel this way," He shouted.

"I ... I-I'm not doing anything. What you're feeling ... it's all you. I can't influence you like you think I can."

He hit his own stomach one more time, screamed out in pain, then slapped her again and left Charlotte. He didn't return to the warm cave, and took off at a quick pace, wanting to distance himself from her, from his family, from his feelings.

*I hate myself.*

# 29

## <u>A New Start</u>

The forest was thicker on the western side of the Kruluver Mountains. Albert preferred the smell of the pines over the bad egg smell of the caves. This high up, on clear days and when the fog had rolled in down in the valleys, the view looked like an endless ocean with piercingly tall mountaintop islands everywhere and in rows. It was a spectacular sight when caught all day long, but the air was still chilly.

Albert had left home, not permanently—though there were some days he wanted to leave forever. It was his second day of being outside and with no one else. He yearned for this confidence, yet he shook when realizing what type of risk he was taking.

"We Metalists must stick together." Jebadia's words always echoed.

He hated hearing the narrow-minded nagging, but worse, he hated repeating it—speaking it aloud. There was such anger that dwelled just under his surface. Anger at his father, Charlotte, and Papa Edwin. They had all failed him in one way or another. Whether it be harsh opinions, hiding life-threatening secrets, or revealing horrific family trauma, Albert had a hard time discerning it all. But none of it seemed to matter anymore. Albert felt betrayed by them all.

Leaving home behind and taking this long walk had helped him forget. Helped him relax. Until nighttime descended. It had been cold last night, and the fire he made refused to stay brighter than embers. Albert missed Charlotte's warmth; her raging fires that never seemed to dim.

*But she uses magic, evil magic. Father says ... Father says. I sound like a child. A dumb clot of a child. She called me a man, but maybe I am still just a child. I have just seen twenty winters, counting this last one. At least, that is what Edwin tells me. He and his stupid counting sticks.*

He snorted and believed he could hear Charlotte rebuke, "They're not stupid. Quite smart, actually. Let's you know things about the world around you that you wouldn't have thought of until you make notches on a stick."

His anger towards her boiled up again. His back muscles felt like thick columns holding up shoulders that were ready to wither. And then an icy breeze found a minor break in his warm clothing at the back of his neck. He shuddered.

*I must stop thinking about all of them.* He grunted and picked up his pace. The sun was about to dip into the foggy ocean; the temperatures were already falling. He had spied an outcropping to camp on, but Albert wouldn't make it there until after the sun was gone.

A few of the stars were quick to appear and guide his way. As he came around a gentle turn in the mountainside, Albert saw a much better, safer place to camp. It was a cave with a crescent moon opening. He was above the tree line, and far above the swampy fog that hadn't left the surrounding valleys for days now.

Excited feelings bubbled forth, and he paused to feel these percolations. They felt reminiscent of how he felt when he first met Charlotte, like having a hiccough caught in your diaphragm, but in a good way. It was these emotions that had been beaten down by his father, yet showered and encouraged by Charlotte, that confused him the most. And asking Edwin about such things would only trigger the old man into 'back in my day' rants that bored Albert. He didn't know that the old man was trying to teach him through such conversations, and would easily tire and just stare off, not paying attention at all! But maybe he should have.

All Albert knew was that when he was by himself, now, he felt more alive than he did when around any of them. Especially now that he had found what he was looking for. A new home.

He was cautious when entering the cave, shouting first. His voice barely echoed, caught the back of the cave too quickly for it to reverberate on and on like it did at home. His breath caught, saddened that this cave wasn't just an entrance into some other new world he could explore.

*No, but it is a place I can make my own. And no one has to know.*
*What about Charlotte?*

He didn't respond to that voice in his head. Hated listening to that voice. What about her? She seemed to be doing fine. Papa Edwin was doting on her last time Albert had seen them. She had the old letch to do her bidding; why did she need Albert?

He pulled off his pack, was glad to not have his donkeys, yet sad that he had brought none of them with him. Albert had taken off with only a few things in his packs, not knowing he would be gone this long. But this walk felt different from the last one. This one he had set into his mind that he would find a cave.

"Found it! This is my cave. No one else!" He cackled and worked at his bundle of branches and twigs he had gathered. With his stash of dead squirrels and bundle of wood, he would eat and sleep better than he had the previous night.

As he sat there cooking up his food, Albert could not recall the reason he hadn't gone back home last night.

*I did not want to. I wanted to feel the cold, feel the same on the outside as I feel inside. Just cold.*

*But last night I got too cold. It was cold; a bitterness I refuse to feel again. Tonight, I want warmth. And I have it.*

He smiled, and those excitable feelings in his stomach surfaced again. He punched his gut. "Stop doing that. I am no longer under your spell. Vile Witchtress. Now stop it!"

"Why do you hit yourself?" Albert could hear Charlotte's questions. "Why are you being cruel to yourself? That is something your father might do, but not you. You don't have to be like this. Be soft to yourself, understand that you don't have to have all the answers. None of us do."

"Shut up!" He shouted, that time his voice did echo, and angrily back at him. "Shut up! Get out of my head. Get out of my heart! You, Witchtress, get out of my life. You have ruined me. My mind, my everything! Go. Leave." He cried, then slumped alongside the warm fire.

The dancing of flames hypnotized him for a short time. He reached his hand toward the hot embers.

"I wish you had not come into my life, twisted my mind. I wish I had never seen your magic; wish you never told me your secrets. I love you, and wish I never knew the word. That way I could forget this feeling I have. I do not want it, yet it wants me. It wants me to remember you, us, how we once were, how I wish we still were. I wish .... I wish ...."

He could still feel her softness, her kindness. He wanted it all back in his life, yet he was afraid to accept the fact that Charlotte was as powerful as he was—maybe more. He wanted to be the powerful one, the one who brought peace, who brought the food. She was the one who had to cook it and tend to the family—at least that was what he had been told yet never encountered in his lifetime. He hadn't known what a woman really looked like until meeting Charlotte.

Images of her smiling at him, at different times in their brief life together, surfaced and brought with it a rush of emotions he wasn't ready to feel. Again, Albert hit himself in the face this time.

"Stop it. Stop it. Stop feeling this way. None of this helps. It only hinders. Leave me alone. Just stop it!"

His voice didn't echo at all that time. He was facing the mouth of the cave and still lying next to the fire. A sob parted his lips, and then Albert hit himself once more.

"No crying!" Albert yelped at himself, as Jebadia spoke through him.

Instantly, Albert fell mute. Once again, his eyes were on the leaping flames and tiny embers that flew up into the chilly air to die. He shoved all those thoughts and emotions aside, concentrating on the fire, ignoring all his other discomforts.

*I should just stay here. Stay here and make my own home. This would be a good place to start. And I can chisel it wider. Though it would be easier to do it with another Metalist, I could probably do it. Make this place into a suitable home for me.*

He forbade himself to think about Charlotte at that moment.

*Yes, a suitable home. And once those babies are out, I will bring them here and they will be mine. And I will raise them better than father or Edwin did with me. I will be a better father than they ever were. And we can hunt mountain goats and squirrels. And I will teach them about our Powers, let them hold as much metal as they want. I will not place such restrictions on them as my predecessors have. I will ... I will ....*

It was the sizzling of the squirrels that brought his attention back into the cave, and the eminent meal.

# 30

## <u>WINTER'S APPROACH</u>

Summer's heat faded, and the valleys were mottled with red, orange, and yellow hues. Most days the sky was occluded by clouds, but sometimes they sat above the fluffy layer. Lately, though, it had been pouring rain, and for many days. Charlotte's belly grew rounder with each passing week. The cave's chill reminded her that winter—and with it, the babies' arrival—was drawing near.

One evening, as Charlotte prepared supper, she noticed Papa Edwin at his usual spot by the fire, carefully adding another notch to his counting stick. That small cutout was longer than most of the notches.

"It is official. It has been four moons since your morning sickness ended," the old man mused. "That means you are now seven moons along. The babies grow fast, like Faith's and Tayla's babies did. Metalist children always grow big and come early."

Charlotte touched her swollen belly. "How can you be sure?"

"I have seen it many times now. I believe it is the metal in our blood that grows them strong and quick. I am sure you will deliver before the deepest snows come."

"I hope so." She chuckled, "Though I really wanted to give birth in that meadow of flowers."

"Indeed, a pretty scene. It is better this way. That way, when summer comes, you can be out enjoying the meadow with those babies, as opposed to being hot and bothered by it all, like you were this year."

"Ugh. Yeah, that was the worst; hot and pregnant. Thankfully, there are those cool pools to enjoy, but you might be right. It'll be nice to be out in the wildflowers when the children are further along."

She paused, her sight far off, looking towards that distant future. She wanted to feel joy, her soul to lift even just a hair width. She dreamed of her and her babies lying in the warmth, flowers swaying, bees buzzing around—giggles galore.

"Indeed, you will enjoy it."

"What was your first wife like?"

He sat back on the rock and peered up at the ceiling, trying to recall her, or maybe trying to forget. Papa Edwin wiped the corners of his eyes. "Her name is a distant memory. I believe it was Malai ... or was it Moli ...." He shook his head. "She had sisters, was the youngest of four, they all had children before she did, so she seemed to know what to do with bearing and raising children.

"Her sisters and her were like a gaggle of wild turkeys when together. Their voices seemed to rise above one another, as if haggling for a piece of meat or something. I can still hear them now, going wild over a trinket I made for Malai. Found an agate, a good-sized one, and placed it into a metal setting. Simple, but there was no way that rock would ever budge. The necklace it was fixed to looked like a single circular piece of silver. It moved but shown off her neckline ...." He grinned coyly. "She had a smile that matched the color of that agate, just as bright.

"Molia ... whatever her name was ... she was meek. She did well serving others, and she took pride in watching over her many nieces and nephews. It was sitting there watching her watch them. That was what gave me the courage to ask her to marry me, to have my children. I could see that she had compassion and an enduring nature, someone who was earnestly in love with being around children.

"She loved our children dearly. Every day, she would kiss their noses and play finger games. You know, sing songs with your fingers, like ... like," He sat there for a long moment trying to recall any of her songs. "We were glad to have her sisters around to support us when she became pregnant. Two of them had twins before, knew exactly what to expect, which was good, comforting for her and myself. I mean, I knew nothing about any of it. She was the first woman I had relations with outside of GnSaan. But maybe that is what drew her to me. My innocent charm," they both chuckled.

"It was the saddest day of my life when our little girl struck down Molia. I came home, and she was there, bled out, our little Gunter wailing at her side; Kebrii was nowhere to be found. I raised hell to find her. But when she found me, I ... I-I did what I should have done to begin with. Her unkempt Power .... A travesty it was."

She could sense his sadness and tried not to absorb it. That he had ended so many little girls' lives was a burden she didn't want to bear, yet it rode her like an ornery donkey.

Charlotte's fingers were warm against the old man's weathered hand. "I hope it's not a burden your family must continue."

"Me too Sweet Miss, me too."

As Charlotte shifted, Edwin's hand automatically moved to rest on her belly, feeling the babies move. His expression was tender, but then one of the twins kicked hard against his palm. Something changed in his eyes—a flicker of ancient fear. His other hand unconsciously drifted to the knife at his belt, fingers tightening around the hilt. Charlotte noticed, and their eyes met. Edwin forced his hand away from the weapon, smiling apologetically. "Old habits," he murmured, not quite meeting her gaze. "The mind knows what the heart sometimes forgets."

· · · · ● · ● · · ·

"Albert, can I have your help?" She called, and he groaned.

"What do you want?" He looked at her, but didn't move.

She was having a hard time reaching the top shelf where the jars of preserves were stored. She huffed, "Are you going to be like this the whole time?"

"The whole time what?"

"While I'm pregnant. Hakra, you don't ever just do things to be nice. Why must I always prod you do to things, to be nice to me?"

Albert only glared at her.

Charlotte tried to wipe the frustration from her face. "Just please, get that jar." She stepped back, hoping he would get up off his seat.

Instead, Albert just stared at her. "When did you become incapable of getting things?"

Her mouth hung; eyes bulged. Charlotte looked for Papa Edwin, who had momentarily left the homestead. She was glad Jebadia was not there either. "Maybe you should do it because I need help. I cannot stand on anything without fear of wobbling and falling. Please."

He ignored her plea.

"What of our children? Do you not care about them? Do you really want something bad to happen to them? To me? When did you stop loving me?"

He blinked and began to move.

"I would like to think that you love our children, even if you don't love me anymore."

"It is not that I do not love you, it is just ...."

"Your actions speak louder than your words, Albert. I can tell that you've fallen out of love with me, or worse, you've been listening to your father and now believe the horseshit he spews."

"Stop manipulating me, you Witchtress."

"I'm not a Witchtress! Why can't you just ...." She watched him leave their hollowed-out home.

Slowly and carefully, Charlotte managed her way onto the countertop, and gingerly reached and grabbed the last canister of blackberry preserves.

• • • • • • • • • •

Charlotte's pregnancy weighed heavily on her, both physically and emotionally. Only Edwin offered her any relief, despite criticism from the others. And when Charlotte reached for Albert as he passed, he flinched away—his eyes cold. Without a word, he gathered his belongings and moved them to the far side of the cave, leaving Charlotte alone in what had once been their shared space.

Charlotte missed the man she had fallen in love with. She cried a lot, but made sure no one ever saw or heard her. At least she had memories of their time together, traversing down the slope reciprocating heartfelt passion. She often wondered if those feelings would ever return. If maybe he was just too overwhelmed by her and when the babies came, things would get better, he would return to normal. She didn't want to use her powers of persuasion to make him love her. She was sure he had always loved her. Or had Albert's love for her had been mistaken for lust? It was too hard to tell, too sad to recall.

Time wore on.

Charlotte slept more now, doing less around the cave than she wanted. Her conscious, and the men, nagged at her, but her body helped resist the urge to move. Yet she knew she needed to move. It was one of the core principles for a healthy pregnancy—under Hakran authority, that is. There were many lessons taught to the girls about reproduction, and how to have a safe and healthy pregnancy was written with high regard for a woman's life. She followed those rules to a fault, not wanting any complications when the time came.

• • • • • • • • • •

Edwin was acutely aware of her pains.

One day in early autumn, he took her to Chinochi. The walk down the hillside was not as devastating as the journey to Kobiton had been. A nice reprieve from the stone walls that generally surrounded. The donkeys carried all their belong-ings. Charlotte appreciated being burden-free, save for the sturdy walking stick in her hand. Although it usually took Edwin a long day to arrive, they stopped often for Charlotte. It was that ravine where they first met, where they made camp for the night. Under a brilliant canopy of stars, they slept. She awoke feeling more refreshed than she had in quite some time. Charlotte valued this time with Edwin; his compassion for including her in this trip to town filled her heart.

They arrived in Chinochi mid-morning the next day, and only stayed long enough to drop off coal, pick up necessary items. There was a new owner to the mercantile, another Telepath, but he didn't look like one. He was young and slender and smiled very little. He watched her and Edwin stalk up and down each aisle. She listened to him talking with the other Telepaths about her. They were all impressed by her belly bulge and speculated about Edwin being the father.

A male voice said, *She was probably a whore and did what whores do.*

*Too bad we couldn't have kept her here.* A deeper masculine voice spoke, *made accommodations for her. She could've coupled with one of the men at the forge, or one of us.*

*Does anyone know what Powers she holds, beyond her Erthin Abilities?* Asked the Merchant. His voice was easy to notice—nasally and annoying.

*We were told she's got telepathic tendencies.*

*A telepathic Erthin ....*

*Breed her with a Clan-Duin, make some future Wardens.*

It was hard to ignore all the mental chatter. Charlotte chuckled at them, and kept her own thoughts focused on the list of foods she wanted to purchase. It was a long list, and their markets had only a few open tables along the main avenue. She missed Kobiton's market, the colorful clothing, spicy aromas and the crowds. She had forgotten about these dirty, muddy roads. Charlotte missed the cobbled streets of Kobiton, free of dust and animal refuse. Her boots were caked in mud and muck and would need to be washed once their trip was over.

Returning to this place made her realize how gritty and stinky and unkempt these people were—comparable to the lifestyle she now lived. Chinochi would never become anything like Kobiton—not in her lifetime.

At least this break from the monotony of her daily routine lifted her spirits and would give her a few happy memories. Charlotte was appreciative that someone in her life wanted to bring her joy, even if it was only momentary. And Edwin did everything in his power to make her happy.

Their trek home was cumbersome.

They paused along the trail often. She was out of breath the whole climb. Edwin took it all in stride. He was happy to make camp whenever she wanted.

It took two and a half days to hike home.

Although she didn't want to return to their cavernous homestead, in the end, Charlotte was happy to curl up in her warm bed. Her back and feet burned from soreness. Only Edwin offered to massage her aches away.

They bought many goodies, including a rocking chair, several reams of warm cloth, and more knitting supplies. All these gifts would keep her spirits up as the light of autumn waned and the drizzling days of early winter cloaked the land.

# 31

## <u>BLOOD & IRON</u>

"What is with her? All those swatches of cloth and her needles and thread and yarn. All of it ... Why?"

"Women need to nest," Edwin calmly replied. "It is an instinct."

"Why?"

"Why do squirrels nest? Why do birds nest? It is all for comfort, boy. All for comfort. Those first few moons, once the babies are out, will be the hardest for Charlotte, for all of us. It is why I will purchase a few extra goats, hopefully ones that are already pregnant."

"Extra goats ... why?"

"Goat's milk. It is what you were raised on. It is good for babies. Keeps you healthy while you are growing."

Albert stared at his grandfather. "Charlotte told me babies drink breast milk. I saw her boob dripping once. It was gross."

"Yes. Oh, yes, we will use her milk, but if she has issues, or cannot make enough .... We will make sure there will be enough milk for both babies." The old man must have noticed Albert's apprehension. "Most likely Charlotte will make enough, but it is good to have extra on hand. You drank your weight in milk every day for many days."

"Was that before or after you killed my mother and sister?"

"Your mother died birthing your sister."

"That is a lie. You told me you killed her with your own two hands. You killed both of them all because she bore a girl. I remember it, remember you telling me everything. I was only eight. Eight! Do not deny it, old man. You ruined me that day, and for every day thereafter. I will always remember those words."

Edwin turned red, and his lips vibrated when he exhaled. "Yes, I killed her. But it was for the best. Your mother was a wretched woman, not a good person. How she was to all of us, but especially to Jebadia ...."

"Was she just like Charlotte?"

"No! Charlotte is a good person. Better than your mother ... she had never been shown kindness. And maybe that is what drew Jeb to her. But understand, Charlotte is a good woman, the best one yet!"

"You are just saying that because Charlotte has your mind. Has since the beginning."

"Charlotte does not have that type of power. She does not control my mind. That is not the type of person she is."

"Yes, she is. And yes, she does! That is what she did to me. She stole my mind! That is why I cannot approach her anymore. She is a Witchtress through and through. She took my mind, made me feel ... made me feel weak. She could have commanded me to do anything!"

The old man held back, studying Albert. "But did she? Did she command you to do things against your will?"

"No. But ... well, yes. Yes, she did. She made me ignore the urge to listen to ... to orchestrate metallic melodies. She made me not .... Okay, yes, Kobiton is not a place any of us should go if we want to be cracked like that, but I should have had a choice."

Edwin reached for Albert, grabbed his wrist, pulsated his magnetic Metalistic Power. "When you own your metal, you own your mind. No Telepath can ever take that from you. Understand. She does not have my mind, nor does she have yours. Now get that ugly thought out of your dumb, clotted mind."

Albert pulled free, glowered. "You are lying. She has your mind. Always has."

Again, his magnetic energy pulsated. "I do not lie. That is what children do when they get caught doing naughty things."

"Bah! Naughty. You are naughty! You never told me about people like Charlotte. Or brown-skinned people. Or the ones with wild, crazy red hair like the sun and dots all over their skin. Repulsive they were. You hid all those truths like a snail sucked up in its shell. You lied to me. Your truths are not factual truths, they are just like the stories you have spun in your mind, old man."

Edwin took a step back, eyeballing his grandson. "You are too much like your father."

"Good! He does not lie, like you have. I have found he is more correct than you, about many things. Should have listened to him more and you less."

"Your father is a naïve man—"

"Shut it, old man." Albert raised his hand, readying to hit the old man.

Edwin pulsated his Power and pushed Albert back, feet raking the gravel. Had he not been prepared for something like this, he would have fallen over. Albert leaned into the magnetic thrust, and threw out his own, but Edwin took it into his own bubble, now pulling his grandchild in close enough that he could have wrung his neck.

Wrinkled fingers wiggled in front of Albert's face. "Charlotte is better than any other woman I have met. Much like River in that aspect. It is unfortunate that she did not tell us about her telepathic Abilities. But not all Telepaths are horrible. Some are kind. You need to respect her. Be kind to Charlotte. Help her when she asks for it. Understand?!"

Albert could barely breathe, but he could still snarl. "Did River have Power over you and fathers' minds? Is that why you constantly compare Charlotte to—"

"I am under no one's spell, boy. Maybe that is what your father wants you to believe. But that is not our reality. Charlotte is not like that."

He felt like he was choking but remained persistent. "How do you know?"

"I have met all the worst types of people, boy. Understand me when I say Charlotte is one of the good ones."

Albert continued to struggle under the weight of Edwin's Metalistic spell. "Are Witchtresses Telepaths? Was River a Telepath?"

Suddenly, Albert could breathe, and gasped and coughed.

"River was not a Telepath. She was a plain young woman desperate to get out of a shithole town, away from her abusive family, to make a better life for herself and those she surrounded herself with. River was a kind soul. She would have been the perfect ...." Edwin inhaled deeply, silvery eyes firm on Albert. "But Charlotte being Telepathic might complicate things a bit."

Albert drew close, wringing his hands and licking his lips. "How so?"

"She better have boys."

They stared at one another, measuring each other's response to that statement.

Edwin's tongue slapped his teeth when he said, "Because if she does not, it will be up to you to make the correct decision."

"Which is ...?"

"No female Metalists shall live. Ever!" In that moment, Edwin's wrath would have matched Jebadia's; his shadow grew behind him menacingly.

"Yes. Of course. I get it." Albert shriveled. "I will remember what to do."

"You better. You do not need to know the wrath of a Metalist woman, but especially one born with telepathy descending from her mother."

"Would the boys have the same defect?"

Edwin's head shook only once. "We have telepathy, but only with our twin. Female Metalist's have telepathy with us all regardless of her relationship to us. Now a female born with magnified telepathy, like yours might have. That would ...." The old man huffed, then snarled, "Just make sure you cut the head off any female, and there will be no problems. Understood!"

"What about Charlotte? If she protests ...."

Again, they assessed one another. "Let her protest. If she does, she can end up like the others. We will have goats for the milk. As long as we get a new generation of miners from her. What she says will not matter in the end." Edwin's grimace was menacing. This was the side of the old man Albert knew all about—Charlotte did not.

He hesitantly nodded. "Yes. Okay. I will do what I must." His hair fell across his eyes, hiding his soul-wrenching thoughts.

*How did it come to this?*

*I will have to murder my child if she is born a girl. And I will have to ... Charlotte. I cannot. I love her, it is just .... What do I do? Do I do what I must? Or ... or what?*

*There is no other way.*

*If a female Metalist is just as powerful as Charlotte is, but as a baby, I must. There is no other way. I refuse to feel like that again. And Charlotte will try to .... I do not want this. I just want ....*

*I wanted a family, but not like this.*

· · · ● · ● · ● · ·

Before Charlotte came into his life, Albert had not ventured far from the caves. But now, the outside world seemed to call to him whenever he felt confused. A walk amongst the pine trees and boulder fields gave him the time necessary to rescue his emotional self. It was on these walks that he forgot all his problems, his family, his wife and their expectant children. He roamed the steep mountain slopes, searching for the serenity he needed to continue living with people he now found inferior to himself.

Out here, his emotions fell away like dried autumn leaves. The cacophony of birds, howling winds, and slapping of tree branches filled his mind now. He returned to his secret homestead that was over half a day's hike away and was slowly—every few days—carving that small cave into a residence to be proud of.

While there, Albert tried not to think about Charlotte. Yet her verbal opinions would pop into his mind, like a nagging wife, insisting he make provisions for all her necessities too. He hoped she wasn't really there in his thoughts, listening in on his ideas, influencing him to do as she bid. But that fear clung tight to his shoulders and kept him rigid even in his sleep.

In this wonderful new residence, Albert now had his own cold storage, and a bed filled with pine branches and covered with a donkey hide. Although he hadn't yet brought any of his donkeys here, there was a space for them to live when the time came. Until then, he continued to toil to cut away from the interior, carving seats around his campfire ring and bedrooms, making it even more luxurious than the cavern he had grown up in.

*If she has boys, we will move here; leave my family behind.*

*What if she has a girl?*

He held his breath almost too long, eyesight blurring.

*She must have boys. If she does not ....*

Every time he thought about what he would have to do, his breathing quickened, and the tips of his fingers prickled as if they had been asleep. He hated to think about what he had to do; what his family had done to every little girl ever born.

*That will not be the case. She will give birth to boys. She must.*

*If she does not. I do not want to have to kill Charlotte too.*

His heart hurt from all the suffering of grief.

*How can I kill her? I cannot look at her. Not now. How could I kill her? She is my ....*

His gut fluttered, and he grabbed it.

*This is not how I wanted this to go. Any of it. We had so many ... were supposed to ....*

*But had she not taken my mind, I would never have known of her Powers, of her deceptions. I cannot allow her to take my mind ever again, making me weak. Yet it feels like she is still there, trying to manipulate how I think; how I feel.*

*I thought Edwin said that if I own my metal, Telepaths cannot harm me. I feel like she is still here with me. What am I doing wrong? How can I keep myself safe from her Powers? Her influence?*

He wanted to cry, but more so he wanted to be angry and scream.

*I hate Charlotte. I must. If I do not, then she has my mind again. She messes with my heart, my head. I must hate Charlotte. I cannot let her win, cannot let her in anymore.*

# 32

## <u>FORGIVENESS</u>

She wasn't sure when it started, but Charlotte noticed Papa Edwin appeared more invested in her condition now. As always, he did much to meet her needs, but this constant attention seemed driven by something she could not define. And when she brushed against him, tried to hear Papa Edwin's thoughts, his mind was still.

Albert, and to a lesser extent Jebadia, always seemed angry now—she suspected jealousy over the amount of energy Edwin gave Charlotte every day. The old man confessed to her he had never been like this with any other woman, including the ones he married. Because of this, Papa Edwin found himself bound to honor her in some way.

Edwin also admitted that he watched Charlotte's growing belly with a mixture of joy and dread. He had seen her fears reflected in previous mothers-to-be—the hope of a new life twisted by their Metalistic curse. She also noticed his hand unconsciously touched the knife at his belt more often, possibly remembering all the times he had to use it on his own flesh and blood. She tried to shake off the dread she felt, but it was claustrophobic at times.

"It's not your fault that I got pregnant, Edwin. It's my fault for falling in love with your grandson."

"I know Albert still loves you. He is just having problems with—"

"He called me a cow! He sounded just like Jeb would've. Exactly like him. I can't take his attitude anymore!"

"Well, it is all so very shocking for him to take in. Your belly has grown much in this last moon cycle. Every day you are larger, larger than any other woman I have seen grow Metalist babies. And for him, you are the first pregnant woman he has ever seen. He just is not used to this. Any of it."

"Are you fooling me? It's not like this just happened. He's been watching me bloat up since the beginning."

"It is a hard adjustment for the boy, especially when he did not understand what being pregnant meant."

She gasped. "It's a hard adjustment for me too. Doesn't he think about that? Ignoring me all the time only makes it worse. And if I tell him how I feel, he snaps at me. I'm done with it all."

"I understand. I too am sad that you were his first ... that we kept him so hidden from the world. It was never this way with Jeb, but I regretted raising him the way I did. I do not regret raising Albert this way."

"I know. I get it. I understand why you've raised him this way." She placed a warm hand on his fuzzy face. "I would too. Albert's a good man; he's just naïve. To be honest, that's what drew me to him. How childlike he was. How much I wanted to foster his growth into adulthood. But then ...."

"You have done much for my grandson, Sweet Miss. For all of us. I am sure he will be a good father when the time comes."

"It'd be nice if he was a good father now and supported me. I don't believe he's been looking for a new homestead for us. Like he said he would. I don't think he cares about any of it anymore, except for finding those damn precious ores. If he had that same determination for me, massaged my aches away, instead of you doing it all, that would be .... He should help me with my needs, our children's needs, as opposed to his own. It's not something you should be doing."

"He fears change, Sweet Miss."

Her cackle echoed around the room. "He's scared of change! He needs to understand that everything's gonna change really quick once these babies are out of me. And I'll never be the same. All of this—" She dramatically moved her hands around her torso. "—is gonna be different too, all stretched out and ugly. Pregnancy marks a woman, you know. There's no lack of change going on here!"

"This I know, Sweet Miss. And I think he now knows it too."

"Well, he surely doesn't act like it." She snorted. "I guess I can only hope for the best." *Meanwhile, prepare for the worst.*

"I will be here for you."

She softened, wanting a hug. "Thank you, Edwin." The old man reciprocated the gesture, but did not remain in the embrace for too long.

All of these thoughts tired Charlotte.

She gazed at her book of Tomes, ran her hand across the leather book cover. "I miss Kobiton. But I don't miss all the Hakran propaganda. You know, when the time comes, I look forward to teaching our children to read and write. But I'll tell them that these are just stories, things conjured by the mind of many people, for us to read, to learn from, to understand. They aren't real things that happened.

"I mean, there's no way it rained red for a thousand days. That it grew so dark and cold that life itself ceased to exist. And that by the gift of one brave soul, one amazingly blessed being that the world was set free from the darkness and life returned. I mean come on; these are all just stories." She held up the leather-bound book. "But they are ways to learn to read and write. That's all that matters to me."

Edwin's expression tightened almost imperceptibly. "Some stories, Sweet Miss, are warnings disguised as history." He studied her with an intensity that felt different from his usual warmth. "When we tell ourselves certain truths are merely stories, we often find ourselves repeating the very tragedies we dismissed." His voice dropped lower. "Trust me when I say some fears are earned through blood." The moment passed, and his familiar smile returned, though it didn't quite reach his eyes. "But yes, teaching the little ones to read—that will be a fine thing indeed. I look forward to that day too, Sweet Miss." He patted her hand, and they shared a long moment of quiet.

"Do you think he'll want to sleep with me tonight?"

"I do not know, Sweet Miss. You can always ask."

"I did last night, and he said no. I don't want to force him. I just wish ...."

"I know Sweet Miss, I know. Back when Jeb and Faith were together, pregnant with Albert and his twin, Faith felt the same way. Back then, Jeb behaved the same way Albert is now. This is nothing new. Besides, this is just a momentary feeling, that is all. It will pass. All of it will, and soon you will be happy and with those babies outside of you."

She knew Papa Edwin meant well, but didn't feel as positive about the outcome as he did.

• • • • • • • • • •

Beyond her rampant fears and insecurities, Charlotte hated her cloudy mind and emotionally wrung soul. She wanted to talk to Albert about how she felt, but since he turned away from her, he was seen less and less by all. It was as if he didn't want to be part of his family at all. Conversing with Edwin only brought up his dusty old memories, spewing the same names and instances over and over. She tried not to engage him without specific goals or tasks to be done. The old man could talk all day if given the opportunity.

Sadly, she went through the motions of her daily routines, meanwhile searching for sprinkles of sanity. She sought to find some sort of light amidst her confusion over who she was about to become.

*I never wanted to be a mother. I know nothing about it.*

*Motherhood. What does it even mean? To me, it means wanting to have a family. I have always wanted a family; to belong. But right now, it seems like the whole thing is falling apart. This's the reason I didn't want to become a mother in the first place. How can I be a good mother if I don't know what it means to have a family? I didn't have a mother as guidance. I had cooks in a kitchen.*

*Oh, Lori.* Charlotte swallowed her sob. *She was correct. I went against something I never wanted, all for what? Love and happiness. I'm not happy. Not right now. As for love ... I don't think it's there either.*

*Albert hates how fat I've become.*

*And so do I.*

*But he hates me. Has said it to my face. Spit at me. And now I ... I never see him anymore. Where does he go?*

*And Jebadia .... He seems angrier than usual. I wanna know what he is thinking.*

*Wait, no I don't.* She shuddered.

*And then there's these horrible hormones ...! I just wanna .... Why can't I stop crying?*

That swallowed sob came up like vomit. She covered her mouth, wiped away her tears.

*Because this isn't what I wanted. I wanted love and happiness. I wanted it with Albert if he really wanted it with me. But he doesn't. I think his father has corrupted what little shards of happiness I uncovered.*

*I wish ... I wish I could .... But everything has changed. I can't go back. Especially after the incident with Master Ikyrus ....*

*Why did I allow myself to fall in love? How could I have let this happen? I knew better. All I ever wanted was to serve Hakra. How could I have allowed myself to ...?*

*Because he was so cute. So naïve. And sweet and innocent ... full of wonder... well, not full of it. He didn't wonder about much, come to think about it. But he wanted to know about me, which was very enduring. How could I not fall in love with that, with him?*

*But what really happened to that love?*

*I feel like Jebadia had much to do with it. Calling me a Witchtress, twisting Albert's mind.*

*Or maybe I'm just overthinking things again, overreacting ....*

*I should've brought Albert to meet Mistress Aluyelian and Doctor Feendy. He wanted to go. But would either of them have approved of him?*

*One can hope.*

*I know Albert's not mean, not bad. Of course, murdering Master Ikyrus wasn't the way to solve the problem of him taking advantage of that child. But his heart was in the right place. He just wanted to protect that innocent child from .... And yeah, he's got impulse issues, wants to control things, but who doesn't want to be in control of their life?*

*Albert's just misunderstood.*

While Charlotte's breaths were measured, she was desperately trying to keep a ripple of anxiety from spiking up her back.

*It's like I'm trying to convince myself that everything's gonna be alright, when I know it's not. But what can I do?*

*I just want this moment in my life to be over. I want Albert and I's relationship to be rekindled. Want us to have a new home away from Jebadia's awful influence. He's beyond reproach. I just .... I'm done with being here. Anywhere would be better.*

*And yet ....*

*I hate the fact that this place has grown on me. It's not like I want to leave this place; I just want to leave Jebadia. If he wasn't such a misguided soul ....*

As she sat there, one hand on her swollen belly, breathing away her emotional turmoil, Charlotte realized that the babies' movements felt different now. One strong and steady, the other quick and light.

"Faith told me she could sense her babies' energies," Papa Edwin had confessed a few days ago. "But I think she was lying, because she gave birth to a girl. She had told me everything felt heavy, but I think she knew what she was going to give birth to. I think you will know too, when the time comes."

That memory chilled her.

*What if the light one's a girl?*

Charlotte had seen the darkness in Papa Edwin's eyes when he spoke of female Metalists. The certainty that there was something inherently wrong with every born female Metalist filled her with such sorrow. These men were too afraid of what they believed, blinded by falsehoods, forever unable to see the real truth.

Even so, the stories Papa Edwin had told her were the warning she hadn't realized until now.

She wondered if Albert would follow previous generations' ways and slaughter their daughter. Or would he perceive the infant as a new life, allowing them to jointly teach their children empathy, love, and forgiveness? Those beliefs had shaped her upbringing, explaining why she didn't resent her parents—until recently, and only her father.

*What if our children are born more powerful than either of us? I mean, I am still learning about my Powers—still don't know what all my father was capable of. And Albert's Metalist Abilities, combined with my own .... I fear for our children, but especially our daughter. All the stories Papa Edwin has shared.*

She touched her belly. "I promise you little ones that I'll keep you safe, that you'll grow up strong and will know about your Powers, will know how to use them for good and not evil. I'll do everything in my power to keep you safe." *But will Albert?*

*Albert's love for our children might not be enough to save our daughter. And I know what Jebadia would do to her. And me. Would Papa Edwin be wise enough to prevent past experiences from influencing our future?*

She rubbed her belly, feeling what she thought was the boy kicking high up. *Feisty one you are.* She smiled only briefly. "I'm trying not to worry, little one, but suddenly I don't think this is a safe place for me to raise you both."

*How did I let this happen?*

Charlotte stood at the underground lake, watching her reflection ripple in the dark water. Her swollen belly felt foreign, like something that had happened to someone else. She had never imagined herself as a mother—had actively avoided it at the Abbey. What did she know about motherhood? Her own mother was nothing but a name scratched out in Abbey records.

"You'll be different," she whispered to her unborn children. "You'll know love." But even as she said it, fear coiled in her chest. How could she give them what she never had? And with twins .... The reality of it staggered her.

Recalling Papa Edwin's words about joy felt hollow against the weight of her doubt. She hadn't felt truly happy since ... she couldn't remember when. Everything she had wanted—to serve Hakra, to cook, to belong—seemed to be slipping away with each kick in her belly.

For the first time, she began to truly understand—she wasn't just planning an escape. She was planning a rescue.

· · · · ●· ● · ● · ·

The next time Papa Edwin was ready to visit Chinochi, with packs full of coal, he asked Charlotte if she wanted to come with him.

"Thank you for the offer, but I don't think I can make that journey again. Not like this. I'm better off here."

He looked solemnly at her. "Is there anything you would like for me to purchase?"

She forced a smile. "Maybe a bag of pine nuts, a jar or two of blackberry preserves, and some apple butter!"

He kissed her forehead, squeezed her shoulder, and took his leave. The trail of weighted donkeys followed in his short footsteps. She watched until the downslope foliage hid them.

· · · · ●· ● · ● · ·

Edwin was gone for three long days.

For Charlotte, each day seemed longer than the last. And when the old man finally arrived, it was beyond dusk.

His breath heaved. "I caught us a buck," exclaimed Edwin as the last two donkeys breached the doorway into the long cave.

It was a large black-tailed deer. The puncture mark was acute. The trail of blood that leaked out the doorway was evident. Albert and Jebadia were quick to unleash the beast from the donkeys that hauled it. They then brought it to Charlotte to carve. This time, no one offered to help. She struggled through all of it. Her belly was in the way most of the time. It was a cumbersome job, and the only time Albert offered assistance was to place the large slabs of meat into cold storage.

She was never thanked and was then expected to cook a meal of venison with potatoes. Her body was sore, beckoning her to rest. Instead, she made up the meaty meal and roasted some potatoes, carrots, and beets—knowing that only she would eat them.

Edwin had taken a nap while waiting for supper. Jebadia leered close by, like a hawk, eagerly expecting his slab of meat and cubed potatoes. Jeb always took the first plate. Albert retrieved his plate and turned his back to her while he ate. When Edwin came for his meal, he patted her shoulder and took a seat on a far-off rock. He was the only one who faced her. She was sure this would be how suppertime would be for the remainder of her pregnancy. Charlotte couldn't help but be sad.

# 33

## <u>Final Preparations</u>

Autumn had been pressured to feel winter's first kiss. This high up the chilly winds brought frequent ice and snowstorms, freezing all the rocks and boulders, making everything slick unless you had the correct gear. Albert had to be aware of these things while en route to his secret hideout. Pine needles glistened in sporadic sunbeams. Squirrels were cozy in their dens.

When escaping the dark and dreary caverns these days, Albert found the same thrill he had felt when first being with Charlotte stealing away for hours in the tunnels, but here out in the icy tundra. It was one of his truest feelings, favorite feelings, of doing something he should not be doing. But no one knew. Not even Jebadia—Albert had made sure of it. Especially after the conversation they just had ....

"I saw where you went," Jebadia hissed. "What are you up to, boy? Sneaking away like that?"

Albert sized his father up and down. "You know nothing."

"What are you doing out there?"

"None of your business," he attempted to move away, but Jebadia grabbed him.

"It will always be my business to know what you do."

"You sound old right now. Papa Edwin old."

As Jebadia struck Albert, he grabbed his father's clothing and tossed him to the ground. Jebadia rolled with the impact. Albert came after his father with his heavy boot, frothing and spitting.

"Leave me alone. You hear me!"

Jebadia managed to grab Albert's boot. The young man slipped backwards, hitting his head on the hard ground. Briefly he saw stars, then the foot flew toward his face. Quickly, Albert rolled away from the impending kick and Jebadia slipped, ending up on the hard floor as well.

Albert was quicker to get to his feet than his father. And as Jebadia stood, Albert advanced. The younger man pointed at his elder. "It is none of your concern what I am out there doing. Got it, old man. Besides, every time I come back, I bring wood or meat. What I do is none of your concern!"

"Yes, it is! You go behind my back. Going and making a place for you and Charlotte. I thought you said you would ignore her until the end of it ... end of her pregnancy. Have you gone back on what you said?"

"No. I am taking time away from all of you." He snarled. "I cannot handle being around any of you anymore. This place. All of you ...." He kept huffing. "I am done with it all!"

"You cannot leave us now, boy. Your children are on the way."

"What good are they if they are born like her?"

"As long as they have our Power—"

"What if they do not?"

"All that matters are the boys. The boys are the ones we want. And we must murder all the girls."

Albert echoed his father's harsh words, "... all the girls. Yes. I know. I know."

"And the Witchtress too." Jebadia stepped into Albert's pointed finger, pressing it into his chest. "She is not allowed to breathe the moment they are free from her womb." He glowered when he snarled, "Understand?! If that Witchtress bears any girls, it is because she wanted them more than boys. Maybe you should go and tell her what will happen if she bears girls; that she will be killed too. That should invigorate her to bear only boys. Besides, I prefer boys."

The lustful heat in Jebadia's eyes was as intense as Charlotte's Erthin made fires. A small part of Albert wanted to shy away from the contact with his father, but only a small part. He pressed his finger further into Jebadia's hard chest. "If you touch any of my children the same way you have touched me, I will cut off your head."

Jebadia cackled when he said, "I would like to see you try!" He pulsated his Metalistic Power at Albert, pressing him back and against the closest wall.

Albert flinched and mimicked his father's angry eyed glare. He tried to pulsate his Metalist energy against Jebadia's magnetism, but his father was able to envelop that energy grab into his own bubble and press Albert harder against the softly carved corridor. "Do not cross me again, boy."

The moment Jebadia relaxed his Metalistic hold, Albert scuttled down the corridor and escaped the bleakness of the caverns for the bright and crisp day outside.

Occasionally he glanced back to see if his father was following him, to see if anyone was watching his quick disappearance down the slope—to his secret home.

*Maybe I should leave them forever. My cave is almost finished, almost secured for wintertime. All I must do is finish stacking the rocks, mud up the spaces between, and the entrance will be complete. Then it will be cozy. A perfect place for ....*

*Oh, Charlotte.* He whimpered, *no. She cannot know of my place.*

*But I do not want her to die. She does not deserve death after all she has endured.*

*What if father is correct, that Charlotte wants and bears girls?*

*Does Charlotte really deserve death for doing that? Edwin said they left River behind. I wonder if we can do that with Charlotte once the time has come.*

He hesitated. The corner of the valley in the mountain slope where he was stopped swept down like the backside of a heavy cloak, long and soft. There were many trees perched in precarious places between hardened rocks and the granite mountain slope. Mosses grew in the shadows, the air smelled of moisture—a storm was coming. Far below, the sunlight gleamed against a snaky river. Puffy clouds of white and gray swam quickly across the blue horizon. In a nearby tree, a squirrel chattered at him, breaking him from his revere.

*I never wanted this. Any of it. I wish I could go back ... go back and ... and tell Papa Edwin not to bring Charlotte home. I wish I had never met her.*

· · · • · ● · ● · • · ·

As her pregnancy progressed, Charlotte found herself restless, seeking distraction from her discomforts. One day, while exploring the lesser-used tunnels, she stumbled upon a small hidden chamber.

Charlotte's fingers traced the silver etched into the walls, feeling the subtle yet intricate designs of metal and stone. "What is this place?" she wondered.

"Ah, you have found it," Edwin's voice startled her. He stood in the doorway, a mixture of pride and sadness in his eyes.

"Found what."

Edwin sighed and entered the chamber. "This is my sanctuary. This is my personal room, my metal. We all have a room like this. Has Albert not shown you his?"

"No. He hasn't. And I haven't stumbled upon it either."

Edwin settled onto a smooth rock, gesturing for Charlotte to join him. "This was where I first felt truly free, where my possessions were mine alone. Where I didn't have to share, where I could just sit and be me." He retold his story of life again. Yet the fever in which he spoke, recalling his time of oppression and rebellion, kept her planted at his feet.

"Why didn't you return? You and Edge could've saved them, all your family." Charlotte asked when Edwin paused. "I mean, how you speak about your brethren ... don't they deserve to live as you do?"

Edwin's eyes clouded. "Because, Sweet Miss, I am sure they are already dead. I cannot imagine the manganese mines of GnSaan would still be fruitful after all these years. We were brought to Urthis for one purpose. Most likely they shipped my people off to another planet to milk us of our Talents."

"They, meaning?"

"Telepaths."

Concern wrought her face, wrung her soul. "I can't believe .... That's just so sad. Your family deserves to be free, to live in rooms like this one, to see sunrises and sunsets. To have families, friends."

Edwin's eyes grew distant. "Freedom comes at a cost, Charlotte. We left behind everything we knew; everyone we cared about. Sometimes I wonder if we did the right thing, if there was another way ...." He shook his head, refocusing on the present. "But then I look at Albert, and you, and I know why we fought so hard to build this life." He looked at the silver and gold inlaid walls—intricate carvings perfectly mottled together. "This room we sit in was built like this to remind me of how powerful we can be."

Charlotte's hand instinctively moved to her swollen belly. "I'd hate to think your family is the only family of free Metalists on all Urthis."

"It is possible that Edge made a family. But who knows? This life is cruel to those of us with amazing Abilities. That is why we must safeguard ourselves. For now, know that what grows within you is more precious than you can imagine."

As they made their way back to the main cavern, Charlotte's mind whirled with new understanding. The cave was no longer just a shelter, but a sanctuary, the last bastion of a dying breed. And she, unwittingly, had become central to its future.

· · · ● · ● · ● · ● · ●

At higher altitudes, the seasons changed in a blink of an eye. It was always chilly, and the barren tundra held little life and no food. Yet winter's harsh breath had come in like a powerful shout that silenced what little sounds there were.

The first hard-falling snowstorm came as Charlotte entered her final moon of pregnancy. Edwin thought it earlier than usual, a harbinger of the harsh winter to come.

It was a heavy snow that quieted the land and didn't take long to stack up along the sides of their exit from the cavernous homestead. Daylight waned. Edwin kept mental notes of these things, always sharing his observations with Charlotte. Every time he went to Chinochi with coal, he knew exactly how many pounds were being hauled—and how much he should've been paid each time. Although old, his mind was still quick. He always had a running list of the items needing to be purchased during his next visit, noted people's likes and dislikes, including Charlotte's. He always bought her extra, of any request.

It had been a year since she had come to live with them. She was well into the last trimester of pregnancy. She couldn't recall the last time she had seen her feet. Putting on boots was now something Edwin did for her, along with rolling her stockings up her thick calves. This was the hardest time in her life. Not even the Warden's mental grasp had been as fearful as her daily interactions with the men and the mountain they lived under.

At this point, Albert rarely spoke to her. And when they touched—a caress on the arm, massaging his shoulders, or a brief hug—his thoughts were full of vicious ideas and worst-case scenarios (where she died in childbirth, or the children were all stillborn, or worse he had to kill her and their baby girls too). She wondered if Albert had been too young when Edwin confessed his life story, explaining everything he had done over the years to be able to raise their family apart from society.

It was a burden to know Albert's biggest fears. And every time he thought about it, and looked at her, he became teary-eyed. Yet, at the end of the day, he didn't want to hurt Charlotte. He truly loved her, but was afraid of her—of what she had become. And he feared for her life and the lives of their unborn children. He wanted to know if they were boys, wondered if she could tell, but never asked. There were so many imagined conversations between them. Never would he initiate, too afraid to know the truth; nor would she instigate, too afraid he would then know she had overheard his thoughts through their touch. And their joint worry about their elders forcing Albert to murder Charlotte after bearing their children grew every day.

As time passed, Jebadia seemed more apprehensive of her, growling and glaring more and more. She was positive he had been plotting how to strain the relationship between Albert and Charlotte. He had been planting seeds of doubt long before she admitted her pregnancy. And though she never would touch the old man, even when passing off a spoon or bowl, she could see his horrific thoughts, his secret wishes on how to dispose of her and the babies if she didn't bear twin boys, in those steely eyes of his.

All this knowledge chilled Charlotte. She, too, worried about giving birth to twin girls; hoped beyond reason only boys would breach her—would mourn the death of any little girl. Part of her wanted to figure a way out of this place, away from these grizzly mountain men. But how? When?

Her desire to have as much telepathic control of these people when the time came was now solidified. And yet she knew her plan was flawed, perhaps fatally so. But with each passing day, Charlotte felt the noose of fate tightening. Snow or no snow, bloated and exhausted or not, she had to try. The alternative—watching them take her daughter—was unthinkable.

# 34

## <u>FALSE LABOR</u>

It was the middle of the night when she woke to shooting pains in her abdomen. The cavern was chilly. Charlotte forced herself out of her bed and saw everyone else sound asleep under their piles of hides and blankets. She went to the firepit and pushed a bout of Erthin heat to stoke the campfire. A kettle was placed aside the blaze, and she stared at the flames while breathing through the pain, waiting for the water to boil.

Edwin heard her and stepped quietly across the cold stone floor. "Is everything alright, Sweet Miss?"

"I don't know." She then grunted. "I don't think so."

"It cannot be time, can it?"

"Shouldn't be. I thought I had another moon to go at least!" Her bloodshot eyes peered up at him.

Edwin had kept track of her pregnancy. By his estimations, her childbirth would happen right before the darkest days occurred—over half a moon cycle away. She had wanted to give birth in the field of flowers but knew that only the bleak snow would be the thing to greet her and the babies.

A cold sweat trickled down her spine and she got up to move around. Everything hurt, especially her uterus.

"I think it's time." She panted, trying to keep a rhythmic cycle to her breathing. Edwin came to her and blew out his breath when she did.

"It will be alright. I will not leave your side."

She crumpled into his chest and sobbed. "I'm scared."

He petted her messy hair and held her like a crying babe. "Do not worry. I will take care of you," Edwin repeated. He took her back to the fire and brought her a hot cup of tea.

"Why can't Albert be like you?" She blubbered. "I just want him to care for me like he did. I don't want this, Edwin. I don't want this."

Albert, nor Jebadia, appeared disturbed by Charlotte or Edwin being awake in the middle of the night. They were as quiet as they could be. The old man remained close to her and soon they went for a walk. Charlotte insisted they go to the cavern where the underground lake lay. He didn't balk and brought many items she had kept in a bucket for this specific day.

She worried that Albert and Jebadia would be mad at her for not remaining at home to make their breakfast. Edwin insisted she not worry about that either and to keep her focus on the task at hand—delivering the babies without too many problems.

Yet Charlotte's mind raced with concern. She knew all the bad things that could go wrong and found it difficult to push those rampant thoughts out of her mind. "Just let it go," Edwin breathed with her.

There was already a comfortable place to be, quiet and back from the lake's edge, yet close enough to retrieve water. They were there for a long time before Albert came looking for them. He was angry until realizing why she and Edwin had shuffled away from the cave.

"Is it time?" For the first time, Albert stood by, humble and in the moment. He came to her as if a dream had washed away from his mind, bringing reality to the forefront. "How come you are here? Why did you not wake me?"

"This is where I want it to happen. The best place for it."

A fire raged nearby; two buckets full of warm water were on hand. Blankets laid about, and for the moment, she was sitting up and didn't feel the pressure of contractions.

An eagerness drew up Albert's lips. "Is there anything I can do? I mean, father woke up hungry, so if I need to make him food I will, but I was hoping you would do it."

Edwin snapped, "She is in no position to make food for anyone. And we could be here a while."

"Just boil up some water and add two cups of oats. It should be enough. Oh, there's ...." She groaned as another contraction wrung her body. "I made ... I made a broth. It's in the big pot aside the fire. I was going to add to it today some meat and vegetables. Ugh. If you could do that, it would help." She panted. "Just ... just slice everything up into bite-sized pieces."

Albert shook. "Should I bring it for you to do?"

"Oh, for shit's sake, boy, you can cut up meat. You can make the meal." Edwin scolded.

"But ... but it will not taste good. Father will be displeased."

"If Jeb has anything to say, send him here to me, and I will set him straight."

She grabbed Edwin's hand. Noticing his anger churning, he softened. Her attention slid to Albert as she passed him her pouch of seasonings, laced with her Coterie spells. "Just sprinkle some of these over the soup. Cook up the meat in the skillet, then place it in the broth with the cut-up vegetables. Then boil it." Again, she grunted and panted. "I know you can do this, Albert." Her eyes were firmly on him. "I believe in you."

He was quick to leave, possibly afraid to upset Jebadia further, but possibly afraid to witness Charlotte giving birth.

Soon, just the dripping of water and her rhythmic breaths were the only sounds that filled the giant cavern. This went on for a while. But there were breaks in the quiet, of her walking and grunting, of Edwin consoling and toiling.

Albert returned much later and with a bowl of now tepid soup. He brought it to Charlotte and said, "Somehow it tasted just like you made it." She patted his fuzzy face, and he took a seat near her.

"When will they come?"

Edwin replied, "Any time now, boy."

"Can I stay?"

"Only if you will help."

Albert cowered nearby for a while before getting up and leaving. He took the now empty bowl but returned a little later with it full again. This time, he offered Edwin the meal.

A spark of hope fluttered forth. They both saw it and wondered if this incident—this moment would change Albert—would make him more receptive to Charlotte and their soon to be born children. Again, he remained until they all heard Jebadia's shouts for his return. Slowly, somberly, Albert retreated home, but said he would return. He said he wanted to be there to witness their children's birth. But when he returned much later, the three of them continued to sit around and wait.

"This could be false labor." Charlotte confessed. "Many women experience this."

"Does it feel false?" asked Edwin. She shrugged, afraid to speak more of it.

Again, the giant chamber went quiet, except for the consistent dripping sounds. Albert came and left two more times before she was sure he was asleep in his warm chambers.

"You don't need to be here with me." She told Edwin as he too yawned and tried to stay attentive.

"Yes, I do. You will not go through this by yourself. I will be here for you."

"I wish your grandson was as kind and caring as you, Edwin."

"We will make sure your children are." A tear clung to his wrinkled face. "Because of you, Charlotte, I know where I went wrong in raising my son and grandson. I know what I could have done better. You have made me a better person, a better man. I can only hope your sincerity will transcend you and onto the babies."

"Thank you, Edwin. Thank you for everything. I know you've tried so hard to make my life here accommodating, and I am forever grateful."

"Oh, Sweet Miss, this has been my pleasure. And my pain. Unlike the others, I will remain here to help you with this burden." He held her hands, looked longingly at her, and his eyes softened. *I hope you bear no girls. If you do, they will be killed. As will you!*

Charlotte recoiled from the thought, but kept her expression neutral. "I know you care for me, Edwin."

Edwin sighed heavily, taking her hands in his. "And that is what makes this harder, Sweet Miss. I have lived long enough to love many things I've had to destroy." His thumbs gently stroked her palms as his voice dropped to a whisper. "Your presence has brought light to these old caves, made me remember joys I thought long forgotten. But some duties transcend even our deepest attachments." He gazed at her with genuine affection—and behind it, unwavering resolve. In that moment, Charlotte understood that his kindness and his cruelty were not contradictions but companions, twin aspects of the same fractured soul.

· · · ● · ● · · · ·

"We should just rip those babies out of her belly." Jebadia snarled. "Toss Charlotte to the vultures."

"But what if they are both boys? I think she would be a good mother."

"She still has your mind. No. She is horrible. A terrible person, a Witchtress of a woman. No. She must die with all the rest of them."

Albert's eyes shook as he stared at his father. "But if she bears boys?"

"I do not care what comes from that Witchtress. They should all die if I had my druthers."

He stepped up to his father's face. "I will not allow you to kill my children, my boys."

Jebadia cackled, "I do not care if she bears boys. Her head should roll just the same. She is not a good woman, not worthy of raising our children. We could do it better than she, and without all the nagging." He spat on the ground. "Good riddance."

Albert reflected on the humble abode he had been working on. Since the blanketing of snow, he had not returned to it, but wished he was there now.

"Then who will raise the babies? Papa Edwin?" Albert spat on the same spot his father had. "He twisted my mind up just as bad as she did. I refuse to let him watch over our babies."

Again, Jebadia cackled, but wilder than before. "I would do a better job than he. Edwin is old and weak. Maybe we should kill him too. Be done with the whole lot of them." The fiery spark in Jebadia's eyes made Albert cower. "Do you disagree?"

"I ... I-I had not thought about it," Albert shivered even though he wasn't cold. "Why would we kill Edwin?"

"He is compromised—has been under her influence since the beginning. He would deserve it for the years of neglect." Jebadia held a far-off look. "We should do it soon. Do it the same day we kill her and her babies."

The shaking Albert felt was now vibrating throughout his whole body. "If you lay one hand on my children, or Charlotte ...." Albert was ready to strike his old man.

Jebadia grabbed his son's hand. "If she bears any girls, they will all die. Mark my words. No Metalist girls will live, and that Witchtress will die just as quick too."

He was not sure he felt up to such a heinous act. But the fever at which Jebadia loomed over him, trying to coerce ideals, was hard to ignore. And though he wanted to trust his father's intuition, Albert remained quiet, not wanting to jump to conclusions. He felt that his father's opinion that all women were corrupt was beyond reproach, yet he, too, was willing to accept that belief now.

If only Charlotte had confessed who she really was, how powerful she could be, before they had traveled to Kobiton—before she became pregnant—things might have turned out differently.

# 35

## <u>BIRTH & BETRAYAL</u>

Those first bouts of labor pains had indeed been false. She went through fantom contractions for two days before her abdomen calmed. During this downtime, she plotted her escape from this place, these people. There were a few trails to take, but only two led down the steep slopes towards civilization.

By this point in her pregnancy, Charlotte was positive that at least one fetus was female. Things she could not explain had been happening between Charlotte and her unborn children. Psychic bonds were in their final phase of solidification, and Charlotte could now sense her children on a deeper level. There was suddenly so much to prepare for, and little to no time to do it in. As long as she had the correct clothing, a stash of food, and the means to carry everything, including the soon to be newborns, it was hard to find fault in her plans.

Until she felt contractions once more, and they were three times as fierce as before.

· · • · • • · • · ·

Nothing had changed from their previous visit to the cavern; it had only been six days since she had last experienced false labor. Now, as the winter winds howled outside, Charlotte knew this time was different. Her journey of nearly nine moons was about to end.

She lay there, grunting in pain, wondering when it would all end. Yet once her body was in the throes of childbirth, it didn't stop, thrusting the infants out into the cold world quicker than expected.

Albert and Jebadia were nowhere to be seen, as she wanted it. Edwin had been helpful the whole time.

Hours blended into a haze of pain and determination. Charlotte gripped Edwin's hand, each contraction feeling like it might tear her apart.

"You are doing wonderfully," Edwin encouraged, wiping her brow.

Between pains, Charlotte's mind raced. Would the babies be healthy? Would they have her Powers or Albert's? Would they ever see the world beyond this cave?

She had been preparing for weeks, testing her herb-based sleeping tincture in small doses during meals—watching how it affected the men's alertness, adjusting the potency. While they slept, she had memorized the cave passages that might lead to freedom, making them in her mind. Small cashes of supplies were hidden near the underground lake, gathered slowly so no one would notice their absence. She knew it was a desperate plan, but with each passing day, the urgency grew.

As another contraction built, she focused on her breath on the life she was bringing into the world

"I can do this," she whispered to herself. "For by babies, I can do anything."

· · · · ● · ● · · · ·

Everything hurt after giving birth to the twins. Alive and healthy, the infants, named Irwin—after her childhood friend/half-sibling H'Eirwyn (but she spelled her baby's name different)—and Lori, were bonding with Charlotte. She was warm, but the air inside the giant cavern was icy. For the moment, the three of them lay undisturbed. Charlotte was captivated by her babies, taking in every new thing about them.

Edwin sat close by, his mind in a haze from a telepathic spell she had placed. Although she wasn't very strong with her Abilities, she had been taught how to make someone compliant to simple tasks. For now, he sat statuesque. She didn't want him to have thoughts, wanted to keep him subdued. In doing this, she was allowing herself time to gain the strength needed for what was to come.

"You should have the rest of that stew while it's still warm," Charlotte encouraged.

Papa Edwin looked at the small pot of stew Albert had brought them earlier that day. The pot sat fireside, remaining warm. He poured himself a bowlful, picked up a spoon, and consumed the meal.

He slurped and smacked his lips. "Tasty, huh?! It's my favorite dish to make." She watched him finish every morsel, drinking the bowl clean.

Watching Charlotte with the babies, Edwin said, "I have spent so long running from the past that I nearly missed the chance for a better future. Those children, they are not just Albert's legacy—they are a chance to right the wrongs of our history."

Her smile widened. "I agree, and I'm glad you realized that. I must thank you, Edwin. Thank you for everything you've done for me and these babies. Just so you know, everything will be fine. You've nothing to worry about. I'm sure I can raise them on my own. And I'll tell no one about you, or your Powers—their Powers. We will live simply. No Hakran influence. We'll find our way." She touched his hand.

He blinked, looking even more drowsy. "What do you mean?"

The Coterie spell she had placed on the herbs sprinkled into the stew was supposed to make every Metalist tired. Hopefully, it would keep them all asleep and for long enough for Charlotte and her babies to escape.

"It's gonna be okay. You're just tired. You can go to sleep now. Rest."

He yawned and looked like he was fighting her sleeping spell. "Why did you say what you said?"

"You, out of everyone here, should know I won't allow anyone to hurt these babies. Not you. Not them. I'll keep them safe. Keep their Powers a secret."

"You should not have ...." Edwin yawned repeatedly before collapsing into a snoring heap.

This was the moment she had been fearing yet waited for.

Her hands shook as she reached for Edwin. This was it—the point of no return. Once she did this, there would be no going back, no chance of reconciliation. For a moment, her resolve wavered. Was she doing the right thing? But then she looked at her innocent babies, thought of the life that awaited them if they stayed, and her determination solidified. With a deep breath, she turned on her Succubus Power and began the energy transfer, silently apologizing to the one person who had shown her genuine kindness in this harsh world. Edwin wasn't as harsh as the Warden had been to her. She had hoped her Succubus Power would've killed the Warden, prayed she would only hurt Papa Edwin.

Charlotte stood over the elderly man. She appropriated much of Edwin's life energy—taking him well beyond sleep, but didn't deliver him to Death's door. He would be unconscious for at least a day. That way, Albert and Jebadia couldn't blame him for what was about to happen. She knew the spell placed on their food would keep them asleep, but for how long? She hoped she had enough time to transcend below the snowline, to find freedom for her and these two new and beautiful babies. Her love for them grew with every moment, every time she peered at them, her face hurt from glee. Charlotte would do whatever it took to keep them safe from this rotten family.

She hadn't more of a plan than this but knew the way to Chinochi and hoped to have a lengthy lead—hoped her spell lasted longer than the spell she placed on the Warden's food.

Every step sent pain shooting through her body. Birth had left her weak, bleeding—she hadn't even had a full day to recover. The babies' weight against her chest made breathing difficult in the thin mountain air. But fear drove her forward, even as her vision blurred.

Since her false labor, Charlotte remained in the giant underground cavern where the water dripped loudest. It was there that she felt safe. During this time, while she lay as comfortable as a pregnant woman could be, Edwin had brought her many provisions. All the blankets and buckets, swaddling clothes, and the warmest of the children's clothing she had made. She knew she couldn't take it all with her, but wanted to be comfortable until then. She hoped Papa Edwin hadn't figured out what she would do with those items. But when he made his questions known, she had perfect excuses.

"I don't know what I'll need once they are outside of me. I just want to be prepared for anything, you know. After that last bout of pain, I think I've got a better plan, but anything can happen. Just gotta be flexible, you know."

"Yes, of course. I cannot imagine your pains, Sweet Miss. Whatever you want."

"This all should be good enough. Thank you so much, Papa Edwin. I'm glad I have you in my life."

Over the last few days, she hadn't felt safe with Albert's sudden interest in their babies. He had made her promise, every time he had seen her; to send Edwin the moment she gave birth. Insistent on knowing immediately if a little girl was born. And how he looked at her, insisting she follow through with his demands, fortified her will to leave this place forever. These men of the mountain weren't good men, weren't good people.

And yet there was a brief moment when Charlotte pondered if she was being brash, overthinking her reason for departing. She had happy memories with these people, appreciated Papa Edwin for showing her fatherly love, yearned to feel as lighthearted as she did when first falling in love with Albert. And the views from this mountain top were serene.

She looked down at her twins, memorizing their faces. Beautiful Lori, so small and perfect. Precious Irwin, already so strong. In another life, they might have grown up together, protected by a family's love. But she had seen too much, heard too many of Papa Edwin's guilt-laden confessions about past daughters who had never drawn a second breath.

Her body screamed for rest, but fear drove her forward. The herbs in the men's food would only keep them under for so long. She had one chance—not just to escape, but to save her daughter from a fate sealed generations ago. Even if they died in the snow, it would be better than watching them murder her baby girl.

The cave's darkness pressed around her as she gathered her cached supplies. Each step felt like walking through deep water, her body still raw from birth. But mothers had done harder things to protect their children. She would do this or die trying.

Rations were stuffed into the buckets, swinging in either hand, along with the baby's clothing and some of her own. She was wrapped up in blankets and cold weather garments; babies warm against her chest—against her heart. They had been crying but now fell limp—finally soothed to sleep. She hadn't a moment to spare and was glad to know the best way out of the underground caves. It wasn't easy slipping between many of the rocks, pushing her gathered belongings ahead of her into dark passages. This made her departure longer than expected and before long, all that extracted energy started to wane. She had to stop more often to catch her breath.

Charlotte's heart pounded as she continued further into the twisting passages. Every shadow seemed to hide a threat; every echo sounded like pursuit. The babies, mercifully quiet, were warm against her chest.

She paused at a junction, trying to recall Albert's lessons about this specific cave system. Left or right? Her choice could mean the difference between freedom and capture.

A distant sound made her jump. Was that a footstep? The scrape of metal on stone? Or just her frightened imagination?

"We're almost there, little ones," she murmured to the babies. "Just a little further, and we'll see the stars."

When she finally reached the enormous gap in the mountainside, it was nice to be greeted by a moderately cloudy day. When the sun shone through and upon her, she was thankful for the momentary warmth, and she tried to suckle as much energy out of the sunbeam too.

Her descent to the tree line proved arduous; the weight of her possessions, the clinging babies, and her aching body slowed her progress. She knew she needed to find the trail that led to Chinochi. Taking this route wasn't the best way to go, but what could she do? She didn't want to believe she was lost and thrust that thought out of her mind. As long as she was below the snowline before dusk, they would be safe.

Her heart beat hard against her chest. Her breath labored, as was every step through the fresh and deep snow.

Soon the infants began crying from under her clothing. They felt smashed against her warm flesh. They were either hungry or just as scared as she was. Charlotte didn't stop. She couldn't.

Even as she fled, a part of her ached for Albert. Despite everything, she loved him still. She hoped that someday he would understand why she had to do this, that he would forgive her. In her heart, she carried the memory of their love, a bittersweet reminder of what could have been.

Soon, exhaustion from it all slowed her. And then it began snowing again. She stopped to catch her breath and make sure everyone was doing well. Taking a drink of icy water, she opened the blanket where her two little miracles were wrapped. They stared at her. She gave each a breast, ate some jerky, and continued to gaze lovingly at her tiny babies.

"I love you two so much. We will make it through this. I promise."

She hated making promises, but worse, she hated the idea of baby Lori being killed because she was a Metalist girl. Charlotte had to continue, no matter the cost.

She had sat around for too long.

Jebadia's voice was faint. "There she is! There is that Witchtress! This way Albert!"

Instantly, panic threw her forward and out of her snowy seat. She wrestled with her clothing, trying to secure her children within the warmth.

*How'd they survive my wickedness? Could their Metalist Powers do more than just channel metal? Can they ward against my spells placed on herbs?*

She forgot her buckets but wrapped up the babies as she scrambled through the knee-deep snow. Once again, the babies were crying. She wanted to soothe them, but more so she wanted to save herself. For now, she had to put more space between herself and the angry miners chasing her down.

Icy tears hurt as they clung to the corners of her eyes. Charlotte kept muttering. "I'm so sorry, babies. So sorry."

She had believed there was a way to tame these Metalists through scrumptious meals, but they somehow warded off her visceral attack. If she were close enough to touch them, could she bend their minds? But they yielded metal—always kept skin deep and ready for use. Metal trumps telepathy every time.

Charlotte heard the metal singing behind her—they were using their Powers to track the studs in her boots. She should have thought of that, should have taken different shoes. But it was too late now. The babies were crying; the snow was deepening, and her strength was failing. She had nowhere left to run.

Suddenly, the wind was knocked out of her. Pain shot along her shoulder blade and down to her lower back. Charlotte was tossed face down in the bright snow. Her once rampant heartbeat was forever silenced.

In that final moment, as she heard Jebadia's approach, Charlotte knew she had failed. Not just herself, but her children. She had tried to outrun fate with newborns pressed against her body and a desperate plan. The metal spike that took her life was almost a mercy compared to watching what would come next.

# 36

## <u>INTO THE SNOW</u>

Jebadia kicked Albert to wake. They lay alongside the fire ring of rocks. "I think she poisoned us, boy." He spat at the ground near Albert's head. "I think she contaminated our food."

The savory cast-iron pot was overturned, stew spilled across the firepit. Their only source of light was immediately suppressed. The heavy iron pot then hit the stone floor; its loud tone, a burst of sound that resonated throughout their meager homestead.

"I should have slit her throat the moment she showed her Powers," Jebadia's voice echoed around the room. "Just like River. They are all the same in the end."

Albert was still dazed. How long had they been asleep?

He stumbled along, weak and physically disoriented. He was still incredibly tired, but his father was not. Jebadia angrily pulled Albert along down the corridors towards the underground pond and birthing ground.

Jebadia was seething. "We will kill them all. Let her Hakra sort them out."

"What do you mean?"

"Edwin. That fat girl. And all her babies."

"Why? Why would we kill Edwin? Or Charlotte? Why kill all the babies? They are my children too!"

"She has pulled the wool sweater over your eyes far too long, boy. She is a Witchtress through and through. I told you to watch out for her. Any Power she has, those babies will have too."

"You do not know that for sure."

Jebadia slapped Albert. "Do not tell me what I do not know. I know more than you. Always have, always will."

His face was hot from the open hand. Albert now trailed Jebadia, muttering, "Please do not kill my babies."

"If there are any girls, they will be slaughtered, just like that Witchtress of a woman you mated with."

"Bah! Old man, I need you to stop comparing Charlotte to River. She was a Witchtress. Messed with your mind."

"Shut it!"

Again, he was hit. Albert then tripped Jebadia, who fell to his knees. They tussled, but their anger over this moment didn't keep them boxing for long.

Both men stumbled into the enormous cavern and over to where Charlotte and Edwin had been. Their lantern light was the only light; the fire near the underground lake had been extinguished. That was where they found Edwin unconscious; though upon first inspection, he appeared to be dead. They attempted to wake him, but to no avail. Slowly, steadily, their energy was returning, and with it, even more anger over Charlotte's attempt to murder all the Metalists and kidnap their innocent babies.

"I know where she is. Can feel the metal studs I placed in her boots," Albert said and turned on his heel. They had to go back the way they had come.

Not runners by nature, in this moment Albert and Jebadia were sprinting back to their humble abode. Swiftly, they suited up for the cold and took off into the ever-white landscape. They took the well-worn trail, heading down the mountain as if going to Chinochi.

· · · ● · ● · ● · ·

They had only been outside for a short time before Jebadia saw her off the main trail, but far downslope. Jebadia's voice echoed when he pointed. Albert had been ahead of him and cut straight down the slope, jumping off rocky outcroppings, trying to get to Charlotte first.

Jebadia couldn't keep up, but that didn't matter. He was quick to use his rage and Metalistic magic.

Albert felt the blade fly overhead, wanting to stop it, but with Jebadia's wickedness piloting the deadly spike, he had no chance. It struck the backside of Charlotte, tossing her forward against the cold snow. She didn't have time to scream out; fell over dead. The white tundra was now splattered with her blood.

He tried to get to the babies before his father did. But Jebadia, like a wild boar in heat, flew down the slope to where Charlotte lay. Albert arrived at the scene a moment after. The babies were wailing from under her deceased and bloody body. She had fallen forward into the snow, and curled her body around her children, trying to protect them even after Death had stolen her soul.

Jebadia rolled her limp body over to expose the wailing children to the bitterly cold air.

Albert stood frozen, watching red bloom across the pristine snow. The woman he had loved, the mother of his children, looked small now—nothing like the Witchtress his father had painted her as. Just a girl who had tried to run.

As he stared at Charlotte's lifeless form, shock and grief battling within him. The biting wind seemed to mock his pain. Charlotte had been his first love, his window to a world he had never known. Now that window had slammed shut, leaving him in darkness.

He remembered her laugh, the way her eyes lit up when she told stories of Kobiton. He thought of all the dreams they had shared, now turned to ash.

A sob built in his chest, raw and primal. It tore from his throat, echoing across the snowy landscape. He fell to his knees beside her, cradling her cooling body.

A new, undefinable emotion clouded his mind—the worst he had ever experienced.

"I am sorry," he whispered brokenly. "I am so sorry, Charlotte. I should have protected you. I should have been better."

As Jebadia loomed over him, Albert felt something harden inside of him. The world had taken Charlotte from him. He would not let it take anything else.

· · · · ● · ● · · · ·

Jebadia produced a thick sword and severed Charlotte's head, kicking it down the slope. "Good riddance Witchtress." The haggard man then shot his son a menacing look.

Albert hunched, nose wrinkled with disgust, yet he complied. Beyond dealing with the turmoil of emotions churning within, he didn't want to be hit again. He took the wailing infant, the female Metalist—the one Charlotte had named Lori—out from the deceased's warm clothing. He stared at her, afraid of her in every way. He then wondered why he should be afraid of something so frail, so small.

His voice shook when asking, "What should we do with this one?"

Jebadia scowled. "Female Metalists are not allowed to live; you know this." Jebadia's hands shook as he recounted the first time he had to dispose of a female child. "It is our way," He whispered. "Since I killed Charlotte, you must kill her. Do it quick." The old man reached for Irwin and lifted him into the cold air; the infant began crying.

Guilt and remorse filled Albert's lungs; tears stung his eyes. It was so hard to breathe. Finally, he spit out, "I just want to leave her to die."

Jebadia shrieked, "In the snow? You are callous. Kill her already! We must return home now!"

Albert's shoulders slumped as he turned away from Jebadia. The baby's cries cut through the howling wind as Albert lifted her. His hands shook—from the cold or something else, he could not tell. He had imagined this moment differently, had told himself he would be strong when it came. But as he looked down at his daughter's face, so much like Charlotte's, he felt something inside him crack.

*I do not want to do this. But I must. This is what we do. We kill them. Every girl. We must. But why?*

This wasn't the place or time to question. As the snow and winds shifted, it would become a total whiteout soon. They had to return home.

Later, they would tell themselves it had been necessary. A sacrifice for the greater good, like all the others before. But in his dreams, Albert would always see Charlotte reaching for her children as she fell, would hear two sets of crying become one, then none.

· · · ● · ● · · ·

Jebadia pressed the baby named Irwin into his stinky clothing. He hissed at Albert, hoping his son would comply.

A moment later, baby Lori's insistent cries were forever silenced.

It seemed colder now. The wind howled louder than before. The snow turned into relentless ice chips, slicing at all exposed flesh. Huddled in their warm yet stinky clothing, Albert and Jebadia retraced their footsteps upslope, picking up the buckets of clothing and food left behind, they brought home the last remains of Charlotte; a little baby boy who would be renamed Samuel Miner.

Papa Edwin would be the only one who would call him Irwin.

# 37

## <u>EPILOGUE</u>

The days following Charlotte's death cast a deeper shadow than any winter storm. In the caves where she had once brought warmth and life, only echoes remained. The space she had carved out for herself—her kitchen tools, her herbs, her paltry attempts at making the cave a home—sat untouched. No one spoke of moving them.

Albert spent his days in the chamber where Charlotte had first shown him her Erthin Powers to create warmth and manipulate water. For hours he would sit with Samuel Irwin, watching his son reach for the metal in the walls with tiny, grasping fingers.

"He has her eyes," Albert would whisper, voice cracking. "Every time I look at him, I see her. See what I failed to protect."

At night, his anguished cries echoed through the stone corridors, a sound so raw it made even Jebadia flinch. But during the day, he threw himself into teaching Samuel Irwin about their Powers, about the metal singing in their blood. He was determined his son would be stronger than he had been, and he would never know the weakness of love.

Edwin watched this with growing sadness. He saw how Albert scrutinized every gesture Samuel Irwin made, searching for echoes of Charlotte. Even the way the baby smiled seemed to pain him—a ghost of what was lost.

"You must be careful," Edwin warned one evening. "Samuel Irwin is his own person, not just a reflection of his mother."

"His name is Samuel," Albert snapped. "Samuel Miner. Not Irwin. Never call him Irwin. Hear me?! Charlotte is gone." But his grip on the baby tightened, belying his words.

The cave that had briefly been brightened by Charlotte's presence now felt darker than ever, her absence a wound that refused to heal. Albert became obsessive in his devotion to baby Samuel Irwin, measuring every woman he encountered against the ghost of his first love. None would ever be allowed close enough to threaten what remained of his heart.

· · · ● · ● · ● · · ·

One night, as Papa Edwin rocked Samuel Irwin to sleep, he felt the weight of all his years press down upon him. "Oh, Sweet Miss," he whispered to the empty air. "If only we had done better by you. If only I had been brave enough to stop it all."

The baby stirred in his arms, and Edwin saw in his tiny face both hope and warning. Samuel Irwin would grow up knowing his mother's story—not the comfortable lies they told themselves, but the truth of who she was and what their fear had cost them all.

In the deepest part of the cave, where the metal sang strongest, Albert had begun carving a new chamber. Its walls would tell the story of their family's power, their legacy. But in the soft silver patterns, if one looked closely, there was also the story of a woman who he had dared to love, and what that love had cost.

For now, though, Papa Edwin simply held his great-grandson close, humming the lullaby Charlotte used to sing, and prayed that this child would grow to be braver than any of them had been.

Above ground, the winter winds howled, and somewhere in the endless snow, Charlotte's final sacrifice lay buried, waiting for the spring thaw to reveal its truth.

If you haven't yet read the rest of the series ... click , or visit .

If you have read the whole series up to this point, please know there's going to be more to this epic adventure. I love Irwin too much to just let him go!

If you enjoyed Bound By Iron & Blood, please leave a review. Thank you for enjoying the journey thus far.

# Epilogue

The days following Charlotte's death cast a deeper shadow than any winter storm. In the caves where she had once brought warmth and life, only echoes remained. The space she had carved out for herself—her kitchen tools, her herbs, her paltry attempts at making the cave a home—sat untouched. No one spoke of moving them.

Albert spent his days in the chamber where Charlotte had first shown him her Erthin Powers to create warmth and manipulate water. For hours he would sit with Samuel Irwin, watching his son reach for the metal in the walls with tiny, grasping fingers.

"He has her eyes," Albert would whisper, voice cracking. "Every time I look at him, I see her. See what I failed to protect."

At night, his anguished cries echoed through the stone corridors, a sound so raw it made even Jebadia flinch. But during the day, he threw himself into teaching Samuel Irwin about their Powers, about the metal singing in their blood. He was determined his son would be stronger than he had been, and he would never know the weakness of love.

Edwin watched this with growing sadness. He saw how Albert scrutinized every gesture Samuel Irwin made, searching for echoes of Charlotte. Even the way the baby smiled seemed to pain him—a ghost of what was lost.

"You must be careful," Edwin warned one evening. "Samuel Irwin is his own person, not just a reflection of his mother."

"His name is Samuel," Albert snapped. "Samuel Miner. Not Irwin. Never call him Irwin. Hear me?! Charlotte is gone." But his grip on the baby tightened, belying his words.

The cave that had briefly been brightened by Charlotte's presence now felt darker than ever, her absence a wound that refused to heal. Albert became obsessive in his devotion to baby Samuel Irwin, measuring every woman he encountered against the ghost of his first love. None would ever be allowed close enough to threaten what remained of his heart.

· · · ● · ● · ● · · ·

One night, as Papa Edwin rocked Samuel Irwin to sleep, he felt the weight of all his years press down upon him. "Oh, Sweet Miss," he whispered to the empty air. "If only we had done better by you. If only I had been brave enough to stop it all."

The baby stirred in his arms, and Edwin saw in his tiny face both hope and warning. Samuel Irwin would grow up knowing his mother's story—not the comfortable lies they told themselves, but the truth of who she was and what their fear had cost them all.

In the deepest part of the cave, where the metal sang strongest, Albert had begun carving a new chamber. Its walls would tell the story of their family's power, their legacy. But in the soft silver patterns, if one looked closely, there was also the story of a woman who he had dared to love, and what that love had cost.

For now, though, Papa Edwin simply held his great-grandson close, humming the lullaby Charlotte used to sing, and prayed that this child would grow to be braver than any of them had been.

Above ground, the winter winds howled, and somewhere in the endless snow, Charlotte's final sacrifice lay buried, waiting for the spring thaw to reveal its truth.

**If you haven't yet read the rest of the series ... start with SECRETS OF URTHIS. Visit https://www.kdlumsden.comfor more details.**
**If you have read the whole series up to this point, please know there's going to be more to this epic adventure. I love Irwin too much to just let him go! If you enjoyed Bound By Iron & Blood, please leave a review. Thank you for enjoying the journey thus far.**

# <u>Also By</u>

**<u>The Metalist's Journey</u>**
0.25 ~ The Last Metalist
0.5 ~ The Metalist's Journey Prologue
1 ~ Secrets of Urthis
2 ~ Elements of Power
3 ~ Sleeper Assassin
4 ~ Land of Cannibals
4.5 ~ Bound by Iron & Blood
(+2 more at least!)

**If you liked this book please leave a review!**

Want more information about Irwin and the world of Urthis?
Join KD Lumsden's newsletter at https://www.kdlumsden.com/

# THE UNUSUAL CREATURES MENTIONED

**ANCIENT DWELLERS**

<u>APPEARANCE</u>: Unknown

<u>UNIQUE TRAITS</u>: Deities who created the universes. They wanted life to happen; to experience love, hate, melancholy, triumph, and sorrow. Everything exists because of them.


**CLAN-DUIN**

<u>APPEARANCE</u>: brown skinned, black hair, hairy bodies, eye colors can be gray/ green/ brown/ amber

<u>UNIQUE TRAITS</u>: shapeshifters, can be feline, canine, raptor, bear, ape, and/or marine mammals. Are very loyal companions, prefer to live in packs, but can be loners. Linear thinkers, they can be stubborn and foolhardy.


**COTERIE**

<u>APPEARANCE</u>: pale-skinned, white to blonde hair, white to blue eyes, but can take on darker appearances if bred with other creatures, such as Clan-Duins or Erthins.

<u>UNIQUE TRAITS</u>: Blended children of the Guru, infused with Mortal DNA. Their abilities are similar to Guru, but can be limited by Mortal blood. They are considered bastard children of the Guru and are impure. Often arrogant and egocentric, they live anywhere/anytime.


**ELEMENTALIST**

<u>APPEARANCE</u>: grey to olive-skin color, auburn-orange to red hair, green-hazel eyes

<u>UNIQUE TRAITS</u>: can harness every element known to exist. They can create elements from within themselves, or through interaction with organic and

inorganic life.  They are known to have the ability to live out in space without oxygen or nutrients, they can oxygen exist inside their lungs without taking a breath. It is said they were the first beings created by the Ancient Dwellers, that they were necessary for creating the known universes.

## ERTHIN

<u>APPEARANCE</u>: grey to olive-skin color, auburn-orange red hair, green-hazel eyes

<u>UNIQUE TRAITS</u>: hybrid Elementalist and Mortal. They can harness the five most powerful natural elements: Air, water, fire, earth, and spirit. They can be pure-bred and have all abilities, or part-breed and have abilities specific to person (ie. the ability to harness only one element).

## GURU

<u>APPEARANCE</u>: white skinned, white-ashen hair, white-blue eyes.

<u>UNIQUE TRAITS</u>: Direct descendants of Ancient Dwellers. They have can use any type of power (teleporting, telepathy, shapeshifting). Considered living gods, they hide in plain sight and across all the universes. They can live everywhere/anywhere/anytime.

## GYPSY

An enclave of like-minded people, usually Talented, who tour Urthis rescuing other Talented people. They often take the rescued to sanctuary cities.

## HAKRA (Urthis's God)

<u>APPEARANCE</u>: black-skinned, blue-eyes, hairless.

<u>UNIQUE TRAITS</u>: considered a living god who resides in Akarah City, capitol of Urthis. Has lain the groundwork for Telepaths to shape Urthis into an interstellar hub; keeps the general population subdue through religion. Every few years produces a Tome for the people to follow, hypnotizes the masses through telepathic ideology; zealot followers are devout enough to turn in their brother or neighbor if they believe they are Talented. Every few years his followers take pilgrimages to Akarah to stand in Hakra's presence with hopes to be bestowed a gift.

## ISHIK EMPIRE

Current rulers of Doas Territory, the Ishik Empire have been in control for the last thousand years. Believed to be the last full-blooded Coterie family, they claim to be purebred; to couple with someone outside the family brings dishonor. They tout their land to be free of Talented people, yet employ Talented people to work at the palace. They maltreat their subjects, taking boys away from their families at 9-10, to work iron mines, daughters are married off by 8-9, families live in small dome-huts, and when compared to the rest of Urthis, Doas Territory is at least one hundred years behind in technological advancements.

## METALIST

<u>APPEARANCE</u>:  ashen skin color, gray hair, silvery-gray eyes

<u>UNIQUE TRAITS</u>: can harness all types of metal including, but not limited to; gold, silver, aluminum, nickel, iron, zinc, mercury, cadmium, cobalt, chromium, platinum, lead, etc.  They can hold up to eight pounds of any given substance within their own flesh, flushed it under the skin to specific places. Their ability to manipulate metal starts with extraction, turning the metal into its liquid form, and integrating it back into its hard form, and can form anything imaginable with any amount of metal. They are known to give off a deathly scent when holding metal within. Direct descendants to Elementalist.

## MORTAL

<u>APPEARANCE</u>: always pale-skinned, brown-eyed, hair light brown to dark-brown/black

<u>UNIQUE TRAITS</u>: Bipeds with no superhuman powers. One of the five eldest beings created by the Ancient Dwellers. They have been exported from their home world, brought to foreign worlds to repopulate but often exploited as cheap labor.

## PLANETAIRY CONSTIBLE PATROL (PCP)

Comprised only of people with Talents. Telepaths are given powerful positions (Admiral, Captain, Colonel, Corporal, Sargent), Erthins can hold powerful positions (Lieutenant, Sargent), Clan-Duins are considered working soldiers or minions, but can be demoted and placed in a "court-yard sitter" position. Also called "Population Control Patrol". They usually patrol in groups of four and are seen riding large "warhorses".

## SANCTUARY CITY

Not necessarily a city, but a place where people with Talents are safe from the PCP and Hakran ideology. Most don't allow Mortals to reside. Most require those looking for permanent residency to prove they are a positive influence, that they will help protect others with Talents, regardless of abilities, and not cause issue within the community. There are rules within each community to adhere, and if someone breaks that main rule they can be banished from one, or all sanctuary cities. (*Note: All Sanctuary cities are interconnected by Telepaths.)

## SHAYOT

A truly talented child, usually male, but sometimes are females brought through the ranks. They are usually multi-cultural (Telepath and Clan-Duin, or Erthin and Telepath, or any unique mixture) and are trained by the worst of the worse in order to understand how to think like murders and rapest, thieves and mercenaries. As an adult they are highly regarded and given positions of power within the Hakra regime.

## TALENT, PEOPLE OF (aka TALENTED)

Any being who possess supernatural powers.

## TELECAPRITIAN

<u>APPEARANCE</u>: pale skinned, white to blue eyed, white to blonde hair

<u>UNIQUE TRAITS</u>: can use telekinesis and telepathy, can shapeshift appearance but only into same gender roles. One of the five eldest beings created by the Ancient Dwellers.

## TELEPATH

<u>APPEARANCE</u>: pale skinned, white to blue eyed, white to blonde hair

<u>UNIQUE TRAITS</u>: hybrid of TeleCapritian & Mortal, they cannot yield telekinesis. There are many types of telepaths; dreaming (they see visions future or past based), some can hear thoughts, some can manipulate beings though 'telepathic' brain waves, others can only do this through physical touch.

## TELEKINESIS

The ability to move objects at a distance by mental power or other nonphysical means.

**URTHIS**

Fourth planet from the sun in the Oska'al solar system and one of the many places in the known universe that hosts supernatural and natural powered creatures. It is the planet on which Samuel Irwin Miner lives.

**VOLATILE**

A derogatory word used against people of Talent. (see: Talent, people of)

**WARDEN**

<u>APPEARANCE</u>: enigmatic. They have the ability to become anyone of the same sex

<u>UNIQUE TRAITS</u>: a Warden is a breed of person (can be male or female—usually male) that is of Telepathic, Clan-Duin, and Elementalist descent. They are considered greatest of warriors and hunters, usually former *Shayot*, and work directly for Hakra and his minions. The only way to kill a Warden is to cut off their head.

# About KD Lumsden

KD Lumsden was raised on a small farm where her youth was spent running away from angry bulls, riding horses, fishing, camping, and daydreaming about fantastic worlds. Born dyslexic, she has learned to use her neurodivergent mind for the good of mankind—creatures on other planets are another story. Though she's not a fast reader or writer, her mind flies with many stories, eagerly waiting to be told. Better with numbers and art, KD became an architectural designer long before it was cool to work from home, and has always enjoyed drawing, creating maps, laying out and designing buildings, and of course other worldly planets with amazing settings and diverse people. She lives on a farm outside Eugene, Oregon, with her supportive husband, imaginative son, and their many two and four-legged animals.

Get to know KD more by visiting her socials ....

https://www.facebook.com/KDLumsden/
https://www.instagram.com/kdlumsden_author/
https://bsky.app/profile/authorkdlumsden.bsky.social
https://twitter.com/KDLumsdenAuthor
https://www.amazon.com/author/kdlumsden
https://www.bookbub.com/profile/kd-lumsden
https://cravebooks.com/author/author-kdlumsden
https://www.goodreads.com/author/show/22489719.K_D_Lumsden

# BLURB

**Charlotte's magic can grow life from the smallest seed.**
**Albert's power can bend metal to his will.**
**Their love might destroy them both.**

Deep in the Kruluver Mountains, where metal sings to those with the right blood, Charlotte finds refuge with a secretive family of miners. As she falls for the youngest son, Albert, she brings warmth to their cold stone world—and unknowingly awakens generations of deadly tradition.

Female Metalists are never allowed to live, and Charlotte's unborn twins will be no exception.

In a cave where ancient fears echo louder than love, Charlotte must fight not just for her heart, but for her children's very existence.

In this stunning standalone novel, KD Lumsden weaves a tale of forbidden love, ancient powers, and the lengths we'll go to protect those we love. Set in a richly imagined world where magic runs deep but prejudice runs deeper, Bound by Iron & Blood explores themes of identity, belonging, and the cost of breaking cycles of violence. This gripping story will stay with you long after you turn the last page.

Perfect for fans of N.K. Jemisin's The Broken Earth trilogy and V.E. Schwab's A Darker Shade of Magic, Bound By Iron & Blood combines intimate character drama with epic world-building in a story that questions what it means to be family - and what it costs to be free.